Barbara Howe lives on the third rock from the sun, while her imagination travels the universe and beyond.

Born in the US (North Carolina), she spent most of her adult life in New Jersey, working in the software industry, on projects ranging from low-level kernel ports to multi-million-dollar financial applications. She moved to New Zealand in 2009, gained dual citizenship, and now works as a software developer in the movie industry. She lives in Wellington, in a house overflowing with books and jigsaw puzzles, and wishes she had more time time to spend universe hopping.

T0288795

Reforging: Book 1

The Locksmith

By Barbara Howe

The Locksmith

ISBN-13: 978-1-925496-50-5

Printed in Garamond and Goudy Old Style typefaces.

IFWG Publishing International
Melbourne

www.ifwgpublishing.com

Acknowledgement

This book would not have happened without the support of my husband, Art Protin, and daughter, Lucy. For all the times they came running when I announced I had a new chapter ready, and their willingness to listen to the same story over and over, I thank them. I also owe Lucy for the contribution of her villanelle, the spell on the Water Office.

I'd also like to thank Tim Jones for his encouragement and advice, Gerry Huntman and the professionals at IFWG Publishing Australia for their support, Donna Garzinsky and Anne Troop for reading it and asking how soon it would be published, and last but not least, my sister, Cindy Howe, for letting me use her good name.

For Art and Lucy, who wanted more.

Kestrel in a Chicken Coop

This is not a Cinderella story.

Under other circumstances it might have been; there are similarities, starting with my name, Lucinda Guillierre. But my stepmother was not cruel, and next to Claire, I was the ugly stepsister. Nor did I, a scholar's daughter, have much respect for our frivolous nobility. I would not have been happy with a prince, no matter how charming.

Not that I ever had an opportunity to turn one down. I was brooding over my lack of prospects, marital or otherwise, and our dwindling cash that day in early April when I walked into Father's study and found Mother Janet eyeing the shelves.

She jerked her hands away from the books. "Oh, hello, dear, I was just dusting."

I snorted.

She flushed, and waved a rag. "I...Oh, all right. I was considering, er..."

"Don't you dare think about selling them behind my back. I would know which ones are gone."

"I have every right to think about selling them. We need the money, and they're my property, and—"

"They are not. Father left them to me."

"That's what you say, dear, but Mrs Miller talked to her cousin, who talked to his sister-in-law, who talked to the magistrate, who said that was rubbish. A man's property goes to his widow."

A cold, hard lump formed in the pit of my stomach. We had argued over the books many times, but she had never threatened me with the magistrate before. I pulled a law book at random off the shelf and began flipping through it. "That's only if there's no written will. Father wrote a letter saying he was leaving the books to me." His hand had shaken; the letter was illegible. If she called in the law, I could lose everything. "Give me a moment to find the section on wills."

Her hands fluttered, the rag waving surrender. "No, no, I'm sure you know. But we have to do something. Soon."

I lowered the book and frowned at her. "We already agreed that if neither Claire nor I have an offer by my next birthday, I'll go to Rubierre and look for work as a cook or housemaid." The knot in my stomach got harder. No one in Rubierre, not even the richest merchant, had a library a quarter the size of Father's.

"That's too far," she said. "Miles. Strangers. You shouldn't have to… But we can't… That is, it's too…" She backed into a bookcase, leaving lint drifting in mid-air. "The money won't last that long."

"Nonsense," I said. She followed me into the kitchen and watched me fumble in the dark cupboard. "We've got enough to—" My fingers closed on the hidden bag, and I went cold. I yanked it out and upended it. Silver and copper coins spilled out across the table. Not a single gold frank in the lot. Enough for three months, maybe, if we were tight with every farthing. I stared. Swallowed. "Where did it go?"

"Have you forgotten Claire's new shoes?"

I winced. I had tried to. Her leather cast-offs would have been an improvement over my wooden clogs, but my feet wouldn't fit in her dainty slippers.

"And then," Mother Janet said, "She needs new gowns. The blacksmith's wife has gone to visit her sister in Gastòn, and I gave her money to bring back fabric."

"Gowns? More than one? Are you out of your mind? And why Gastòn? We can get perfectly good wool and linen in Rubierre. You're not wasting money on silk, are you?"

"Er…"

I leaned on the table and glowered at my stepmother. She retreated into the hall.

"I know, I know," she said. "I shouldn't have. But it seemed like a good idea at the time.".

What did this woman have for a backbone? I had wondered that before, and never come up with a good answer. If I ever had children, be damned if they would push me around.

She said, "Claire needs to look good, you know. One of you girls has to make a good match, or we're doomed. And… Oh, dear."

My cheeks burned. "Go ahead, say it. I'm an old maid." I groped for coins, stuffing them back in the bag. "Old Mrs Barnes is only too happy to remind me of my character flaws: nosy, truculent, and the never-ending stream of why-this and why-that would drive any man to distraction." Besides, Claire had mesmerised, and then spurned, everyone who had ever come courting me.

"And they're all too scared of you," Mother Janet said.

"Scared. Of me?" I fumbled for the chair and sank into it. "They're my friends. They can't be scared of me."

Her brow puckered. "What do you expect, when you act like a fire witch?" She held up a hand to forestall my protest. "I know you aren't one. It's a shame. But why can't you let someone else win an argument once in a while?"

I dropped in the last shilling and stared down at my hands. The flowers Claire had embroidered on my cuffs were being worn away. The dark red of the roses had long since faded to a dull pink. I picked at a loose thread. "I don't mean to argue. It's just wrong to let somebody get away with spouting rubbish."

She sighed and shook her head, then started talking about the books again. Panic clawed at me, and I listened with only half an ear. Was it true that the young men in the Camptons were afraid of me? Mother Janet was, but she was afraid of her own shadow. I was fit and sturdy, but no match for a farm boy. They couldn't be afraid of me; it made no sense.

She called from Father's study. "I thought we would just sell a couple. You wouldn't miss just two, would you? Edward said these were the most valuable."

I bolted across the hall, yelling, "Not those." I snatched the two volumes out of her hands, dropped the one onto the desk, and opened the other. Shoved the endpaper under her nose and tapped the words written there with my fingernail. "This is mine. It says so right here. If you try to sell this, I'll charge you with theft."

She fled back to the kitchen. I sat down at the desk, clutching the book to my chest, and waited for my heart to stop racing. Once I calmed down I would have to apologise to Mother Janet; my disrespect was appalling, even to my own ears. And she was right, too; these two books were the most valuable objects in the house, but they were indisputably mine, and I would never sell them. I lowered *Fire Wizardry in the Ancient World* to the desk and read the inscription: For Lucinda, who burns for knowledge, on her 12th birthday. Your proud and loving father, Edward Guillierre.

I wiped my eyes on my apron. I had already read *Fire Wizardry* once before he gave it to me—it had been in his library for decades, and by then he couldn't afford to buy a pristine first edition. I had reread it, several times. I closed the cover and admired the red leather, the gold leaf. That volume, and its companion, *Seventh Century Flame Wars*, were the only ones we had by the flame mage, Jean Rehsavvy. I closed my eyes and dreamed about owning another of his works. *Roman Warlocks*, that would be the one.

Years ago, the pastor had accused Father of cruelty for teaching me to read. I had earned a caning for calling the dear old soul half-a-dozen nasty names, but now I admitted the validity of his charge. If I went to work in Rubierre, I would never read another new book. Nineteen years old, and my life was as good as over.

Claire had come down the stairs and was in the kitchen, cajoling Mother Janet to sell the house and move to Paris. Even with two walls between us, I could see my stepmother's hands fluttering. I shook my head. Claire might as well wish for the moon. Or a fairy godmother.

"I wish," I muttered, "I wish there was a gate nearby."

Fool. I would have to get out of this suffocating backwater on my own, if at all. I reshelved the two histories and took out pen, paper, and ink. On the first sentence, I broke the pen. I got out another quill, cut a nib, and jabbed holes in the paper. Flung the pen down, and splashed ink across the desk. Got it on my sleeves while cleaning up.

I gave up then, and went back to my chores. For the next four days I cleaned the house, rafters to root cellar, scrubbing imagined stains from gleaming floorboards, and working myself into such a state of exhaustion that I could write my letters without savaging the paper.

The first letter, to the clerk in Rubierre, asked for his help in selling Father's law books. They were the only ones in the house I hadn't read, but I had no Latin, and they were full of it. I had been deluding myself that I could someday make sense of them.

The letter to the Scholar's Guild, begging for a position as a servant at a university or in an educated man's household, lay on the desk unfinished. I had no idea where to send it.

I trudged through the village on a damp, grey morning, looking for someone to take the completed letter to the Rubierre town clerk. Mrs Wilson, the miller's wife, called to me from the butcher shop, saying she had news. I went in, glad to be out of the cold wind.

She said, "Have you heard? The Fire Warlock opened a gate in Rubierre."

In Rubierre? Almost in my own backyard. I blinked as if in dazzling sunlight.

The butcher said, "Morning, Miss Lucinda. What can I get you?"

"Lamb chops."

His eyebrows rose.

"No, sorry," I stammered. Where had that come from? I hadn't meant to go to the butcher at all. But a new gate, in Rubierre! I could be extravagant. "One link of pork sausage with fennel, please."

While he worked on our orders I plied Mrs Wilson with questions. "Why there? Why now? How long has it been open? Who's gone through?"

She waved me off. "All I know is what I heard from a peddler on my way here. He said Baron D'Armond has been causing trouble. The Warlock sent him an invitation."

The baron deserved a reprimand, but I winced. "Summons, you mean. The nobles call it an invitation only because they don't want to admit how much he scares them."

The butcher snorted. "Maybe the baron will start behaving himself, knowing the Warlock's got an eye on him."

"We can hope," Mrs Wilson said. She chattered on about the baron's misdeeds, but I stopped listening.

"Miss Lucinda, do you want this or not?"

I took the sausage the butcher held out, apologising for my inattention.

Mrs Wilson laughed. "It's my fault, Jack. I started talking about the Fire Warlock when she walked in."

The butcher rolled his eyes. "For Pete's sake, Miss Lucinda, the way you go on about fire witches and wizards all the time you ought to be one.

I'm tired of all the stories you tell the youngsters, filling their heads with all kinds of nonsense. They don't need to know the names and life histories of all hundred-and-some-odd Fire Warlocks."

My hackles rose. "Don't call me a witch. And there have only been seventy-three Fire Warlocks, not a hundred."

"Who cares? Why don't you do something useful, missy, instead of reading all them silly books? There're things a girl should know, like how to sew."

"Let her be, Jack," the butcher's wife called from the back room. She walked to the doorway and wiped her hands on her apron. "I'd eat her cooking any day, and she keeps a neat house. If she wants to read her father's books after her work's all done, it's no skin off my back. Besides, she's too old to keep climbing trees and running breakneck through the woods with the boys." She smiled at me. "Promise me that after you get back you'll tell me all about it."

I went rigid. "Get back?"

"You're going to Rubierre to see the new gate, aren't you? I expect a full report on it tomorrow night."

I tried to sound sheepish. "Yes, ma'am."

"That's a long walk just to look at something," her husband said.

"Two hours," I said. "That's not so bad."

"Two hours each way. And what're you going to do when you get there? Spend five minutes looking at the blooming thing, then turn around and come home? Stop wasting your time."

I followed Mrs Wilson out, leaving the butcher still grumbling. I asked, "What's the matter with him? I know he thinks Father spoiled me, but he doesn't usually mind my stories. He's even thanked me a few times for keeping his children out of mischief for a while."

She said, "I expect he's worried that half the young men in the area will walk the challenge path to see the Fire Warlock. The nearest gate had been so far away that nobody thought much about it. But now, with a gate that close, it's more tempting, and with all the stories you've told, it's more on their minds than it would be otherwise. Insisting that no one dies on the Fire Guild's challenge path hasn't helped, either."

"Now, wait. I never said that no one has died on it—accidents can happen anywhere. I just said the stories about men dying right and left are nonsense."

"How do you know—because you've read it in a book? Sorry, dear, but I don't believe you. There are too many stories about boys leaving home and never coming back."

"It's common sense. Why would the Warlock kill his own supplicants? Most of the ones who never came back didn't want to. But it doesn't matter what I say. Even without the risk of dying, the challenges—and having to work for him for a year—make most shy away. I know all the boys within an hour's walk, and I can't name any who'd go—at least, not to the Fire Guild. Within a day's walk there'll only be a few who are brave and ambitious enough, and most of them will be troublemakers and malcontents. That's the way it's been every other place he's opened a new gate."

"I know, and I'm not worried about my son going. But Jack's just heard the news. He'll calm down when he's had time to think about it a bit."

I said, "Even if the rubbish about people dying doesn't scare them off, the thought of facing the Fire Warlock will. Everyone here went out of their way to avoid Gladys, and she only had a sharp tongue."

I never fathomed why even the burliest farmers sidled out of the old fire witch's way. Gladys could light a candle at will, but not much else. When she dropped by to chat with my mother—almost a fire witch herself—I would run to her and tug at her skirts, begging for stories about the Fire Warlock. Hers were even wilder than the ones in Father's books. The Fire Warlock figured in so many tales of magic and derring-do, some real, some nonsense, that he was both more respected and more feared than our sorry excuse for a king.

Even the witch could not answer all my childish questions. Can the Fire Warlock really shoot sparks out of his eyes? How long is his beard? Is his hair all grey or is some of it still red? He was old. They all were, I had known that much. But she had never seen the Warlock. She would say, "He never comes down out of the Fortress, you know, 'cept for when he has to haul the king's arse out of trouble. He stays up there on the mountain, keeping an eye out for danger. Anybody as wants to see him has to go to him, he doesn't come to us."

I said to Mrs Wilson, "With both Gladys and my mother dead for ten years there's no one left with an affinity for the Fire Guild."

"Except for you. Too bad the Fire Office has no use for girls."

She waved goodbye, and I walked down the lane, following the rock wall. If only the Fire Guild was not so one-sided. There were witches as well as wizards in all four magic guilds, and there were women in the top ranks of three. The Air Guild had its enchanters and enchantresses, the Water Guild its sorcerers and sorceresses, and the Earth Guild its mothers and fathers. But the Fire Guild, charged with defending the Kingdom of Frankland, had nothing but warlocks and mages on its guild council, and even in the lowest ranks there were more wizards than witches. There were stories of both girls and boys asking the other Officeholders for aid, but all the stories of supplicants asking for the Fire Warlock's help were about boys and men.

Mrs Wilson was out of sight. I climbed the rock wall and danced along the top, my letters forgotten. The butcher's wife wouldn't have been so sympathetic if she'd known I wasn't planning to come back. So what if no girl had gone before? I would walk the challenge path myself, and take my case to the Fire Warlock.

We're Off to See the Warlock

Should I be worried about the challenges ahead? I went through the motions of fixing dinner like an automaton. Each of the magic guilds maintained a challenge path by which a supplicant could gain an audience with the head of the guild. In the case of the Fire Guild, both the folklore and Father's books agreed there were three challenges, although no one seemed to know what they were. I shrugged. I couldn't force myself to fret. There wasn't enough to go on to make any planning worthwhile, and the stories said a clever head and a stout heart were all one needed to get through them. I thought I had both of those, although I would never know for sure if I stayed in Lesser Campton.

If I did pass the challenges, what then? I conjured up an image of a peevish old man asking me the question that made my chest tighten, Why should he help me?

The Warlock would have no sympathy for a mundane girl who wanted books. Rumour said his library had a copy of every book on magic ever written, but I wasn't a witch, I didn't need to read spells. Father had kept all his books on magic locked up, and never allowed me near them.

Please, Your Wisdom, I don't want much—just to eat, sleep, and breathe in your library. The old man scowled and chewed me out for getting above myself. I asked for adventure; he scolded me for not acting respectable. I asked him to help me find a husband; he jeered at me.

I put down my knife and leaned on the table. Losing a finger would not augur well for walking the challenge path. After I stopped trembling, I took a deep breath and picked up the knife, not letting my attention waver. Mother Janet would complain the chunks of carrot were too big. Too bad.

So what if he laughed at me? The purpose of the Office of the Fire

Warlock was to protect the nation's women and children. I was harmless; he wouldn't harm me. The stories said that he approved of boldness, at least in boys, so he might help me. But if I asked for help in finding a match, small blame to him if he did laugh at me. If that's what I wanted, I should go to the Earth Mother or the Frost Maiden for help, not the Warlock.

I had considered going to one or the other. A day's walk would take me to a gate leading to the Frost Maiden's Crystal Palace, but the thought of asking that chilly witch for aid left me, well, cold.

I would rather go to the Earth Mother. Both she and the Fire Warlock had gates in the city of Gastòn, but a three-day walk through forest, sleeping in the open and depending on the kindness of strangers, would have been a desperate venture even for a boy. There were too many stories of robbers setting on solitary men, beating them, stripping them of their clothes, and leaving them to die in isolated places. An unescorted girl could not expect even the courtesy of being left to die.

Besides, if I could have gotten to Gastòn, I would not have gone to the Earth Mother. I would have made a beeline for the Fire Warlock's gate, pulled like a moth to a flame, as I was being pulled now to the one in Rubierre.

⸺❦⸺

Mother Janet went upstairs to take her nap after dinner. I was in the kitchen washing up when Claire came sweeping in. "Lucinda, our prayers have been answered. The Fire Warlock has opened a gate in Rubierre!"

I studied her for a moment. Her blue eyes sparkled and her skin glowed as if she had a new beau. Why did the news excite her? If her affinity wasn't for the Water Guild, I'd cook one of Father's law books and serve it for breakfast. "So?"

She pouted. "You already knew, and didn't tell me?"

"Why should I? You don't have an affinity for the Fire Guild."

"No, but you do, and you're going to walk the challenge path to see him, aren't you? Unless you are happy about being an old maid?"

I scowled at her, but didn't answer.

"You are going to see the Warlock, aren't you?" she repeated. "You have to, if we're ever going to get out of this God-forsaken little village."

We? Conversations with Claire often left me feeling muzzy-headed. I hadn't won an argument with her in years.

"Claire, girls don't go to the Warlock."

"Then why do you always talk about the Fire Warlock whenever I mention one of the other gates? Lucinda, please say you're going. Pretty please?" Her eyes brimmed with tears, ready to spill out if I said no.

"All right, I know you won't tell Mother Janet. I'm going tomorrow."

"Wonderful!" She beamed at me. "I'm going with you."

I dropped the handful of cutlery I'd been about to toss in the dishpan, and gaped at her.

She giggled, showing her dimples. "Lucinda, you look so funny with your mouth open."

I closed it, and looked down at the spoons littering the floor. They could wait. "Claire, that's ridiculous. The Warlock won't be interested in finding you a husband. You'd be better off going to the Frost Maiden."

She waved my objection away with a flick of her hand. "She's too far away. He's a man, even if he is a wizard. He'll do whatever I want once he sees me."

Probably true. Everybody turned into a mound of quivering jelly on meeting Claire. "Have you forgotten the three challenges? You're not going to get close enough to talk to him."

"Of course I will. We'll walk the challenge path together, and you'll help me."

I gaped at her again. She laughed—the merry, tinkling laugh that made men grovel—and said, "Are you going to pick up the spoons?"

"Spoons? Oh." I picked up the dirty spoons and shoved them in my apron pocket. "Claire, I have never heard of two people going to see him together. Ever. It's always a one-person quest. And if we make him angry, well…"

"Well, what? You keep reminding everybody he's there to protect the country's women and children. What's the worst he'll do to us—send us home?"

Hoist by my own petard, I was. Through clenched teeth I said, "He'll give us a good tongue-lashing, at least."

"Since when has a scolding ever bothered you? Besides, the peddler who brought the news said I should go, and I shouldn't be afraid. He said His Wisdom is really an old dear with a soft spot for pretty girls."

"What? Who is this peddler and why is he spouting nonsense about the Fire Warlock?" I shook my head, but it didn't help. Was Claire that naïve? "Getting through the challenges just guarantees an audience with the Warlock. You'll still have to convince him you deserve his aid, and if he does condescend to help you, you'll have to work for him for a year."

She said, "But we'll be together and can help each other out. It'll be easier and more fun than working alone. Please, Lucinda, let me come with you. If you go away without me, I'll be stuck here forever. I'll never get out of here without help." Her lip trembled; her eyes brimmed with tears again.

I said, "I don't know if I can get through the challenges myself."

"Of course you can. You're the smartest person I've ever met, and you're even braver than the hostler in Old Campton."

She smiled her most winning smile. My head fizzed as if I'd downed three glasses of champagne. I was smart, I was brave, and I marvelled at how perceptive she was. My objections drowned under a wave of affection, and I promised we would go together. We made plans to leave at dawn, and then she waltzed away down the hall and up the stairs.

As soon as she was out of sight the surge of affection evaporated. My blood boiled. It seemed strange there was no steam rising from the dishwater my hands were in. If we spent the next year together in the Warlock's fortress she would captivate every man there, as she had here. I would have no more chance of finding a good match than I would in the village, even with the Warlock's help.

I was the smart one, was I? Then why did I let her talk me into something I didn't want to do? I slammed the cast-iron skillet into the dishwater, sending a fountain cascading down the front of my dress and onto the floor. Getting drenched did not make me feel any better. Or smarter.

Hypocrite. I shouldn't call other people mounds of jelly when I couldn't stand up to Claire either. This wasn't the first time. Or was it? As I mopped up the water, I groped for memories that stayed stubbornly out of reach, and seemed to recede further the more I struggled.

I sat back on my heels, and discovered the mess the sticky spoons had made in my apron pocket. I flung them in the dishwater. Why did I think I had what it takes to get through the challenges? I couldn't even congratulate myself on my audacity; Claire's idea was more daring. What would the Fire Warlock say when two girls came together? And what if I was wrong, and the challenge path was life threatening? What right did I have to risk not only my own life, but Claire's, too?

I wasn't making her go. If she got scared, she could turn around and go home, but I would go the whole way, and I would see the Warlock and his fabled Fortress. I went back to my chores with a light heart. Even if the Fire Warlock refused to help me, I'd have a day of glory and come home with a story to tell my grandchildren. I wasn't afraid of the challenge path, and I had more sense than Claire. I would avoid anything truly dangerous, such as imagining the Fire Warlock was an old dear with a soft spot for pretty girls.

Nerves kept me from sleeping well, and I was up well before dawn. Getting Claire up was another matter. I couldn't make much noise with Mother Janet in the next room, but whispering didn't work. Neither did pinching Claire, nor shaking her.

Let her sleep. I would go without her. I started down the stairs, but stopped and paced a tight circle on the landing. Father had gotten angrier about broken promises than for any other transgression, and I couldn't do it. I bolted down the stairs and out to the springhouse to fetch a pitcher of cold water, and dribbled it onto her face while holding my hand over her mouth. She glared at me as she awoke. I couldn't suppress a smirk.

When I was confident she wouldn't go back to sleep, I went to the library and pulled out the two histories Father had written my name in. I had spent most of the previous afternoon there, caressing one book after another. If we passed the challenges and the Warlock accepted our requests, Mother Janet would sell them all in the year we were away. I ran my fingers over the spines of my other old friends with burning eyes and a tight throat. They seemed to shrink from my faithless fingers. I turned and fled.

The two books, wrapped in my other dress, went into a bundle with bread and cheese, and the rest of my belongings—a hairbrush, and a few small trinkets of my mother's. I waited for Claire by the back door with the light load slung over my shoulder. She came down the stairs carrying nothing besides a small purse that jingled as she moved. I ground my teeth. In a louder voice than I intended, I said, "Aren't you taking anything? Food? Clothes? A hairbrush?"

She said, "When we're living in the Warlock's castle I'll send for my clothes."

"Mother Janet won't be happy about the expense, or the work involved."

She shrugged. "Mother won't be happy about us leaving either, but we won't be here for her to yell at." She walked out the door without a backward glance.

I lingered for a moment, taking a last look around the kitchen. I had done all the cooking and cleaning because I couldn't have stomached living here if I hadn't. My mother's gleaming pots reproached me for my treachery in leaving them to Mother Janet's slovenliness. I wiped away tears and hurried after Claire.

The sky was lightening as we passed the village commons. In Old Campton I pushed a note under the pastor's door asking him to let Mother Janet know where we had gone. Going home to her hurt feelings and the villagers' jeers would be unbearable. Whatever happened, I could not turn back now.

The Gate

The morning was cold when we started out, but the sun came up in a cloudless sky, and once we were out of the shadows the walk was pleasant, enlivened by the fresh green hint of new leaves in the trees and the yellow of daffodils bobbing by the side of the road. I bobbed back at them, and laughed when Claire giggled.

A mile short of Rubierre, a farm wagon came up behind us. I was tired and my skirts muddy, so I hailed the boy driving and asked if we could ride.

He shook his head. "Sorry. My dad said not to stop for nobody."

Claire turned and smiled at him. She looked as fresh as when we had started out. "I'm sure your dad wouldn't mind if you let us ride."

He gawked, and drew rein. "No, I guess he wouldn't."

Everyone acted that way on meeting Claire. Even to my jaundiced eyes, she was lovely—small and delicate, like a china doll, with long lashes, and pale skin. She brought out the most chivalric behaviour in men. I had overheard several of her suitors making wild promises about protecting and taking care of her. Nobody made promises like that to me.

The boy climbed down and helped Claire up onto the seat, then climbed back up.

There wasn't room on the seat for three. I tossed my bundle in the back and clambered over the side. I was lowering myself to the bed of the wagon when it started moving, and I sat down with a thud on the hard floorboards.

As I rubbed my rump, I said, "Today isn't a market day, is it? Where are you headed?"

The boy didn't answer. He just stared at Claire.

Claire asked, "Where are you headed?"

The boy started telling her about his errand.

I fumed. Did I need to look helpless in order to get some attention? I was taller than Claire, with muscles in my arms and browner skin from hard work and playing outdoors. I doubted I could look helpless, even if I wanted to. I'd laugh at any man who thought I should. And I'd rather be a servant than marry one of Claire's halfwit suitors.

When Gladys, the old fire witch, had visited my mother she would usually hand me a sweet and say, "Pity you have no talent, the guild could use clever ones like you." I once protested that I was glad I was not a witch, and she tsked at me. "Eh, maybe you aren't so clever. If you were a witch, you could earn your own way. You wouldn't have to marry if you didn't want to. Think about that, now."

I had, and knew she was right. I would have been better off as a witch, but some part of me, impervious to logic, proclaimed I was glad I was not one.

The boy dropped us off a block from the town square. I thanked him, but he didn't seem to notice. He was still staring at Claire as he drove away.

I suggested we go to the square and ask directions, since we didn't know where the gate was. We walked around the apothecary's shop on the corner, and discovered we didn't need directions. A massive wrought iron gate, with the Fire Guild's flame emblem picked out in gold leaf in the centre, stood directly across the square.

Claire and I had been to Rubierre many times before. The town square consisted of a small lawn with a gazebo and a few trees, surrounded by cobblestone streets, with shops and merchants' houses on three sides. On the fourth, the north side, the church and town hall sat side by side. Now this gate, wide enough to drive a coach and six through with plenty of room to spare, separated the church and the town hall. How could even magic squeeze a gate that wide between them? The two buildings looked no different, neither did the square.

I had read stories about magic all my life, but I had never encountered any substantial displays. I set down my baggage, and we looked at each other. Claire's eyes were round. She asked, "How did he do that?"

"I don't know. An illusion spell? But illusions are the Air Guild's domain. Doesn't matter, I'm impressed."

We crossed the street to the gazebo and took stock. The bundle that had weighed nothing at all in Lesser Campton had become an instrument of torture, and I dropped it with a grateful sigh. I kicked off my shoes, too, and sat down. Claire had complained more than once that her new shoes pinched her toes, but she didn't sit. I massaged my shoulders and arms where the cord had dug in while studying the gate ahead of us.

The gate itself was in two pieces that opened inwards, each half mounted on a pillar of the same light yellow stone used in most of the local buildings. A thick stand of trees lay behind the gate—there had been no wooded area in the middle of town before—with a cobblestone drive curving away to the right and out of sight. In front of each pillar a guardsman, dressed in the Fire Guild's red and orange livery, stood at attention with a pike in hand. A third guardsman, older than the other two, paced between them.

"What do we do now?" Claire asked.

"Talk to the guards, I suppose."

"Let's go, then." She swept out of the gazebo, leaving me fumbling with my shoes and baggage. She was halfway across the lawn, turning towards the guard on the right, before I got my shoes on.

I hurried to catch up with her, glancing at the guard on the left as I went. He was watching me. Had I met him before? Impossible. I'd never met any guards.

He winked at me, and I recognised, under the guard's gaudy hat and uniform, one of the boys from the large flock of children raised on the farm down the lane from us. "George!" What was he doing here? I hadn't seen him in several months, since he'd left the village looking for work.

"Shhh," he hissed. "I'll be relieved at eight o'clock. Wait for me."

I glanced at the church tower. Its clock read twenty till eight. I mouthed, "Thanks," at him.

Claire had reached the other guard, and glared at me over her shoulder, snapping, "Lucinda, hurry up!" She turned to the guard and smiled. "I am on my way to see the Fire Warlock. Open the gate and let me through."

The guard did not move. "You'll have to talk to the sergeant, miss."

The sergeant was apparently the third guardsman, the one pacing between the two pillars. He came to a halt in front of Claire.

Claire gave him the blinding smile that turned all males to mush and repeated her demand.

He asked, "Do you have an invitation?"

Invitation? "Sir," I said, "isn't the challenge path open to all comers?"

"No invitation," Claire said. "The Warlock doesn't know I'm coming, but I'm sure you'll let me through, won't you, Sergeant?"

I gasped when the sergeant scowled. "Nobody gets through this gate without an invitation. Good day, Miss."

Claire's eyelashes fluttered. "Really, Sergeant, I'm sure that rule wasn't meant for me."

He said, "You won't talk to me or the boys again if you know what's good for you."

Claire's smile vanished. "I am not used to people talking to me like—"

The sergeant took her by the arm and marched her across the street. She struggled with him, so that when he let go she was off balance and fell on her knees in the grass. She got up and stalked away, her very gait expressing outrage.

For several seconds, I stood frozen. I had not seen anyone, male or female, refuse a request from Claire in more than five years.

I bobbed a curtsey to the sergeant and ran after Claire, intending to give her a piece of my mind for being so rude. I caught up to her, but my tongue wouldn't say the angry words. We walked across the square without speaking. Should I go back and talk to the sergeant? If he treated Claire like that how would he treat me?

I looked back at the guards. A conversation with George would be more satisfying alone.

"Claire," I said, guiding her by the arm back around the apothecary's. "I know you're tired. Why don't you go to that coffee house we passed on the way and have a better breakfast? I'll see if there is another way in. You can relax."

After she settled in with a cup of coffee and breakfast on order at a table out of view of the square, I walked back to the gazebo and sat down to wait. The fact that I, too, was tired and hungry was irrelevant. I had no money, and persuading Claire to part with any of hers on my account was a lost cause from the outset.

A new trio of guards arrived on time, there were presentations of arms and salutes all round, and the old trio sauntered away. George carried on an earnest conversation with the sergeant, with glances in my direction, and then he loped across the square, grinning.

"Hey, Miss Lucinda, it sure is good to see you. Are you both trying to see His Wisdom or just Miss Claire?"

"George, you have no idea how glad I am you're here. We both want to see him. How do we get through the gate without an invitation?"

"I don't know, but you can ask Sarge now that he's off duty. I told him you were nicer than Miss Claire, and he said you could come have breakfast with us if you wanted, as long as you didn't bring the witch. Meaning Miss Claire, that is."

"What? That doesn't make sense. Claire's no more a witch than I am."

He shrugged. "I don't know about witches, but it would explain things, wouldn't it? So how about breakfast? And where is she?"

"She's in one of the coffee houses. I'd love to have breakfast with you, but I don't have any money."

"Don't worry about that, it's on me."

"No, really, I can't—"

"Course you can. It's the least I can do. I'd do the same for anybody from Lesser Campton, except maybe Miss Claire, who never gave me the time of day unless she wanted something from me."

I followed him down one of the side streets, admitting that yes, it would be nice to relax and eat breakfast with them. "What are you doing here? The last I had heard you were working on the wharfs downriver."

"The work wasn't bad, hard but not any worse than working a farm, but I didn't like my boss. When the guards came to town I heard they had a couple of holes in their ranks, and jumped at the chance. It seems like a fair deal to me. They'll train me to fight with a pike, and most of the time all I have to do is stand up straight and keep an eye on things. I can do that well enough, and if things get nasty and there's a fight, I think I can do alright there, too."

"I've heard rumours of you emerging with honours from a few dust-ups."

He grinned. "And it could get real interesting if we go to war."

I recoiled. "War?"

He shrugged. "The guards are saying the emperor wants to be Europa's most powerful wizard, and just thinking about our Fire Warlock pisses him off. They think he's looking for an excuse to say the Warlock's insulted him, and it won't be long now until he finds something."

I knew empires didn't appreciate obstinate nuisances like us on their flanks. They had no chance against our Fire Warlock, of course, but far too many wars had triggered Scorching Times. I shivered. We could do ourselves far more damage in a decade than the Europan Empire could in a century. We reached the inn and a more urgent problem drove worries about war out of my mind. I had to face the sergeant that Claire hadn't charmed.

The Guards

I followed George to a table with the sergeant and the other guard. George ordered a big breakfast for me, over my feeble protests. The sergeant looked me up and down coldly, but I kept my chin up. I was going to see the great Warlock, wasn't I? I couldn't let a mere sergeant put me off.

George told a story about one of my childhood pranks that made the sergeant's lips twitch. I relaxed a little. The food came, and as we dug into our bacon and eggs I started to tell a story in retaliation about one of George's less sensible escapades. Better not, the voice of reason said, and I changed it mid-sentence to a story about his pluck and daring. George and I took turns telling stories about our childhood days, mostly at my expense. By the time we finished eating the sergeant was laughing outright.

Over coffee I dove in. "Sergeant, I know my sister got off on the wrong foot demanding that you let her through the gates, but how can we get to the challenge path if we have to have an invitation? Is there another way in? Or some other test I don't know about?"

The sergeant cleared his throat. "Miss, I never heard of two people going together. As far as I know everybody has to get in by theirselves."

The other guard added, "I never heard of girls going either."

George said, "If any girl can do it, it's going to be Miss Lucinda. Everybody in Lesser Campton was sure she was going to be a fire witch after the Guillierre's made a trip to Gastòn and she screamed bloody murder the whole time she was on the ferry."

I had kicked, bit, and punched, too. It was a shame I was too old to crawl under the table. That had been fourteen years ago, and I had still not lived it down.

"Drown her," the ferryman, a low-level water wizard, had said.

My mother, white-lipped and rigid in the centre of the boat, had snapped, "How dare you! Can't you see she's going to be a fire witch?"

"All the more reason to drown the brat."

My father had been furious, and proud. When I had displayed no magical abilities by the age of twelve, he had taken me to be tested. The bitter disappointment on his face when the wizard told him I had no discernible talent still stung.

George was saying, "Doesn't hurt for her to try, does it?"

The sergeant shrugged. "Beats me."

George said, "But I think he's right about going by yourself. You'll have better luck with His Wisdom without Miss Claire along. Besides, if you get through and she doesn't, you won't have to put up with her anymore. For a year, anyway."

I stared down at my coffee cup. Claire had once been my best friend. What had happened to her? The Claire I once knew would have been a prize for any wealthy, shallow nobleman.

"George, I made a promise and I'm going to keep it. Who knows? Maybe the Warlock can help her. If he does, I'll be glad. I don't want her to get her comeuppance and live out her life as a nasty old maid. I'd rather have the old Claire back than just be rid of the new one."

And if she didn't marry well, I'd be stuck supporting both her and Mother Janet. I wasn't sure I could even support myself.

There was silence. I looked up from my coffee. All three men were staring at me.

I asked, "Uh, does that make any sense?"

The sergeant said, "Well maybe it do and maybe it don't. I can't say what the Warlock will make of it, miss. If you want to try, I won't stop you. I just didn't like your sister trying to use magic on us."

"But Claire doesn't have any talent."

"She was doing something, miss."

"What?"

He shrugged. "Don't know, but the Warlock doesn't let much of anything work on us. Anyway, I don't mind telling you that there's another way to get in. There's another, little gate. A door in a wall, see, on past the church. There ain't no guard there, but anybody that has regular business at the castle—the lieutenant and a few other people—they've got keys. Just ask nice and the lieutenant will let you through."

"Oh, bless you, sir. That's wonderful."

"Don't sir, me, miss, I'm not a gentleman. I'm a sergeant. Just doing my job."

"Where can I find the lieutenant? I'll go get Claire and then we'll ask him to let us through."

"Uh, miss, maybe you'd have better luck with the lieutenant if you was to go by yourself."

"You're probably right," I said. "Do you know anything about the challenges? I've read that there are three, but I have no idea what they are. Is there any advice or hints for getting through them?"

The sergeant stared up at the ceiling. "Yep, there are three. As for anything else, everybody as has been through comes out magicked and can't tell anybody else. You'll just have to find out for yourselves, miss."

"I was afraid you were going to say that."

He stood up. "All right, we'll take you to the lieutenant. Let's go."

"Yes, sir. Thank you!"

"Told you not to 'sir' me. Go on with you."

They led me to the lieutenant's office and waited outside while I went in. The lieutenant was a young man, not much older than George or me, with a thin beard. He listened in silence to my request, then studied me with his arms folded across his chest for at least half a minute longer. I waited. If he'd been as old as the sergeant, I might have been nervous, but despite the fancy uniform he looked like just another farm boy, trying to look older by growing a beard.

He said, "The Warlock makes people he agrees to help work for a year. If you aren't willing to work hard, you should go home."

What could the Warlock make me do that would be harder than being a farmer's wife? I shrugged.

"What kind of work can you and your sister do?" he asked.

"Everybody needs to eat, and I can cook. My sister can do laundry. We can both clean and sew and do other housekeeping chores."

"Ha," he leered. "There are other services a pretty girl can provide, and you wouldn't even have to get out of bed to do them."

What was he talking about—work in my sleep? Or… Oh. I laughed. He drew back as if I'd gone mad.

I'd heard of sleeping one's way to the top, but this was ridiculous.

23

"Seduce the Fire Warlock? I'm not stupid. Or suicidal."

He turned bright red. "I meant you could do things for the guards. You might as well. What's a year among us going to do to your reputation? If you value it, don't go."

"Witches spend years at the Fire Guild's school without damaging their reputations. The whole purpose of the Office of the Fire Warlock, and the guards and everything else associated with it, is to protect the women and children of Frankland. If members of the guard spread malicious rumours about an innocent girl, he wouldn't like it."

The lieutenant blanched.

"The Frost Maiden wouldn't like it either," I added.

"Ahem. Well. I don't have to let you through if I think you're going to waste the Warlock's time. Why do you want to see His Wisdom?"

"I'm sorry, sir, but we don't have to explain our quests to anyone but the Warlock. That's what the rules have always said, and you ought to know the rules as well as I do, if not better."

He sniffed. "Maybe the rules have changed. Maybe the Warlock doesn't want all kinds of riffraff and silly girls coming to see him, and he's told us to only let through sensible people."

I bit back my first response—in that case, the Warlock needed to find someone sensible to sort them out—and said as meekly as I could manage, "But the challenges are designed to weed out the people who aren't sensible and serious. The lore says the Warlock doesn't appreciate anybody else putting obstacles in a quester's path. You should let us through, sir. I wouldn't want it on my conscience that he got angry with you for stopping us."

He stared at me through narrowed lids. I struggled to keep a straight face.

He said, "If you get through, which isn't likely, he'll just send you home again without even listening to you. You shouldn't waste your time and put yourself in danger for that."

"No, sir. He's obligated to listen to anyone who makes it through the challenges. Then he might send us home, but he has to listen first."

"Even to a couple of girls?" he sneered. "Girls don't go to the Warlock."

"Even to a couple of girls. If no girls have come to him before then maybe the sheer novelty will amuse him."

"I doubt it. You aren't likely to be the sort of person he wants to see."

24

Interested, I asked, "What sort of person does he want to see?"

"A brave one," he snapped, "or an educated one, who wants to talk about books and ideas."

I laughed again, and pulled the two books out of my bundle. I laid them on his desk with a thump. "I'm a scholar's daughter, and these are my treasures. If he wants to talk about books I would be in heaven."

He gave up. He shooed me out and called the sergeant in to give him the key.

The Warlock loves to talk about books, does he? I ran down the street, laughing. What kind of a man was the reigning Warlock? *The History of the Office of The Fire Warlock* in Father's library was two hundred years old. I knew little about the current one, other than the stories Gladys told about the wars he had fought, and his *nom de guerre*, Quicksilver. An odd name, surely, for a member of a breed noted for violent tempers and stubborn grudges.

Claire was where I had left her, looking cross. "Where have you been?"

I said, "I've been talking to the guards. Supplicants go through another gate, an ordinary door. George just joined the guards. He and—"

"Who?" She looked blank.

"George Barnes. From the farm down the lane. He left Lesser Campton a few months ago looking for work. Remember?"

"Oh, yes. He's one of the rowdies who always smelled of pigs, right?"

I closed my eyes and counted to ten. "Right. Well, he and the sergeant are going to meet us at the door and let us through."

"Good."

"We need to be polite to them."

She sniffed. "Why? They're guards. If you get along with them so well perhaps you should do all the talking."

"Claire, that's brilliant. I'm glad you suggested it."

She glared at me, and started to retort, then closed her mouth and sniffed again. She followed me around to the back of the church, where George and the sergeant were waiting. She nodded at them, gave George a smile, and didn't say anything. Why had the sergeant turned her away? He had said why, but I had already forgotten. I shrugged. It didn't matter; he was going to let us both through.

We followed the sergeant down the alley to a wooden door with an iron handle, and no markings to distinguish it from any of dozens of other wooden doors in the same town.

He held up a key, and said, "Now, miss, this here door is locked on this side, but on the other side it has a latch, and it's been magicked so that if you need to come back you can pull the latch and walk right on out. But if you do, you won't never get no second chance."

I nodded. "That's what I expected."

He unlocked the door and pulled it open. "Are you sure you want to go in?"

"Yes, s…I mean, yes, Sergeant." He grinned.

Claire said, "Thank you, George. Thank you, Sergeant," and walked through.

I walked past George, then turned and kissed him on the cheek. I whispered, "Wish me luck." He gave me the double thumbs up and a big wink. I thanked the sergeant again, and kissed him on the cheek too before walking through.

Behind me, as the door closed, the sergeant said, "Good luck, miss, with the other two challenges."

A Sticky Situation

I whirled but the door had already clicked shut. I stared at it for a moment, then turned to look around. We were in a wooded park with a path through it. Pine trees thinned out before a curving hedge, its top about eye level. Beyond it, in the distance, the path ended at another door in a wall. We looked at each other and shrugged. Walk in one door and out the other. What could be hard about that?

The path led downhill, so that when we reached the hedge it towered over our heads. We stepped through a gap, and saw another hedge, also with gaps in it. Paths went off to the right and left, curving around and out of sight. A maze. I had heard about them, but had never been in one. Without a ball of string, I had no clue how to find our way through.

We stepped into the maze. Claire said, "We're going to get lost, aren't we?"

"Um—"

"Which way?"

I looked up at an overcast sky. What happened to Rubierre's cloudless blue? "Going widdershins would be unlucky, I suppose." I started down the path to the left.

We must have wandered around for more than an hour, before we stumbled upon an exit with a path leading up the hill towards a door in the wall. Claire set off up the path at a brisk pace. I trailed behind, relieved to be out of the maze, but troubled that we'd gotten through it simply by luck. I glanced down at the path, and gasped.

"Claire, wait!" I shouted.

She stopped a foot from the door. "What is it?"

"We're headed towards the same door we came in through. Look!"

I showed her the fresh footprints in the damp dirt, two sets leading from the door; two sets the same size and shape going towards it. Her shoulders sagged as she agreed they were ours.

I sank down onto the pine needles and studied the maze. After a few minutes I turned and studied the trees. There was one not far away that had branches lined up on one side like a ladder. Too old to climb trees? We'd see about that.

The trees I had climbed as a child had been hardwoods with smooth bark. The bark on this pine was rough, and sticky with sap. I surveyed the other trees, but they were all pines. None of the others would be any better.

I set my jaw and started up.

The branches that had, from the ground, seemed like rungs on a ladder, were not close enough together to make climbing easy. I had to get a solid grip on each branch with both hands, and swing my legs and then the rest of my body up onto it. On the second branch, my skirt caught on the rough bark and tore a two-inch rip front and centre.

I said, "Scorch this despot of a Fire Warlock and his flagrant bias for boys."

Claire gasped. "Lucinda, you can't say that. What if he's listening?"

"We're not important or talented enough for him to pay attention to. And what if he did? He'd laugh at us."

My dress and petticoat—both threadbare and easily torn—were going to be in ruins, but I kept climbing. By the time I got high enough to get a good look at the maze, I had scratches on my arms, legs, and face, and I was sticky all over with sap.

There was even sap in my hair. My hair was the feature I was most proud of, even if it was ordinary compared to Claire's golden halo. Mine was the colour of polished oak, thick, glossy, and fell down below my hips. It caught and pulled on several branches, and would probably acquire more sap on the way down. It came loose and fell in my face, but there was so much sap on my hands that I didn't dare touch it to put it back up again. Would it wash out, or would I have to cut it out?

The possibility of dying on the challenge path had not stopped me, but I had not anticipated losing my hair. Maybe dying was better. Dead, I wouldn't care about my hair.

I took a good look at the maze, and my heart sank. The curving paths were obvious, but even once I had worked out a route through them, I would have trouble remembering when to turn left or right. I couldn't draw the plan of the maze without anything to write on. Even if I'd brought paper, ink, and a pen, my bundle lay on the ground and I couldn't endure climbing this abomination of a pine tree more than once.

A gap in the hedge on the far side of the maze, opposite the one we went in through, opened onto the path leading to the gate in the far wall. There were at least two, maybe three paths through the maze, but only one went through the open space in the centre. I couldn't see the ground from my perch in the tree, but the centre must be important, and I tried to memorise that path.

I called down to Claire about what I saw, and looking down, I noticed, as if for the first time, that her dress had a long fabric sash, long enough that it wrapped several times around her waist.

"Claire, take off your sash. I want you to put knots in it to help us track which turns to make."

"What? Why? What kind of knots?"

"It doesn't matter what kind, as long as you use one kind for right turns, another for left turns, and a third for gaps to skip."

I explained this several times, and when she understood, she tied knots as I called out directions. Then I climbed down, acquiring more scratches and rips on the way, and leaving behind a lock of hair that tore right out of my scalp. When I reached the ground Claire looked me over with a wrinkled nose.

"You look like a street urchin."

"This explains why the stories all have the boys arriving on the Warlock's doorstep in tatters." I rubbed my sore scalp with the heel of my hand. "Come on, let's go. The sooner we get through this cursed maze the sooner I can get clean."

With the knots in her sash, we had no problem finding our way through the maze. We had not gone halfway when we came across a door set in the hedge. The door looked just like the one we had come through to get into the park. We stopped and stared at it.

"Do you think this is the way out?" Claire asked.

It was tempting, but I shook my head. "No, we have to get to the centre. It would be good if we could remember where this door is. You could use a hairpin to mark its place on your sash?"

29

"And have my hair come down and blow in my face? I'd rather not."

My hair was already blowing in my face. I reached up to grab a hairpin, and remembered too late the sap on hands.

Through clenched teeth I said, "Here." I bent my head. "Pull out one of mine."

She stretched out a dainty hand, and without touching me, pulled out a hairpin to add to the sash.

We were soon standing in a gap in the innermost hedge. A pond, nearly covered over with lily pads, filled the inner circle. There was no space to walk around it. We could not avoid it to get to the gap on the other side.

I glowered at it. I'd been expecting a test of courage. What was this nonsense?

Claire asked, "Do you think we're supposed to swim?"

She could swim. I couldn't. I sniffed. "To get to the Fire Warlock? Not likely."

I took off my shoes and socks and added them to my bundle of belongings, leaving them and my cloak in the gap with Claire, then hitched up my skirt and started poking under the lily pads with my toe.

Claire asked, "What are you doing?"

I said, "Looking for stepping stones."

No stones. Should I try wading? Keeping an eye on the far gap to make sure I headed in the right direction, I took two cautious steps out into the pond and realised I was not in the water, but on it. I looked down, startled. How could I have missed the stepping stones? I felt around for the other stones that must be there, but couldn't find any. Magic. I straightened up, and couldn't see the gap on the other side of the pond anymore. I stared for a moment, then took a deep breath, stepped off the stepping-stone, and fell onto my hands and knees in two feet of water.

I came up spitting out a mouthful of weedy water. If I were a fire witch, I'd turn the whole damned pond into a cloud of steam. I stood for a moment in the water, cursing the Warlock and his asinine challenges. What was the point of all this, anyway?

I clambered back to the gap in the hedge, where Claire was struggling, without much success, not to laugh at me.

I said, "That does it. I don't care what it takes. We are going to get through these ridiculous challenges and we are going to see the Fire Warlock. If he sends us back home I'm going to demand that he use his magic to fix the rips in my dress, so I don't have to go home in disgrace."

"Lucinda, you can't do that."

"Why not? What would I have to lose?"

I could once again see the gap in the hedge on the far side of the pond. I was already soaked, how much worse could it get? Fixing my eyes on the gap, I charged out across the pond. Halfway across I slowed down, and strolled the rest of the way on stepping-stones.

I called back to Claire, "Here's the secret. You can walk on the stepping-stones across the pond, but you have to do it without looking down. You have to trust that they will be there. Keep your eyes on me all the way across. And you have to carry my bundle and cloak, too. I don't dare come back for them."

The rest was easy. We soon came out of the maze onto a path with no footprints, leading to the far door.

Claire said, "Was that one challenge, or two?"

"If that was two then we're done."

"Do you think?"

"Can't be. That was too easy, and we've not had the only challenge I was sure we'd meet on the Fire Warlock's path."

"What's that?"

I looked at the door and gulped. "A test of courage."

Going to Blazes

"How do we get up there?" Claire whispered.

We huddled together in the recessed doorway from the park. "I don't know," I whispered back. "There has to be an entrance somewhere."

A featureless wall dominated the view from the doorway. I stuck my head out from under the overhang, and got a good look. Arrow slits near the top, and flanking towers some distance away provided the only variety. By craning my neck, I got a glimpse of a second battlement-encrusted wall higher up and further in. The walls spanned the gap between two snow-laden shoulders of mountain extending out on either side. We were boxed in—easy prey.

If it noticed me, it would crush me like an ant, as it had crushed all other threats to Frankland for more than a thousand years.

Threat? Merciful Heavens, where had that come from? I was harmless. The Fortress protects women like me. Why should I be afraid of it?

Why shouldn't I be afraid of it? This stronghold was Frankland's shield; the rock all armies came to grief upon. The gates scattered all over the kingdom let the people of the land come with our requests and homage, but that was not their true purpose. They channelled all attackers, invaders and rebels alike, towards this place so that they must first attack here, no matter where the danger arose.

The castles in Rubierre's gentle river valley that had so awed me as a child were nothing compared to this. The fairy-tale castles that the nobles now built only for show, even the much older fortifications, now in ruins, were but toys, built of a child's blocks, which one could knock over with a sweep of a hand. We needed no standing army; we needed no other strongholds. Only scholars and Fire Guild enthusiasts remembered this castle's original name, Citadel de Fortunatus. To everyone else it was simply the Fortress, and had been so for centuries.

The mountain at its back frowned down at me. I had seen mountains before—insubstantial blue shapes in the far distance that stirred vague romantic yearnings, when I thought about them at all. If I served my year here, would I ever forget that a volcano—Storm King, the source of the Fire Warlock's inexhaustible power—loomed over me? The yearning it stirred was to run back in the park, and escape. White slopes faded into grey cloud with no discernible boundary, but even though I could not see the broken cone, that silhouette so familiar from the many drawings of this place, its hulking reality pressed against me. I was the phantom, not it.

I would have been disappointed if there had not been a test of courage on the challenge path, but this was not what I had expected.

I pulled my head back into shelter and shivered, pulling my cloak tighter under my chin. My wet dress would feel good in August, not April. We needed to move soon, my teeth were starting to chatter. Who knew that on my way to see the Fire Warlock, I risked freezing to death?

I edged further out, and gazed at the curtain wall, spellbound. No wonder we had been blessed with such peace while the forces of chaos swirled all around us, empires rose and fell, and our enemies coveted our lush pastures and wealthy cities.

Looking back, I realise I glimpsed many fragments, but not the complete picture. I did not yet understand the dangers that lay in its strength and rigidity, nor did I comprehend the human toll it took on the Warlock who served it, and not it, him.

Claire poked me in the arm. "Is that Blazes?" she said, pointing

I forced my attention down to earth. We were on the edge of a small rock-strewn meadow, perhaps a hundred yards wide, separating us from the base of the Fortress. A path led off to our right, and some distance away, a low, rough rock wall extended perpendicular to the Fortress, with a gate halfway between the Fortress and the park. Slate roofs on buildings of dressed grey stone peeked over the rock wall.

Blazes, the home of the Fire Guild. I quivered like a foxhound on a tight leash and the scent in its nose. Gladys had twice gone to Blazes, and had brought back fantastic tales. I wanted to see for myself the bubbling pools of mud, and the school with its rock walls and metal furnishings where young wizards and witches practiced setting and controlling fires.

Had the old witch been telling the truth in her stories about children keeping baby dragons for pets? Or about the fountain of boiling water that spouted so regularly you could set a clock by it? She must have made that up.

I said, "Yes, that has to be Blazes," and returned to studying the Fortress.

Claire said, "Maybe someone there can tell us what to do."

"I think we have to get through the challenges by ourselves."

"Do you have a better idea?"

"No."

"Then let's go." Claire gave the wall another wide-eyed stare, then squared her shoulders and set off down the path towards the gate.

My shoulders ached. I massaged them before following, my attention still on the looming Fortress. I had only taken a few steps before I was nearly startled out of my wits by a fierce roar. Claire screamed and turned to run back towards me. A brown mound I had taken for a boulder was a male lion, bounding towards us.

Run, hide! My heart was about to burst out of my chest, but I couldn't move. The lion was on the path to the gate. There was nowhere to hide, except back in the park.

Claire tripped and sprawled on the path. My world shrank. All that mattered was my terrified stepsister and the lion charging towards her. I raced towards them, screeching like a banshee, my cloak billowing in the breeze. I reached Claire seconds before the lion did. She was struggling to rise. I trod on her back, sending her face down again in the mud, and flung my only weapon at the lion. The bundle with the two heavy books hit him square on the snout. His roar changed to a yelp, and he stopped.

He's just a big cat. A cat—

I grabbed my cloak with both hands and held it as far over my head as I could reach, shaking it, and screaming all the while. The lion backed up a step, snarling.

Our cat, hissing and spitting, with back arched and fur puffed, had once scared away a bigger dog. If I ever got back to Lesser Campton, I would feed that cat all the cream it could eat.

I got off Claire's back. She rolled over and scrambled to her feet. I grabbed her by the arm before she could start running again and spun her around to face the lion. She screamed, and the lion backed another step.

"Hold your cloak up," I said. "Yell. Don't run." The lion, still snarling, paced a full circle and a half around us until it blocked the path back to the park with the maze. The gate to Blazes was standing open, with somebody watching us.

"Claire," I said, "we are going to walk—*walk*—to the gate. If we run we are dead."

I took a few steps forward, keeping a tight grip on Claire's arm. We reached my bundle, and I dived for it, coming up swinging. The lion backed away. We walked towards the gate, with the lion following twenty paces behind until we were within ten paces of the gate, where it turned its back on us and stalked away. The iron gate began to swing shut. We ran. I fell, rolling as I went through, and the gate clanged shut behind us.

I still half expected lion claws in my back. The rage that had carried me across the meadow evaporated and I lay face down in the grass, whimpering. The Fire Warlock doesn't kill his own supplicants. I had said that, hadn't I? Maybe not, but he'd done a bang-up job of scaring us half to death.

When I could move, I raised my head. Claire crouched behind a boulder, showing only wide eyes over top. I rolled, following her gaze, and fetched up at the feet of a red-haired, smiling giant.

I scrambled to my feet, ignoring a proffered hand, and attempted a deeper curtsey than I'd ever bothered with before, stammering, "Your Wisdom." My shaky legs gave way, and I fell on my rump in the grass. I should have known better—curtseying has never come easily to me—but I couldn't stop my cheeks from burning. So much for making a good first impression on the Fire Warlock.

The wizard grinned and doffed his hat. His mane was as big as the lion's. He made an elegant bow, rumbling, "Welcome, welcome. Congratulations on making it through all three challenges."

I whooped like a boy, and a warm glow settled in the pit of my stomach. Claire came out from behind her rock and made a deep, graceful reverence. He returned the salute with aplomb, then offered me a hand a second time.

I took it and let him pull me to my feet. My hands made a futile brush at my skirt, and I gasped. My dress was dry, and I was warm.

The wizard said, "You're not the first I've had to dry off after a tumble in the pond. Wouldn't want you to get sick. You're not the first, either, to call me 'Your Wisdom', but I'm not him."

"You're not? But…" I gulped, and stared. His Fire Guild emblem had more dancing flames than I had ever seen on one hat before. He wore an ordinary tunic and trousers, but the cloak slung over one shoulder had a silk lining and fur trim. His bushy beard had only a few streaks of grey. Of course. What was wrong with me? He was decades too young. The Warlock never left the Fortress, either. At least I'd get another chance to make a respectable curtsey.

The wizard smiled. "Let me introduce myself. I know who you are, the Guillierre sisters, Lucinda, and Claire," inclining his head to each of us in turn, "but you do not know me. I am Warlock Arturos, member of the Fire Guild Council, Practical Arts teacher, and Keeper of the Challenge Path. I am indeed a warlock—little a, little w, but not The—capital T, capital W—Warlock. I am an ambitious man and someday I may be the Warlock, but not yet, no, perhaps not for some time yet."

I looked up at his massive shoulders. Arturos. The bear? I am tall for a girl, but next to this man I was a midget. "Arturos sounds like an appropriate name for you."

His smile turned into a grin. "Ah, an educated young woman. Of course, Warlock Arturos is my war name. My parents named me Beorn."

I groaned, and his grin broadened. Claire looked confused, but she didn't ask for an explanation, as I would have.

I said, "Keeper of the challenge path? Then, that beast—"

"I hope my little pet—"

"Your pet?"

"—didn't frighten you too badly. One badly perhaps, since that is his job, but not two."

I couldn't suppress another groan, and he laughed. My "Thank you" as he took my bag was a reflex action. He hadn't commented on two girls coming together to see the Fire Warlock. He seemed more amused by us than angry, to my relief. An angry warlock would have frightened me more than the lion.

I pulled my cloak tight so my dress wouldn't show as we walked into town, even though getting the cloak clean was going to be a devil of a job. I had been filthy even before I rolled on the ground, and the grass sticking to the sap was hideous. What right did the Fire Warlock have to ruin my clothes? I'd like to give him a piece of my mind.

I gulped. I'd get my chance soon enough, and I couldn't even get up the nerve to growl at Warlock Arturos about his infernal pet.

Warlock Arturos ushered us into an imposing building in the centre of town. "The Warlock has other business this morning, and can't see you until after dinner. You've had a strenuous morning, but we have comfortable chairs and good food here at the Guild Hall, so you may as well relax until he's ready to see you."

He eyed Claire. "You can both get cleaned up, too."

I snorted. Claire looked, as ever, immaculate, not a hair out of place. It wasn't fair.

A brisk, middle-aged witch led us into a small room and started pulling brushes and other items out of a cupboard. "These brushes are enchanted. Use them to get the sap off."

I swiped my skirt. The sap hardened and crumbled as the brush touched it, falling to the floor like sawdust.

"Don't forget to brush your hair or your petticoats, and when you're done, sweep it all up and put it in this bucket. Here's salve for your scratches. When I come back, I'll take your measurements. We'll give you a new dress to replace this ruined one, even if he sends you home. Which isn't likely—he's a bit of a soft touch, the current one is—especially when it comes to girls," she said as she walked away.

A new dress? Girls? The Fire Warlock, a soft touch? I stood for a moment gaping. Then I recovered and ran after her. "Wait, wait! Other girls have walked the challenge path?"

"A few," she said. "Not often. It's been close to twenty years since the last one. Most girls go to the Earth Mother or the Frost Maiden. All the girls I know of who came here were fire witches whose talent wasn't identified early enough, or whose families wouldn't let them come to the school when they should've. He always sends them to do their year's labour in the school, learning how to use their talent and helping out with the younger children."

"I'm not a witch."

"I can see that. What he'll do with you, I have no idea."

Claire scrubbed at her face and clothes as if she'd rolled in the mud, and insisted that I give her back a good brushing. I shrugged. It seemed to make her feel better, and she brushed mine without complaint.

My anger at the Warlock crumbled to dust along with the sap as I brushed my hair. A glance in a mirror confirmed that my hair looked better after I got it pinned up again than it had when I started out in the morning. A new dress for one day's work? That was a bargain. Even if he sent us home, I'd done what no one else in Lesser Campton had ever attempted. The warm glow that had started in the pit of my stomach suffused my whole body. I felt as light as a bit of ash drifting up a chimney.

I was clean, and the room tidy, when the witch came back. She led us to a table in the hall and directed a young witch to bring us dinner. The food may have been excellent, but I didn't notice what I shoved in my mouth. Claire stared down at her plate and picked at her food, responding to everything I said with one-word answers. I stopped trying to talk to her, and examined the bas-relief frieze running around the interior of the hall—no flammable tapestries here—to take my mind off the impending interview.

After dinner, the witch suggested we wait by the fireplace. The dancing fire evoked memories of stories about the Fire Guild, and I relaxed. After a few minutes I was entranced, dreaming of glory waiting around every corner and danger lurking in every shadow. A hand dropped on my shoulder. I started up with a shout and fell over the footstool.

The big wizard caught me and set me on my feet with a grin. I followed him out of the Guild Hall with a hot face, praying I wouldn't embarrass myself in front of the Fire Warlock.

"No, I'm afraid there are no dragons here—pets, babies, or otherwise," Warlock Arturos said. "They're too dangerous for anyone, even the Fire Warlock, to keep as pets. Yes, the geyser shoots up a spray of steam and boiling water higher than my head every two hours and fourteen minutes, as regular as clockwork. Yes, all level two fire wizards and fire witches can walk through the flames unharmed. The spell for protection against fire is one of the first things we teach the youngsters, but only the most powerful—level fives—can use the fire to travel from one place to another."

I had dozens of questions about Blazes, the Fortress, the Guild. We got to the base of the Fortress long before I ran out of questions, and, thank God, before he ran out of patience. A gate at the right end of the curtain wall, closest to the town, stood open. Despite the cool air, I sweated, but the guardsmen on duty saluted the big wizard and let us through without a challenge. I walked at the wizard's heels through a tunnel dozens of feet long before coming out into the open air inside the walls. He led us over towards the mountain wall, where three parallel sets of steep stairs led up and out of sight.

Claire said, "Sir, how many flights of stairs do we have to climb?"

He grinned. "You don't have to climb any. After you," he said, gesturing for us to take the stairs. "Please hold onto the handrail."

Claire looked confused but stepped onto the first step, and let out a squeak, clutching at the rail, as the stairs began to move. I followed, and laughed as the stairs carried us up the mountainside. The wizard got on two steps below me. I still had to look up.

He said, "The stairs on the left go away from you, the stairs on the right come towards you, and the stairs in the middle do not move, so you can walk if you want to."

"Who would do that?" Claire asked.

"The Warlock usually does," the wizard said. Claire and I both stared at him.

"What? Why?" I asked.

He shrugged. "Says he doesn't get enough exercise otherwise."

What an absurd idea. I paused in my catechism and looked around. There was a roof over the staircase but no walls. Off to the left, the curtain wall sheltered stables and other buildings tucked into the side of the mountain. Above us, the second wall, further back, drew closer. We walked across a landing at the base of the wall, and rode the stairs on up. The Fortress rose up the sloped face of Storm King in tiers, not built onto ledges as other castles have been, but carved out of the solid mountain wall itself by the magic of the second great power, the Earth Mother, the Fire Warlock's staunchest ally. The windows, and the shutters hanging beside them, grew bigger, and my heart lighter, with each tier.

Why had I been afraid? I was safer here than anywhere else in Frankland.

We reached a tier as impressive in its opulence as the first tier had been in its stark defensive strength. Huge windows with shutters as big as barn doors and mouldings decorated in gold leaf hinted at large open spaces.

Ballrooms? A wide courtyard, covered in snow, sat at the base of this tier. A glassed-in section held trees in pots. Lemon trees? Oranges?

Overhead, the roof had changed from slate to glass. The clouds had lifted, and snow on the ramparts glittered in bright sunlight. Blazes and the surrounding forest dwindled beneath us, and a bare expanse of rough lava fields stretched out to the southwest.

I nudged Claire, and pointed, but after a quick glance over her shoulder she turned back to face the stairs, clutching the rails with both hands. I shrugged. She could miss the view if she wanted, but I wasn't going to waste my time being afraid.

At the base of the next tier, the wizard led us away from the stairs and waved us through a door, saying, "Please wait in here, the Warlock will be with you soon."

Claire trod on my heels as I stopped in the doorway and stared.

The Warlock

Would the Warlock let me in his library? My God, I never dreamed…
The room dwarfed any I had ever been in before, even the church
in Rubierre, and bookshelves covered every square foot of wall space.
Freestanding bookcases divided the space into smaller bays, uncrowded
tables and chairs in each one. My knees buckled and I grabbed onto the
doorframe. I could spend a lifetime—"What was that?"

"I can't see around you," Claire said. "Please move."

"Sure." Ahead of us, through an open doorway, a corridor stretched
off into the distance, with more bookshelves in the rooms beyond. My
father's collection would not have filled even one of the small bays.
When I had daydreamed about the fabled library at Alexandria, my paltry
imagination had not made it so—"Ow!"

Claire's second poke in my back had been much harder. "You're still
standing in the doorway," she said. "Move!"

I lurched towards the first bay, and came face to face with a bust of
Warlock Fortunatus, the first Fire Warlock. I curtsied, as a girl should on
meeting one of the four Officeholders, and did a decent job of it for once.
The fixed smile on Fortunatus's face beamed his approval at me.

I scanned the titles in the first bookcase, and my throat tightened. Σ,
Ω, π—it was all Greek to me. I moved on, and found a section with titles
in Latin. I had expected that, but it didn't help. I rounded the corner, and
gulped. I didn't even recognise the alphabet on the books shelved on the
back wall. Please, let there be books in Frankish here. Please?

Startled by a noise overhead, I looked up, and watched a man dressed
in scholar's robes scurry along a gallery above me, scanning the shelves.
He was intent on his search, and didn't appear to notice me.

I craned my neck and discovered, further up, a second gallery. I gawked at the arched ceiling, decorated with stars in gold leaf on a dark blue background. I turned in a circle, taking in a globe, charts, maps, alcoves in the outside wall with heavy curtains of dark red velvet, drawn back to let in the light from floor-to-ceiling windows. My eyes came back down to a shelf nearby, and I spied words in Frankish.

I flew towards the shelf. My first love, ancient history, welcomed me. There were books I had read, translations of works by Livy, Tacitus, and others I knew only by reputation. Thank you, I breathed aloud. I reached for a book by Pliny the Elder, then pulled my hand back, gasping at my own presumption.

And there—oh, glory—was Rehsavvy's *Roman Warlocks*, calling to me. I snatched my disobedient hand back, inches from the coveted book.

My pulse raced, and I trembled. I closed my eyes, but I could not undo that one glimpse. If only I dared take it off the shelf. I wouldn't even open it. I would run my hands... My hands were damp. That would never do. Never. I rubbed them on my skirt, and clasped them together behind my back, to keep them out of mischief. I would hold the creamy leather against my cheek, sniff the pages, and trace a light finger across the top, where minute flakes of gold leaf would decorate my fingertip like fairy dust... Enough of that.

I walked away with a tight chest, scanning the titles on other shelves. Where were the books on magical theory and practice? Father had said the Fire Warlock had a copy of every book ever written on magic. Every book ever written, more likely.

I came to the end of the first bay with my eyes still on the shelves, and almost walked into the young man standing there. I jumped back with an exclamation, made a shallow bob with a hasty "Excuse me," and walked on around him.

How long had he been watching me? Was that fur border on his silk robe sable? Somebody important, maybe even a prince. I swung back around with another exclamation, attempted a deeper reverence while still turning, and came close to falling on my face. He reached for me, but I grabbed the bookshelf and righted myself. I stammered, "I'm sorry, sir."

A handsome prince? Well, no. He was rather thin, not tall—I could look him in the eye—with black hair, dark eyes, and a clean-shaven plain face. I would not have given him a second glance if he had not been in fancy clothes.

He looked as if he was struggling not to smile, and my face, even my ears, got hot. At least he was polite. I would almost have preferred that he be offended, so I could justify being angry. I was tired of being embarrassed.

He said, "I am sorry I startled you. But now is not the time to lose oneself in books. Come." He turned and walked away without looking back.

Acted as if he owned the place. What was a nobleman doing here, anyway, and what did he want with me? Maybe Claire was right, I should have paid more attention to who was who in the upper classes.

I followed him towards the windows where Claire was waiting, noting the embroidery in silver thread on the black silk, and the heavy silver and opal belt. Wait, opals? But opals are Fire Guild tokens.

Claire turned at the sound of our footsteps and her eyes widened. She made a deep reverence, with more grace than I have ever managed, saying, "Your Wisdom."

My stomach dropped to my toes. The Fire Warlock. It couldn't be. My face went from hot to ice cold in an instant. I'd nearly ignored him? I'd wanted him to be offended? Oh, dear God.

Claire waited for him to come and raise her. I would have forgotten that nasty little bit of protocol even if I'd known who he was. He led us towards a small table with several chairs in one of the windowed alcoves. There was a silver tray on the table. We sat in the bright sunlight and poured tea.

The Warlock was ancient. This man looked younger than Warlock Arturos.

He picked up his cup and saucer, and the Token of Office of the Warlock of the Western Gate winked at me. I stared. I had seen illustrations of that ring: ornate, old-fashioned, with a gold dragon cradling an enormous ruby. The stone—the focus of the spells and bindings constraining and directing the Fire Office, and the conduit by which he could draw on the power of the volcano—sparkled, flashed, and glowed a velvety deep red. There could be no mistake, this was indeed the Fire Warlock. I clutched at the arms of my chair, and fought off dizziness.

The Warlock and Claire made small talk. I contributed only "Yes, sir" and "No, sir" in response to direct questions. Then he leaned forward to put down his cup, and moved out of the partial shadow cast by the telescope in the corner of the alcove. Direct sunlight hit the ruby; flashes of brilliant scarlet splashed across the table and dazzled my eyes. He leaned back, into the shadow, and the stone resumed its deep inner glow.

I breathed a drawn-out sigh. This was why the wealthy lusted after gemstones. Were the mundane stones they could buy, not lit by magic from within, one-quarter as mesmerising as this?

The conversation had stopped. I looked up. Claire was staring at the ring with her mouth half-open, cup in mid-air.

The Warlock said, "A fine spring morning is a good reason for a vigorous walk, but you did not come here by accident or whim. What do you wish of me?"

He addressed the question to me rather than to Claire. A flock of butterflies took wing in my stomach. I drew in a deep breath. How could I explain our errand without it sounding ridiculous? Father's stern voice admonished me, "Never, ever, lie to a warlock."

Claire's tea cup rattled on its saucer. "Your Wisdom, Father died before he could ensure good marriages for us, and there aren't any suitable young men nearby. I'm not resigned to being an old maid, even if my stepsister is."

I splashed tea onto my skirt. "I am not an old maid!" The Warlock's glance flicked to my face and then back to Claire's.

Claire said, "You know all the nobility and wealthy merchants in this kingdom. Will you please help me find a good match?"

I cringed, and fumbled for words, but something seemed to have control of my tongue.

The Warlock regarded her over steepled fingers for a few moments. "You are setting your sights rather high. Why should one of even the minor nobility consider you? And why you and not your sister?"

"Because I'm beautiful and Lucinda isn't."

Thank you, Claire, for pointing that out.

The Warlock's black brows drew together.

She smiled at him. "I need to marry a wealthy man so my beauty won't be ruined by the drudgery of housework."

The Warlock's frown deepened. I slumped in my chair, and wiped clammy palms on my skirt. Shut up, Claire. Please, just shut up.

He said, "This is a working fortress, not a pleasure palace. How do you intend to perform your year's service without some drudgery?"

"Oh, there isn't anything I can do for you, so I don't expect that you'll keep me. Lucinda can cook and do other housework. She can do the year's service for me."

I gasped. His glance flicked to me again. I met his eyes, and got a hint of the power he held in check. From his relaxed demeanour he could have been on a Sunday picnic, but his eyes were smouldering, and vividly alive.

He said, "While I agree your sister—"

"Stepsister," she said.

"Ah, yes, thank you for the correction. I agree that your stepsister will be a more interesting addition to my staff, and she should be encouraged to keep her distance from you, but it is a requirement that supplicants sacrifice a year's labour in return for my aid. If you are not willing to do so I cannot help you."

I stared at him. Me, more interesting than Claire? My heart leapt. Reason said, I don't believe it.

Claire smiled her most bewitching smile at him, the one showing the dimples. "I'm sure that's a minor difficulty."

The Warlock still looked relaxed, but his voice was stern. "Certainly not."

I sat up straight. Claire looked shocked.

He said, "It is a requirement of the Office, and not one I can change, so your attempt to enthral me with a glamour spell would be wasted even if I had no shield against it. You failed at the challenges I set. You are here only because you abuse your sister's, ah, stepsister's generosity, and as I expect you will similarly abuse any man you marry, I will not have that on my conscience."

A glamour spell? That would explain so much. Why had that never occurred to me? I wanted to believe it, but it made no sense. Father had had her tested for magical talent, too. She had none.

Two guards appeared, out of nowhere. "Guards, escort this young woman—" the Warlock ordered.

Was he dismissing both of us? I started to rise, but he waved a finger at me. "You, stay there." He turned back to the guards. "Escort her out of my presence before she becomes any more tiresome. She may wait by the stairs until I am done with her stepsister."

They took her by the arms, and she tried to shake them off, snapping, "How dare you? Get your hands off me!" They took no heed and marched her away, chittering like an angry squirrel.

I sank back into the chair, and stared at him, my stomach turning somersaults. A single rebuke from the Fire Warlock would hurt worse than all of Mother Janet's ineffectual scolding, but I deserved it.

The Warlock picked up his cup again, and waited until the clamour died away. "Now, my dear, what can I do for you?"

Requests

What could the Fire Warlock do for me?

I blurted, "Aren't you going to scold me for bringing Claire?" I bit my lip. I had been sorry, at the age of five, after I asked Mother why she hadn't punished me for biting the ferryman.

The Warlock said, "Berate you for falling victim to magic you have no defence for? That would be unworthy of me, surely? You succeeded; she did not. What do you wish for?"

That question again. I looked down at my shoes. "Your Wisdom, I know I shouldn't waste your time on something silly."

"Yours will not be the most ludicrous request I have heard in the past century. All who come this far have some strong purpose driving them, even if they cannot articulate it or it seems trivial to others. It is important to them, and that is what matters."

I looked up and met his eyes. They had been smouldering, but were now tranquil. He regarded me calmly over the rim of his cup as he took another sip.

"But, Your Wisdom, you make it sound as if the challenge path was an ordeal. Those challenges weren't as hard as I expected. Why?"

Both eyebrows shot upward. "Not hard? You do not consider a lion charging you a threat?"

"Well, of course it is, sir, but you have a reputation for being fair, not wicked, so you must have bewitched it to keep it from actually attacking us. The lion was supposed to frighten us back into the park, but if we went back in we'd have failed."

He smiled. "You are too clever by half. Did you see that when he charged you?"

"No, sir. Only the part about not going back in the park. He did scare me, and I wanted to turn and run. It was only after he stopped that I realised that was the purpose."

"So, you stood up to him even while you were frightened. You have courage. Now what of the other two challenges?"

"The maze was a test of clear thinking and trust, and the test with the guards was about dealing with people and having good manners. My grandmother always said that good manners were more about treating people with respect and putting them at ease than knowing which teaspoon to use."

"Quite so. It is remarkable how few people understand that. Your surmise is correct; the challenge path is easier now than in the olden days. If not, few nobles would succeed. Not that it seems to matter, too few these days have the drive or courage to come."

He sighed, and set down his cup. "The reputation alone is sufficient to filter out most commoners. For most supplicants, the biggest challenge is overcoming the fear, inertia, and self-doubt that afflict them before they even reach the gate. Commoner or noble, all who reach me are worthy of my attention.

"I studied your history this morning while you were in the park, and was displeased to find a scholar's daughter in such straits. You fit in among your uneducated villagers as well as a kestrel among pigeons. I am afraid your father has done you a great disservice."

Stung, I protested, "Father wasn't trying to spoil me by teaching me to read. He thought I was going to be a witch."

The Warlock waved that aside. "It is to your credit that you stand up for your father, but that is not the disservice I meant. When you were ten he should have taken you with him to the annual meetings of the Scholar's Guild in Gastòn. There you would have been introduced to, and evaluated by, the elders in the community, and you would have met the boys and young men who would now be your natural suitors."

Ten? My throat tightened. Father had not been able to take care of me as he had wanted in his last years, when he had been too ill. But that was after I turned twelve. He had still been able to travel when I was ten.

The Warlock said, "If the Scholar's Guild Council had known about you, they would have looked after your marriage prospects after your father died, but your father had a falling out with the Guild Council about that time, and never repaired the breach. Indeed, it seems that by the time you were twelve he had lost any interest in doing so. Did he not try to dissuade you from exercising your curiosity, whereas before he had tolerated it, if not actually encouraged it? And began to talk to you about marriage to one of the local farmers or tradesmen?"

"Yes, sir. Do you mean there are men who would be interested in me in spite of my education?"

"Not in spite of, quite the opposite. Many will be interested in you because you are clever and literate. You see, a man who wants to have intelligent sons must marry the most intelligent woman who will have him." He waved a hand towards the shelves of books. "The lore is quite clear about that. The councils of the magic guilds, as well as the scholars' and several other of the more intellectually challenging trades, are well aware of that, and search for promising young women to match up with their more ambitious young men. Indeed, I do not hesitate to speak for the other members of the Fire Guild Council in expressing our gratitude that you came here. It will be to our benefit if you marry one of our wizards.

"So you need not worry about that. Despite your advanced age of nineteen," he smiled, taking the sting out of his words, "I foresee no difficulty in finding you a husband who shares your curiosity and love of books." His smile widened. "If further inducement is required, marriage to either a scholar or a wizard will give you rights to most sections of your husband's guild library, history among them."

My fascination with the Fire Warlock bloomed into a full-blown case of hero-worship. If he had asked me to die for him, I'd have done it without hesitation. I would even have cut off all my hair if it would have helped him.

The Warlock waited while I scrubbed away tears and blew my nose. "That is not all you want. What else troubles you?"

Why did he think that? He had already given me more than I dared hope for. But if... Cravings I had not dared put into words blazed like a stirred fire. I closed my eyes for a moment. Mustn't be greedy, and one mattered to others beside me. "Your Wisdom, about Claire..."

A slight frown formed on his face. I got out in a rush, "Isn't there anything you can do for her? I'm sure she doesn't know what she's doing to herself by using a glamour spell. Couldn't you make her stop?"

This time the sigh was much longer and drawn out. He gazed out the window, his fingers drumming on the arms of the chair. I leaned back and took a deep breath. He didn't look angry. I made my hands let go of their death grip on the chair arms.

When he turned his attention back to me he asked, "How much do you know about basic magical theory? You have read the classic text, of course, Protin's *The Four Magics*, but—"

"No, sir, I haven't," I interrupted. He looked startled.

"Father had that, but he kept it locked up in the glassed bookcase with the other books on magic. Mother Janet sold those after he died, and I couldn't argue, since he had said it wasn't appropriate for me to read any of them."

The eyebrows shot upwards again. "Why ever not?"

I had asked Father that, more than once, and had never gotten a satisfactory answer. I swallowed my frustration. "I don't know, sir."

"What other books on magic did he keep with it?"

"There was a four-volume set, *Practical Healing Arts*, a fat one titled *Creative Cookery*, and quite a few smaller ones on potions and spells and the like."

"I see. He was prudent in keeping that lot locked up. Someone with latent talent and no understanding could cause quite a bit of damage with those. But I am surprised a scholar's collection should run so heavily towards the practical arts instead of the theory." He frowned briefly, then raised a wand—where had that come from? He hadn't had one over by the bookshelves. He made a small flicking motion in the direction of the topmost tier of shelves. A book flew off one of the shelves and dived towards us.

"There are gaps in your education. We must correct that."

The flying book made a graceful arc, slowed, and came to a stop, then settled into my lap. I touched the blue binding and it sprang open to the first page on its own. The strongest of the unexpressed cravings satisfied, a knot of tension in my neck and shoulders I had not known existed began to relax. The sunlight pouring in through the windows warmed me, body and soul.

"Here is your first reading assignment. I see little reason to lock up any of the theory texts. The worst reading that one could do is put you to sleep." The corner of his eyes creased into not quite a smile. "And you do need to know at least the basic theory to avoid causing trouble here."

I gulped. "Yes, sir. I don't mean to cause trouble, Your Wisdom. Thank you very much, sir."

The ghost of a smile deepened. "No, of course not, but you do anyway, just by existing."

I swallowed again. "I'm sorry, sir."

The Warlock's eyes danced. "Sorry? For existing?"

My face got hot. "No, sir. For causing trouble."

"You need not apologise for that either, but we have gone off on a tangent. You asked what I could do for your stepsister. I cannot do much without Claire desiring a change, and she has not demonstrated that desire. The principle is the fourth magic, the magic of the self-fulfilling prophecy. Without that, a powerful wizard can force a personality change on someone, but it amounts to soul murder. What is left afterwards is a body inhabited by something that is no longer quite human. I have never needed to do that. I hope I never do." The eloquent eyes were quite sombre.

I shuddered. "No, sir."

He smiled again. "Now, we have covered your education, your marriage prospects, your stepsister... Is that everything? No, I see by your expression it is not. What else? Come on, out with it."

How far could I push my luck? "Your Wisdom, all the old stories are about the adventures boys got to go on, but the girls had to wait for their knight to come rescue them. Why can't a girl have an adventure and see some of the world, too?" I bit my tongue. Did I just say that to the Fire Warlock?

He laughed, but he clearly did not mean it to wound, and I took no offense.

He said, "I cannot blame you for wanting adventure; I did at your age, and it is hard to deny that boys have more fun. But you do realise," he said, sobering, "that the boys in the adventures were more likely to be hurt, perhaps even die, than the girls?"

I said, "Except for the girls that were dragon bait."

"True, true. And further, the questers of both sexes that returned to tell their tales were the successful ones. You do not often hear about the young men that died on the attempt, or the girls who were not rescued by their heroes."

"Yes, sir."

He sighed. "In the span of a year in the Fortress there may be more than one opportunity for an adventure, and given your history I would have difficulty in keeping you out of it. We will let events take their course and see what comes your way. At the very least, you may visit several of the cities and meet a number of colourful characters. Whether that will satisfy you or only serve to whet your appetite remains to be seen. For the moment though, can you cook?"

Mrs Cole

Could I cook? At last, a question I could answer with confidence. "Yes, sir."

"Can you follow a recipe? Bake bread? Pies? Cakes?"

"Yes, sir. All of those."

"Excellent." The Warlock stood. "I seldom take on young women—they tend to be too disruptive to this predominantly male enclave—but we do need another cook."

A servant appeared, on cue. The Warlock said, "Casper, take Miss Guillierre to Mrs Cole, and tell her that she will be helping in the kitchen and will need a room."

I executed the most graceful curtsey I'd ever achieved, one even Claire would have pronounced acceptable. The Warlock's smile warmed me as I floated out of the alcove, hugging *The Four Magics* to my chest. Behind me, the Warlock murmured, as if to himself, "Cinnamon rolls with raisins and icing. Oh, that would be so nice."

I followed the servant to the moving staircase, where Claire was talking to Warlock Arturos. He listened with furrowed brow, stroking his moustache with one finger. Was she using the glamour spell on him? But hadn't he told her to clean up at the guild hall, when she had looked spotless to me?

Tears streaked Claire's cheeks. Claire, crying? She never cried in public. She often employed tear-filled eyes to get her way, but they did not spill over; red eyes and a blotchy face horrified her. I suspected that she did cry sometimes, but alone, where no one else would see the ugly after-effects.

Long-term use of a glamour spell wasn't healthy for anyone. Wasn't there anything I could do for her? I sighed. Who did I think I was, when even the Fire Warlock couldn't help?

I said, "Claire, are you all right?"

She nodded. "Did you get what you wanted?"

"Oh, yes. More than I ever hoped for."

She sighed. "I suppose I must tell Mother that you won't be back."

I winced. That was going to be a distressing scene. Claire would calm Mother Janet more easily than I could have, but it didn't seem fair that she would have to.

"And it will be a long walk home by myself. I'm not looking forward to it. My feet hurt already." She tried to laugh, but her lower lip trembled.

Arturos said, "You don't have to walk the whole way. I can take you as far as the Earth Guild house in Old Campton."

"Thank you, sir," she said, "I would appreciate that, sir."

She did look grateful, an emotion I didn't remember seeing often on Claire's face. I added my thanks.

"Claire, tell Mother Janet I'm sorry. When I come back…"

She looked surprised. "You won't come back. Not to stay, anyway. Why would you? I wouldn't."

She was right. Given the Warlock's assurances, I would probably not be going back there to live, but Mother Janet had tried her best, and I didn't want to offend her.

I swallowed hard. "There's a letter on the desk in the study listing Father's law books." I had to pause and swallow again. "Send it to the clerk in Rubierre. He'll know where to go to get a good price for them."

Claire's eyes were enormous. "Oh, Lucinda. I'm sure Mother will be pleased. I know how much the books mean to you."

Arturos nodded at me, and after offering Claire his arm, drew a circle of flame in the air around the two of them with his wand. As soon as the circle was complete, the fire roared up in a column chest high.

I bumped into Casper as I reeled backwards, away from the flames. "Oh, I'm sorry."

"No need to apologise. I've been here ten years and it still makes me nervous when they do that."

Claire and Arturos had vanished. I was shocked that I felt bereft.

The flames had left a minute ring of ash on the stone floor. I eyed it as I followed Casper onto the stairs.

I forgot about Claire as soon as Casper introduced me to the cook. Mrs Cole was a plump, grey-haired witch with square spectacles and a laugh like a twittering sparrow. She reminded me of my grandmother, and I warmed to her on the spot. She didn't seem to mind my questions, and chattered away down three flights of stairs and along several seemingly endless corridors.

"I'm the housekeeper and chief cook, you see, but the place nearly runs itself. Long ago, we started building up spells that would do as much of the work as possible without supervision, and since they're all stable, it keeps the magical noise level down to a low hum. Jacques, the caretaker, Master Sven, the tutor, and I are the only magical staff here, and frankly, Jacques and I are as much house parents as we are caretaker and cook. There are only a half-dozen others, all non-magical, for this whole huge place."

"Why?" I asked. "I knew it was mostly empty. I read about the guild members moving out of the Fortress and building Blazes during the reign of the sixth Fire Warlock, but the histories didn't say why."

"Because of the interference with the spells for looking for trouble. When the Fortress was built, they thought the Guild and the school would be here even in peacetime, but with all those wizards and witches, the magical activity going on right under his nose blinded the Fire Warlock, so to speak. You would think that somebody would have noticed before they all moved in here, but no, and three of the first five Fire Warlocks died in surprise attacks before they figured out what the problem was. So, we built Blazes, and put a shield over it to protect his eyes and ears.

"Don't they move in here when there's a war?"

"Yes. The Fortress is big enough that every fire wizard and witch in the country, and all their families and relations and servants, can fit in, but it still gets crowded, or so I've heard. The last war was before my time. If the rumours are true, we might have to deal with a siege while you're still here. I hope not!" She shuddered.

That was the second time today someone had talked about war as if it was coming soon. Would I get to see the Fire Warlock call down the lightning? I shivered.

Mrs Cole waved her hand. "Enough of that. That's months away, at least. The only people living here now, besides the staff, are the guards and their families in the bottom tiers, visiting scholars and supplicants in the middle, and Himself all alone up at the top."

"If the castle runs itself why does he want a cook? Or need any servants?"

"Cooking is one of the few things we haven't figured out how to set up spells to do completely for us, especially since folks want some variety in their diet. Cooking is still an art, depending on the type and quality of the ingredients available, and some things—like baking—depending almost as much on the weather as anything else. Most of the actual work can be done magically, but somebody has to keep an eye on things, and make decisions about what to fix, which seasonings to use, and so on.

"And then, too, we're a bit old-fashioned and frugal here. The spells that run by themselves draw on the volcano, so that's no problem, but any magic that Jacques or I do drains our reserves. The ideas that you mundanes have about witches and wizards sitting around all day waving our wands are nonsense. There's usually a fairly steady stream of supplicants to help out. Several of them work in the pantries and get food brought up from the town, but I've been doing the cooking by myself here for a few months, and it will be good to have a young pair of hands helping in the kitchen again. Especially as I've had to pretty much cut out cakes, pies, and the like, and the Warlock does have a bit of a sweet tooth. Now here's the kitchen." The kitchen was large enough to feed Rubierre. The fireplace, big enough to roast a flock of sheep, dwarfed two pots of soup bubbling away over a small fire. I walked over to the fireplace and gawked. Warlock Arturos would be able to stand upright inside it.

Mrs Cole said, "I should warn you. The kitchen is the only place in this part of the castle where there is always a fire burning, so Himself will sometimes come out of the fireplace on his way to somewhere else. He used to do it all the time, but he doesn't do it as much now since one helper I had screamed and dropped a platter of ham on the floor. She said she thought it was Old Nick himself. Humph." She added "Idiot woman" under her breath.

I shivered. Tales of demons and wicked wizards striding out of the fireplace intent on doing harm were all too common. He seemed kind, but if he came out of the fireplace towards me, I might panic, too.

Mrs Cole talked about the daily routine as she showed me where things were. "You and I will need to get up early to start breakfast. Then as soon as that's out of the way, we'll start working on dinner, which is promptly at one o'clock. We also have to start some soup, and figure out what else should be put out along with it for a light supper—bread, cold meat, cheese, fruit, and so on. The kitchen will take care of putting it all out on the buffet, and everyone helps themselves to supper whenever they want. So, we're through by dinnertime. You can do whatever you want for the rest of the day.

"The Earth Guild's burn treatments are in this cupboard. Do you know how to use them?"

"Yes, ma'am. I would be scared to work in a kitchen that didn't have them."

"Good. That's sensible of you. Now let's go find you a room. We'll put you up with the staff, around the corner from me. It wouldn't do to have a chick as pretty as you down by the barracks or in with all the male supplicants and scholars."

The room she led me to was five times as big as my attic room at home, with a bed big enough to sleep four. I was turning circles in the centre of the room when she called me into the tiled closet next door. It had a large basin built into the floor, and when she turned a knob, hot water gushed out of the wall and began to fill it. My knees almost gave out. I had heard of such marvels, but had never expected to see them.

"You mean I can take a bath every day if I want to? And where does the hot water come from?"

She smiled. "You can bathe twice a day if you want to. We're living on Storm King, remember? Getting hot water piped in is no problem; there's plenty of it in a volcano. The part that impresses me is the magic that filters out all the sulphur and other nasties. If it didn't, this bath would stink to high heaven."

As I soaked in a tubful of hot water that night, I recalled my interview with the lieutenant in Rubierre, and laughed. Hard work? When all I had to do was cook for a few hours every day? I'd fallen into the lap of luxury. I fell asleep in the most comfortable bed I'd ever been in.

I had no forewarning that I would wake in the wee hours, disoriented and thrashing in the bedclothes, too short of breath to scream. I had dreamed that the Office of the Western Gate, looming like Storm King overhead, held me in thrall as its shadow advanced, seeking to blot me out. As it had blotted out all other threats to Frankland for more than a thousand years.

René and Master Sven

Mrs Cole knocked on my door early the next morning with her arms full of clothes: two new dresses, a shawl, an assortment of undergarments, a comfortable pair of shoes, and the promise of another summer dress to come.

All this for me? Servants in our district got an allowance for two changes of clothing a year, and only the wealthiest of women had more than four decent dresses. The clothes were well made of sturdy fabric, but quite plain, not at all fashionable. Claire would have been disgusted. They suited me to a T. I stammered out my thanks.

She smiled. "Magic does have its advantages. And don't think this is special for you. We fix up all the supplicants so that you can't tell whether somebody had been a farm hand or a prince by looking at them. You can tell, perhaps, when they open their mouths and start talking, but not by their clothes."

"Why?"

"Everyone comes here looking for a fresh start. Having decent clothes helps get them into the right frame of mind, and keeps other people from jumping to conclusions about them. Or if it's a noble, looking like everybody else means he has a harder time lording it over other people.

"You were in better shape than a lot of people who arrive here, you know, in having a change of clothes with you, but I'm afraid that threadbare dress wouldn't have done for dining with Himself and the scholars."

"Dining with him?" I squeaked, and sat down hard on a chair.

"Oh, yes, honey. You and all the other supplicants and visiting scholars, and Himself, and me—we all sit down and have dinner together. Of course, he doesn't get to dine with us every day, but he wants to know how the scholars are getting on, and what you youngsters are up to. It's his way of keeping an eye on how everybody's doing."

I followed her to the kitchen with butterflies in my stomach, but once there she kept me so busy I had no time to think about making a good impression at dinner, and I forgot to worry. I had never before worked in a kitchen that fed so many people, but the basic breakfast was something I could do well, and I enjoyed the bustle.

As soon as breakfast was over, we plunged straight in to working on dinner. Mrs Cole chattered away while we worked, and I paid no attention to the time. I was startled when the Warlock himself walked into the kitchen a few minutes before one o'clock.

"Good day, Lucinda. Good day, Rose. How is your new helper working out?"

"Quite well, Your Wisdom," Mrs Cole said. "If she keeps going like she's started I'll be sorry to see her go when her year is up." She turned to me. "Now, honey, it's time for you to take off your apron and head on into the dining room."

The butterflies came back. Despite the apron, I had gotten flour on my new skirt, and I suspected I had flour on my face as well; a suspicion only deepened by the arching of one of the Warlock's eyebrows and the twitching of the corner of his mouth. My attempt to brush the flour off my skirt only spread it further.

Mrs Cole said, "Don't worry, dear," and flicked her wand at me. The flour disappeared.

The Warlock said, "Much better," and gestured to me. The Fire Warlock was offering me his arm? I didn't move.

He said, "Despite the stories, I do not bite, or at least, not often."

Mrs Cole winked. "And if he does, we have the Earth Guild cure for rabies on hand." I goggled at her.

He took my hand and placed it on his arm. "More to the point, one never gets a second chance to make a first impression. You will begin on a sounder footing with the rest of the menagerie if you let me escort you in and introduce you than if you try to slip in unnoticed by yourself. It would not work anyway."

"Yes, sir. Menagerie?"

"Not literally, of course," he said, as we walked down the corridor, "but when an otherwise distinguished and urbane scholar is jealous of

62

another's work he can give the impression that he is a wild animal going for the other's throat. That was what I dealt with this morning, sad to say."

The doors at the end of the corridor opened by themselves and we walked on through. The three dozen or so men in the antechamber to the dining room watched us walk in. A tall, fair-haired man with a neat beard caught my eye and I stared. Now there was a handsome prince. He met my gaze and bowed.

"Gentlemen," the Warlock said, "it is my pleasure to introduce to you Miss Lucinda Guillierre, our most recent supplicant."

They bowed, in varying degrees of elegance and depth, and most of the glances seemed either curious or appreciative, although a few seemed hostile. I looked around at the scholars, but aside from the fair-haired man who'd quickened my pulse, there were so many I could not begin to distinguish one from another. Claire would have been in her element. I tightened my grip on the Warlock's arm. I hoped I could get through this without blushing. I had embarrassed myself too many times yesterday.

"Miss Guillierre will be assisting Mrs Cole in the kitchen, for the nonce. Master Thomas, Master Sven, René, please join us at the head of the table."

The Warlock led me through the crowd and into the hall, where he seated me to his right before sitting himself. A stocky, older man wearing a scholar's robe sat down on my right. One of the supplicants I had seen that morning working in the food stores, a boy, about eleven or twelve years old, filled the seat at the Warlock's left, directly across the table from me. The man who had caught my attention in the antechamber sat down next to the boy. He smiled at me, and I fumbled with my fork, flustered.

The Warlock said, "There are no assigned seats at this table, and I encourage all of my guests to move around so that I have an opportunity to talk to them all and no one is slighted. However, for today, I specifically wanted you to meet these three gentlemen. Starting with Master Thomas." He indicated the scholar to my right, who nodded and smiled.

"Master Thomas is a librarian on the castle's staff. He will help you find whatever you need there."

Whatever I need? As if I was a scholar? *Roman Warlocks* called to me, and I didn't even need the librarian's help to find it.

The Warlock indicated the younger man. "Master Sven's stated ambition is to become his generation's preeminent mage."

Being designated a mage—one of the select group of top-ranking talents who were also distinguished scholars—was a high honour. I would have been interested in a prospective mage if he had been fat, fifty, and bald. The fact that he was young—late twenties?—and the most attractive man I had ever seen made my heart flutter.

The Warlock said, "Since I believe that the best way to ensure one's own mastery of a subject is to teach it to another, I have employed Master Sven to tutor supplicants, such as yourself, who need a better grounding in the theory and history of magic."

He indicated the boy to his left. "René is one of the youngest supplicants to ever arrive here."

The boy stared at me curiously. I tore my eyes away from Master Sven to return the stare.

"René has magical talent, but for reasons that we need not go into," the Warlock shot me a piercing look and I understood the message: none of my business, so don't ask, "he is studying magical theory here in the Fortress rather than the practical arts at the guild school in Blazes.

"You will be done with your work in the kitchen after dinner, Miss Guillierre, so I encourage you to spend your afternoons either in the library or in the classroom with Master Sven and René."

"Yes, sir," I breathed. "Thank you, Your Wisdom."

"Hey," the boy René said. "A girl? Can she keep up?"

The Warlock frowned at him. "René, where are your manners?"

René said, "Oh, sorry, sir." He scowled at me. "Can you keep up?"

The Warlock groaned and hid his face in his hands. Master Sven seemed to be trying to kick the boy under the table

I said, "You haven't given me any reason so far to think that I couldn't."

The Warlock winked at me through his fingers, and Master Thomas said "Touché."

Master Sven said, "Please forgive my young friend. He isn't normally either so rude or so dense. I don't know what his problem is today. If he were older I'd ascribe it to being flustered at sitting across from a pretty girl."

My cheeks got hot. For the first time I could remember, I didn't curse my face for blushing at the slightest provocation.

The Warlock said, "No, he does not want your time with him encroached on, and has had so little exposure to anyone, male or female, who is as intelligent as he is, that he assumes the worst of everyone he meets. However, having her study with you will be good for him as well. René, what did I say about Master Sven's labours?"

"The best way to learn a subject is to teach it to someone else?"

"Exactly. Therefore, I challenge you to make sure that Miss Guillierre does keep up, by assisting with the teaching when and where you can." Looking at René with a baleful eye, he continued, "She has passed through the same three challenges you did, one of them with rather more cleverness than you exhibited. Everyone at this table has earned the right to be here. I beg you to remember that."

The boy scowled, and studied me in earnest.

The Warlock turned towards Master Thomas. "There are others here as well who could use a gentle reminder of that fact. I think you know which ones."

"Yes, Your Wisdom, I do. I will see to it."

The Warlock changed the subject, and I was glad for the reprieve. After all the years with Claire, I was not accustomed to being the centre of attention. He had given me much to ponder, too. I was flattered and exhilarated that not only was he giving me access to his library and a tutor, he was actually encouraging me to use them.

On the other hand, the Warlock's interactions with the boy René laid to rest any notions I might have had that I was unique. It was evident that the Warlock enjoyed his role as master teacher, and that he had had many such students over the years. I would need to be careful not to let his attention go to my head.

Settling In

Master Sven handed out assignments to his other students with a lack of fuss, then sat down across a table from me and interrogated me far more thoroughly than the Fire Warlock had done. My familiarity with Frankish literature was pronounced limited but sound, my knowledge of magic judged inadequate and the other sciences little better, but I was only a third of the way through the list of histories I had read when he stopped me with a whistle.

"I may have to appeal to you as the expert on ancient history. You don't need to read any more—"

"But, but, sir, I saw several books in the library I want to read—"

"Don't look so alarmed. If they appeal to you, I'd be the last to stop you. I'm only suggesting you spend more time on other subjects to become well-rounded. You've got a good foundation."

He left me reading *The Four Magics* in a state of warm contentment, and made the rounds of the other students, answering questions, and steering back in line those who had gone astray. He came back to me an hour later, and gave a satisfied nod over the progress I had made. When he dismissed us, I lingered, but after giving me a smile and saying "You're off to a good start," he walked away with his nose in a book.

I watched him go with mixed feelings. He'd treated me the same way he'd treated his male students—with patience, competence, good humour, and a lack of condescension. That was good.

On the other hand, he'd treated me the same way he'd treated his male students. That was too bad. Even without Claire around, was I still going to have trouble getting a man's attention?

I gave myself a mental shake. There was less than an hour of daylight left, and I was wasting time. I picked up my skirts and ran to the library. I pulled *Roman Warlocks* off the shelf, but hesitated for a moment, stroking the soft leather. I was among friends, both old and new, and it seemed fitting to acknowledge the presence of the others. I ran a finger along the edge of the shelf, and looked around at the library. I had never seen this place before yesterday, but I had come home.

I carried the book to a window seat, and settled down to read.

The feeling of being at home grew as I learned my way around and settled into the daily routine in the Fortress. I'd only been there a week when Mrs Cole said, "You don't need me looking over your shoulder. You do the baking and I'll take care of the mains. Fix whatever you like for dessert." The storerooms held every flavouring I'd ever wanted to taste, and many I'd never heard of. In spare moments in the mornings I drooled over Mrs Cole's recipe books, making lists of new things to try.

I got to know nearly everyone—scholars, supplicants, staff, and guards—and no one seemed offended that I claimed a window seat in the library as mine.

It was only late at night that I felt ill at ease. I wanted another girl to talk to. I confess I missed Claire. Why had the Fire Warlock sent her away? He had said why, hadn't he? It nagged at me, but I whenever I struggled to remember what he'd said, I fell asleep.

More alarming, the sense of suffocation that I had expected to lose once out of Lesser Campton got worse. A few times I dreamed that I was trapped in a glass cage. I woke gasping for air, frantic that time was running out.

I didn't tell anyone about my dreams or feelings of suffocation. They seemed so silly in the bright daylight, and I would have been mortified if the Warlock had thought I was ungrateful for what he had given me.

I didn't sit at the head of the table with the Warlock again for several weeks, but two or three days a week I would look up from my work and discover him talking with Mrs Cole. I soon realised that it was part of how he kept abreast of the scholars and supplicants. Mrs Cole would frequently have something to tell him, in low tones that I couldn't overhear, and he would stroll away looking thoughtful. He never seemed to be in a hurry, and would usually stop and ask how I was doing.

One morning I was struggling to get cake pans in the oven on time, and the bread smelled about to burn. Out of the corner of my eye I glimpsed someone in servant's livery come into the kitchen and stand by the door, watching. Over my shoulder I said, "You there, if you're not busy, could you please put the cakes in the oven?"

I ran to rescue the not-yet-burnt loaves and put them on the cooling racks. I turned back, and stopped dead. The Warlock, dressed as a servant, was putting the last cake pan in the oven. I stammered an apology.

He smiled. "Since I dressed as a servant this morning to pass unnoticed where a warlock would not be welcome, I can ill afford to take offense when I am treated as one. You were more polite than several others who ordered me around today."

I said, "But you didn't have to do what I said."

"I may not have to, but I should. When I am dressed as a servant I should act like one, using the fourth magic to help me seem like a servant, you see. And the magic is stronger if you or anyone else treats me according to the way I am dressed. If I make a mistake in the Fortress and ignore an order, it is not a serious problem, but it could be somewhere else. Besides, I am in no hurry, and I will enjoy having cake for dessert, too."

"Why did you need to pass unnoticed? No one in their right mind would attack you, would they?"

He raised a sardonic eyebrow. "No, but few welcome my attention. How do you think the king would react if I asked to speak to his servants?"

"Oh. I guess he'd throw a temper tantrum."

"Indeed. There are many among the nobility that wish they could bar the door to me, but would not dare. However, even though they would reluctantly let me in, that would not serve my purpose. I was after information, and servants talk more freely to other servants than to warlocks."

"I thought you had other ways to gather information, and never left the Fortress."

"There are a number of ways. Talking to people is only one of several, but it is one of the best for keeping a finger on the nation's pulse. Besides, if I did not venture out at regular intervals I would go mad. Can you imagine being trapped inside this pile for a century? You would not like it either."

"I could spend ten years in the library without ever needing to leave."

"Oh? Then why were you not there instead of in the midst of that snowball fight between the supplicants and the guards?"

I started. "Oh! Sir, I am sorry about Scholar Ebenezer's thesis getting soaked, but he wasn't paying attention to what was going on, and walked right into the middle of it."

He leaned across the table towards me, his eyes dancing, and said quietly, "I could have fixed it for him easily enough, but that version had serious problems. I had been trying for weeks to get him to tear it up and start afresh. He may not thank you, but you have done him a great service."

"Yes, sir. Thank you, Your Wisdom."

"And if you did spend all your time in the library I would tell Master Thomas to chase you out occasionally. Everyone needs exercise now and then."

Warlock Arturos was a frequent dinner guest. He came on business with the Fire Warlock and stayed to talk with René, sometimes until late afternoon. After watching them a couple of times, I invited myself to sit with them and listen. The big warlock's grin made up for the boy's dirty looks.

"Another student?" Arturos boomed. "Good, maybe you can help me knock some sense into this young whippersnapper's head."

"Me? What about, sir?"

"About control. He wants to talk about power; I want to talk about control. Listen René, they have to go together. Power without control is dangerous, like trying to fix a broken clasp on a lady's necklace with a sledgehammer. Control without power is ineffective, like using a pocketknife to cut down an oak tree. A good Fire Warlock combines power with control so that he can run the whole gamut. A great Warlock, like the current one, uses the minimum power needed to do the job, and makes both extremes look equally easy."

René said, "If he's so great, why haven't I ever seen him do anything?"

Arturos smacked the table with his fist. Sparks flew and I jumped. "Burn it, René, you ought to know better than that. The Warlock's office is all about control. Most wizards and warlocks struggle to conjure up enough magical energy to do what they want. But the Warlock can tap into Storm King. His biggest challenge is tamping down the energy he brings to bear on a problem so that he doesn't overwhelm it. How many stories are there about some Fire Warlock trying to solve a small problem and burning it and everything else for five miles around?"

"Hundreds," René said.

"And how many of them have died from calling up more power than they could control, and being burnt up themselves along with everything around them?"

"Uh, most?"

"Good, I'm glad you understand that. The Warlock's power is dangerous, and the person in most danger is the Warlock himself. The Office wants a young man who isn't yet set in his ways, while also wanting a man old enough to have some sense about when to use the power. We were lucky this time to get a young mage in the Fire Office. That's why he's lasted as long as he has. Most of what he does is keep control of situations so that they don't blow up and require him to fix them."

I said, "So the better the Fire Warlock is, the less we see him doing anything?"

He grinned at me. "A star student." René glowered.

Arturos said, "You don't see what he does, but I do, and I'm in awe of him. Most Officeholders haven't been able to switch into that frame of mind. They have all that power to work with, and still act like they need more.

"I want you to understand something," he said, speaking slowing and enunciating each word carefully. "When, or if, I become the Fire Warlock, I will fear for my life every time I draw on Storm King. Plenty of ignorant people will think that because I'm flashier, I'm a better Warlock than Warlock Quicksilver. And they will be wrong." He emphasised the word wrong with a thump on the table. "Maybe towards the end I'll approach his level of control, and those folk will think I'm losing my touch. But I won't care. I will be proud."

Later, when I recounted this conversation to Mrs Cole, she snorted. "The person in most danger is Himself, is he now? Well, maybe that's true a lot of the time, but I don't think either Nicole or Terésa would agree with that, would they?"

I knew about Nicole and Terésa, of course. The two tragedies were the basis for our greatest works of poetry, drama, and art. Every villager had seen the plays put on by the travelling troupes of actors, or heard the bards singing. About Nicole, the young peasant girl who had dared to love the third Fire Warlock, and who died in the flames of passion on her wedding night. And about Terésa, the fire witch who thought her shields would protect her, but who fatally misjudged the fierce heat of the volcano.

To me, Nicole seemed so naïve, so passive—a minor character in her own story. I had always preferred the story of Terésa, the fire witch, who was as inflamed by passion as her warlock. She had gone after what she wanted. That was a woman I could look up to.

I shivered. There was no point in following that train of thought. Like René, I wanted to see the Warlock use his magic, but Arturos was right. Far too many of the old stories ended in death and destruction. The Fire Warlock's kindness and urbane sophistication was a veneer over a primal power I could only begin to guess at. I did not want to see that veneer stripped off. At some gut level, I knew that if I ever stopped being afraid of him, I could find myself in mortal danger.

Studies

A polite cough was followed by, "Excuse me, Miss Guillierre."
I looked up from Mrs Cole's cookbook. One of the more quiet scholars stood by the kitchen door, twisting the hem of his sleeve.

"Yes? Scholar Andreas, isn't it?"

"Yes, miss." He coughed again. "Those cinnamon rolls were wonderful, and so were the cream puffs."

That sounded rehearsed. Had he never spoken to a woman before? "Thank you. I'm glad you liked them."

"Master Thomas said you made the cream puffs after he suggested them, and I was wondering…"

I had been trying out new recipes—breads, pastries, pies, cakes, and sweets of all sorts. The throng at dinner gobbled up with delight even the experiments I considered dismal failures. And now men who had never set foot in the Fortress kitchen before were coming looking for me. Bless you, Mother, for teaching me to cook.

I smiled at the scholar. "There's something you would like me to make?"

"Yes, miss. If you don't mind. My mother used to make these little cakes with walnuts, and I…"

"Chopped fine, and sticky with honey?"

"Yes, miss." He was almost drooling.

I'd seen a recipe for them. I flipped back through the pages. "I can make those, but they'll cost you."

He took a step backwards. "Cost me?"

"Yes. You'll have to sit here in the kitchen while I make them, and tell me what you're working on."

His eyes widened, and he edged towards the door. "You wouldn't be interested."

"Try me. You'd be surprised what I'm interested in."

After listening to him stammer through half-a-dozen false starts, I made out he was working on a revised classification scheme for spells. That was timely. I had flown through the basics of magical theory in a few weeks, so Master Sven had directed me to study spellcraft with René. Reading about the individual spells was fun; understanding where they fit was not.

I said, "I hope you're going to make it easier to understand. The scheme we've got now looks like somebody mashed together work by two people interested in different things."

The scholar gawked. "You know? It was three, actually. I started from first principles to make a new system that's coherent and obvious even to a layman."

Well. He might be shy around women, but there was nothing diffident about that. I pulled out mixing bowls and spoons. "I am interested. Talk. And sit down, you're going to be here a while."

A couple of hours later, the hoarse, beaming scholar left the kitchen with a plateful of warm pastries, and a stern order from Mrs Cole to not eat them all before dinner and spoil his appetite. I was enlightened, on more than one subject: the structure of spellcraft, and how to entice a scholar. Ample reward for a morning's easy labour.

"My dear…"

I dropped a bowl. The Fire Warlock caught it and handed it back to me. "I beg your pardon. I did not intend to startle you."

"No harm done, Your Wisdom." Did he have to sneak up on me like that? Fire wizards were supposed to be loud, but he was as quiet as a cat on the prowl. "Did you want something, sir?"

He reached for one of the cakes. "One of these, if I may. And to commend you for feeding the scholars' souls while feeding our bodies and your own curiosity. Well done, my dear."

The scholars on either side of me at dinner asked what I was smiling about, but I shook my head and didn't answer. When René asked the same question in the classroom, I had an answer ready. "One of the scholars described a new classification scheme to me, and it's a lot better than the old one. It works like this—"

"What do you think you're doing? I'm supposed to be teaching you."

"Do you understand the classification scheme?"

"Well, no, but—"

"Then listen, will you? This new scheme—"

"It doesn't make sense. You—"

"How do you know? You haven't even let me explain—"

"Not the classification rubbish. I meant it doesn't make sense that you're not a witch. You've got to be one. You wouldn't be so interested in magic if you weren't."

"I am not a witch. A wizard tested me and said I have no talent. Will you please get that through your head?"

"You keep saying that—"

"Every day for the past month. You're making me wish I could be one, so I could flame you and make you shut up. Now let's get back to the new classification scheme. Will you listen?"

"New classification scheme?" Master Sven sat down beside René. "You've been talking to Scholar Andreas."

"Yes, sir. His scheme makes so much more sense."

"Does it? Explain it to me."

I talked. René doodled, and appeared uninterested, but when I finished, he looked up and said, "You are annoying. It's bad enough that you're a mundane, and then you had to go and be a girl, too. You're not supposed to make sense."

Master Sven laughed. "Are you worried she's going to catch up with you? She picked up a lot about magic from all the history she's read. She might catch up, if you're not careful."

Might? Hah. Will.

René said, "Fine. I get the point. But about this new system, can we use it?"

"It is tempting, isn't it? But no, you have to know the old one. I prefer the new taxonomy, too, but there's not a snowball's chance in a volcano it will be adopted."

"Why not?" René and I said together.

"Why not?" Master Sven's voice rose. "Because this is Frankland, and nothing ever changes in Frankland. We'll keep on using the old one because that's what we've been using for centuries, and if it was good enough for our ancestors, it's good enough for us. Change is dangerous and frightening, and we don't want it. The way it was is the way it always will be. So be it, amen."

He leaned back in his chair, flushed and breathing hard. We stared at him. He had always been so calm and cool I had begun to wonder if he really was a fire wizard, but there had been plenty of heat in that outburst.

"All right everybody, I'm done. Get back to work." The other students gave him furtive glances over their shoulders before turning back to their own papers.

"Sorry," he said. "I shouldn't have vented like that. Forget I said anything."

I said, "It's not true that nothing ever changes in Frankland. The aristocracy has been in decline for, oh—"

"Centuries. True, but not comforting. Our class structure and legal systems are ossified, the obsolete treaties our hidebound diplomats insist on are killing our trade, our—"

René said, "So why doesn't the Fire Warlock do something? Especially about treaties. He can do anything."

I said, "Not so. The Fire Office limits what he can do."

Master Sven said, "And he has to work with the other three Officeholders, and they don't always cooperate. The Air Enchanter, for example. The sixtieth Fire Warlock tried to make some changes…"

I fidgeted. Showing interest in a scholar's knowledge was easy when he was talking about something I didn't already know, like spellcraft. But I could have done as good a job of retelling this story.

"…and so the Air Enchanter showed he could be as stubborn as a warlock. After getting nowhere for five years, the Fire Warlock gave up."

"Wait," I said, "the Enchanter wasn't being stubborn. He didn't have any choice. The Air Office wouldn't let him."

"If he had been amenable, the Fire Warlock could have overruled the Air Office."

"Only on matters of the country's security, and that obviously wasn't."

Master Sven's voice sharpened. "The Fire Office is the strongest of the four. Cooperation makes for more potent magic, but the Fire Warlock can force the others—"

"Nonsense. If he could, he'd have fixed the broken legal system centuries ago."

Sven glared at me. "Where are you getting this rubbish?"

"It's all in Gibson's *History of the Office of the Fire Warlock*."

His eyes bulged. "You've read that tome? Good Heavens."

"It took me a year, the first time through, but yes, I—"

"You read it more than once? Good God. I'm sorry to say it wasn't worth the effort. It's obsolete, and considered misleading. No one bothers with it anymore."

"Oh." My shoulders sagged; the warm glow in my chest I had carried around since mid-morning faded. "It was the most complete history my father had."

"Let's find you something more up to date."

On my way through the library with the text Master Sven had suggested, one of the older scholars waylaid me. "Miss Guillierre, I have a proposition for our mutual benefit."

I followed him into one of the windowed alcoves. What was his name? I had paid this one little attention. He always looked tired, and never laughed, as far as I could tell. He described what sounded to me like a business arrangement, with himself as senior partner. I listened in growing confusion. Scholar Elias, that was his name.

I finally interrupted him. "I'm sorry, sir, but what exactly are you asking me to do?"

He looked surprised. "Why, be my wife. Wasn't that obvious?"

I cringed. "Oh, thank you, sir. I beg your pardon, sir, but, uh, I don't think I can make a decision now, since I just started my year here. Will you excuse me, please?"

I bolted, looking for Mrs Cole.

Her reaction was a hearty laugh, followed by a deep sigh. "Oh, dear, that man has not an ounce of romance in his soul. My guess is he wants a cook and housekeeper and a warm bed, and any woman who could give them to him would do. But I'd not have him, and I don't think you should either, honey."

"Mrs Cole, I've never had a serious beau. The Warlock didn't think I'd have any trouble finding somebody suitable, but how do I know who's suitable? I'd rather be an old maid than settle for a business deal like that, but how can I be sure that I'll ever get a better offer?"

She looked me up and down over the rims of her spectacles, and said, "I agree with Himself on that score. Your biggest problem is going to be deciding which offer to take. I've seen the way they flock around you at dinner. As pretty and good-natured as you are, and as good a cook, it's just a matter of time until they all wake up and start proposing right and left. When word gets about that somebody has already made an offer, the rest of them will line up to get their bids in. Take my word for it."

"If they do, what do I say so they don't get angry while I wait for a better offer?"

"You had the right idea with Scholar Elias. For each one whether you like him a lot, a little, or not at all, thank him for his interest and tell him you can't make a decision now. Tell him you'll be happy to entertain the question next spring, when your year is almost up. If he's serious, he'll be back, and you'll have had time to sort out which ones you like and which ones you don't. Don't let any of them pressure you or sweet-talk you into making a decision too fast. You've got lots of time, honey, to make up your mind."

As word spread that Scholar Elias had proposed, other scholars did make offers. The atmosphere at dinner became rather tense, as the various suitors eyed each other and jockeyed for position, and generally acted like peacocks vying for the attention of a peahen.

I said to the Warlock one morning, "I guess you weren't joking about young women being disruptive. I'm sorry, sir, for the trouble I'm causing."

He smiled. "I expected it. They will calm down soon, once the novelty wears off."

The proposals themselves ranged from a flowery speech full of allusions to romance to a written note from Scholar Andreas. I was touched by the note, and sought him out to thank him. I made a point of sitting next to him at dinner at regular intervals, but getting him to talk about anything besides his classification system took effort, and I couldn't keep that up for a lifetime.

Another scholar wrote me a poem running to four pages, but the woman he extolled bore only a passing resemblance to me, and I had little interest in becoming the paragon of gentleness he seemed to want.

Several of the proposals I would have jumped at, if they had come my way in Lesser Campton, but the calibre of the men I had met since coming to the Fortress had raised my expectations. Master Sven seemed to find my suitors irritating, but made no move of his own to propose. I hinted that an offer would be welcome, and he began to avoid me outside the classroom, watching where I sat in the dining room, and seating himself some distance away.

Maybe I shouldn't have argued with him over obscure historical details, but what could I have done instead? He would have discovered, some day, that I couldn't sit still and listen to anyone say something I believed was wrong.

Mrs Cole watched me brood over him, and clucked at his caution. "I suppose it's to be expected, though. Girls have been chasing him since his university days, and there are a couple of young witches down in Blazes who have their hearts set on him. It may be just as well he's not interested in you, honey—a jealous fire witch can make a mundane girl's life a misery."

I stopped kneading the ball of dough and stared at her. "They couldn't do anything to me here in the Fortress, could they?"

"Well, no, but you're not going to spend your whole life shut up in here, are you?"

"No, ma'am." I went back to kneading with a hollow feeling in my chest. I missed having a girlfriend my own age. I hadn't considered that the fire witches in Blazes might not be friendly. The only people from the town I'd met were Warlock Arturos and two witches at the guild hall, and they'd all been cordial.

Arturos seemed to find my suitors amusing. I often caught him eyeing me. He would wink and not look in the least abashed.

"Mrs Cole, is Warlock Arturos married?"

She shot me a sharp glance. "He's not a scholar, honey—doesn't seem like your type."

"But he is a fire wizard."

"He is that. A perfect example of one, warts and all. Meaning—"

"Meaning he's loud, nosy, stubborn, with a foul temper…"

She laughed. "Of course, I don't need to tell you that. Anyway, he's a widower. His wife was the town's healer, but she broke her neck in a fall, poor thing, a couple of years ago."

"Oh, dear, and without another healer nearby…"

"Wouldn't have done any good. She was dead before anybody reached her."

When I met Arturos in the corridor later that day he seemed glad to see me, and stopped to chat.

"Please, sir," I said, "I want to know more about the rules for the challenges and which people are accepted as supplicants."

His eyebrows rose. "Why? You were accepted; what's bothering you?"

"It's Claire, sir. She needed help, too. It doesn't seem fair that I should get everything I wanted, while she didn't get anything at all, even though we went through the challenges together."

He looked even more surprised. "Did she help you with the challenges? I was under the impression that she was no help to you in the last challenge, and put an obstacle in your way in the first one."

My cheeks got hot. "No, sir, that wasn't what I meant. I would have gotten through them just fine without her." A cold chill ran down my spine, and I heard my father's stern voice: Never, ever lie to a warlock.

I looked down at my feet while my entire face and ears burned. "That's not right. She made the challenge with the guards harder, but she did help with the maze. I'm not sure how I would have handled the lion if I hadn't gotten angry at him for threatening her."

The cold dread evaporated. I looked up. "Wait—doesn't the magic keep me from talking about the challenges?"

He grinned. "You can talk to me. I'm the Keeper of the Challenge Path, remember, and I asked you a question about them. But you said that wasn't what you meant. Go on."

"Yes, sir. All the old stories say you can bring along whatever—tools, food, or anything—you think will help you get through the challenges. I didn't bring anything along; all I have is my head. I was planning to come by myself even before Claire heard about the new gate. But the only thing Claire knows how to do is manipulate people. She knew she wouldn't get through the challenges by herself, so she insisted on coming with me. I was the tool she needed to be able to get through. So I think that ought to count for something. Shouldn't it?"

"Ah," he said, stroking his beard for a bit. "Hmm. Well," he said, pausing again. "I had never considered that. Maybe, just maybe, you have a point, but even so, she doesn't belong here. A glamour spell isn't—"

My stomach lurched. "A glamour spell? But... Oh. The Warlock did say that. I'd forgotten." The conversation with the Warlock about Claire's glamour spell came back clearly. How could I have forgotten something so important?

Arturos tugged at his beard. "Odd. Something going on I don't understand. But it doesn't matter—glamour spells aren't in the Fire Guild's domain. If it's any comfort to you, after I delivered her back to Old Campton, I had a chat with the local earth witch, who promised to keep an eye on her. Maybe she can help where we can't."

I warmed towards the big wizard. "Thank you, sir."

He shrugged, still smiling. "Don't get your hopes up."

I took a deep breath. Time to stop stalling. "Arturos, have you ever considered remarrying?"

The pleasure drained out of his face. "Sure, Lucinda. I've thought about it. A lot. But it's no good. It wouldn't be fair... Well, it just wouldn't be right."

He turned on heel and strode off down the corridor in the direction he had come from. I watched him go with watering eyes and a lump in my throat.

Despite efforts to avoid it, René and I became familiar with the old system of spell classification. We spent days reading through the six major categories and dozens of subcategories of spells, in page after page of detailed descriptions. And then, at the end, almost as a footnote, was the category of locks. All the text said was "specialised spells for hiding things, both physical and intangible."

"What does that mean?" I asked.

René shrugged. "I don't know. I'm glad that's all we need to know about them."

Master Sven, when questioned, said. "Don't bother with that. The study of locks is very esoteric. They don't come up in normal practice."

"Why not? Can't you at least tell us a little more about them?"

"Why do you want to know?"

"I... I don't know."

"I beg your pardon. I didn't mean that the way it sounded. You have every right to ask if you're curious, but you're the first student I've ever had ask about them. So I'm curious about why you're interested."

"I'm not sure. It just seems they deserve more attention than that. Wasn't one of the members of the Great Coven known as the Locksmith? Aren't the locks he devised when the Offices were created considered one of the reasons they've held up so far?"

"That's true, although even most guild members have never heard of him. I studied the history of the Great Coven at university and I don't know much more than that, or about locks. All I know is that they can hide very abstract things—ideas, emotions, other spells—and few witches and wizards can use even the simplest of locks."

"Then how do you hide things?"

"With illusions, mostly. I've never tried to use a lock spell, and I don't know where I'd find much about them. If you want to know more, we can ask His Wisdom for help."

"No, no, I don't want to bother him."

"Why not? He's happy to answer questions about magic."

Why did asking the Warlock seem like a bad idea? I hesitated, then shrugged. "It isn't that important."

I didn't think about locks again for the rest of the day, but that night, I once again dreamed of the glass cage, and woke gasping for breath. For the first time I saw the cage had a locked door, and the lock was on the inside.

The Earth Mother

"We've got to make an extra effort to make sure everything goes smoothly today, honey," Mrs Cole said, "because the Earth Mother will be here for dinner."

The Earth Mother? Was apple crumble good enough? I straightened up and slammed the cupboard door on my finger. I stuck the injured digit in my mouth and sucked on it. Not off to a good start.

When dinner was ready, I hurried down the corridor to the anteroom, anxious not to miss her appearance. The rumours had spread that she was coming, and the scholars were abuzz. Everyone wanted to sit at the head of the table and there would be little chance that I would be one of the lucky ones.

I tugged at Master Thomas' sleeve. "Why is she here?"

The librarian shook his head. "She has lots of business with His Wisdom but we never hear the details. Maybe it's a social call. She's one of the few people he can really let his hair down with."

"Is she as old as he is?"

"Not quite. She's only a hundred. The Frost Maiden's older."

I snorted. "Right. And Storm King will go cold before she comes here for dinner."

At one o'clock the door opened and the most beautiful older woman I have ever seen walked in on the Fire Warlock's arm. Even today, after having seen her many times, I cannot say with any accuracy what she looked like. The only detail I remember is the heavy coil of grey hair, but she looked like someone I loved. Mother? I smiled at the memory, but she had died young. Mother Janet? I hadn't realised I missed her. Grandmother? The butcher's wife, who was forever bandaging skinned knees? Or Mrs Wilson, who had held me tightly and let me sob on her shoulder when my own mother died?

"—and Miss Guillierre at the head of the table."

I snapped to attention, but the Warlock had finished talking. The two guild heads strolled into the dining room, the scholars—a few glaring at me—falling into line behind them. From the other side of the room, Warlock Arturos winked at me.

I looked at Master Thomas. His eyebrows rose. I spread my hands and shrugged.

Arturos came over to offer me his arm. "That put a few noses out of joint," he said with a grin.

"Gee, thanks."

"Don't mention it."

I sat across from the Earth Mother, and the Warlock introduced me. "Lucinda and her stepsister Claire came together to ask for my help. I approved of Lucinda's quest, and she is serving her year in my kitchen. She made the apple crumble for today's dessert, and I expect it will be as excellent as everything else she has produced."

How did he know I made apple crumble? He hadn't been in the kitchen.

He continued, "But she has pointed out that I was wrong in sending her stepsister away."

"I never said that, Your Wisdom." I bit my tongue. Contradicting the Warlock was not a good idea.

"You were more tactful, but the import was the same. I hope I never become so arrogant that I cannot admit I have made a mistake. I know that I do; I make them all the time." Turning back to the Earth Mother, he said, "Her stepsister attempts to enthral everyone she meets, including me, with a glamour spell. I would like you to listen to Lucinda's story, and see what you make of her stepsister's problem."

I told the Earth Mother about our quest. She asked questions, and before long I was pouring out my life story and everything I knew about Claire's.

Claire was younger than I, and we had been good friends before Father remarried. She used to listen, wide-eyed, when I told the younger girls the magical stories of far-off lands and strange people that I read in Father's books. We got along well enough in the same house, once we had each staked out our territory and left the other's toys alone. Aside from Claire my taste in friends ran more towards the boys who let me trail along with them to play Hide-and-Seek or Soldiers-and-Wizards in the woods, than towards the other girls Claire played with who were more interested in dolls or playing house.

I hated rainy days but she loved them, splashing through puddles in her boots and shaking off the rain like a duck. She didn't want to cook but didn't mind, when younger, doing the dishes or the laundry. Her attempts at baking were pitiful failures, and she couldn't stand getting her hands dirty in the garden, but she would carry water from the spring and water the plants.

"An affinity for the Water Guild," the Earth Mother said.

"Yes, ma'am, that's what it seemed to me."

"Odd. Water witches don't usually have much truck with glamour spells. Go on."

As she grew older, Claire became so beautiful that all the boys flocked around her, and even my friends chased after her and ignored me. Everyone who met her, men and women alike, young and old, wanted to do nothing more than please her. Anyone Claire wanted something from would be dazzled into believing she was the best friend he could ever have, then she would turn her attention to someone else, leaving the first victim burning with jealousy. I watched this pattern play out many times in her relationships with other people. She had gotten lazy and arrogant, and didn't understand that everyone around her resented being used. The boys who had courted her got too angry to come back, and she had driven away all her girlfriends.

"Except me. I don't know why she didn't mistreat me, too."

"But, my dear, she did." The Warlock's tone was quite gentle. "Many times."

"But, Your Wisdom, she…" My protest died, half-formed. Fragments of memory came back to me. Claire talking me into bringing her with me on the challenge path. Telling me what a good sport I was when she shirked all her chores. There had been other times, too, I was sure of that.

I had talked all the way through dinner and dessert. Everyone else had finished and gone. The only people left in the dining room were the earth witch and two warlocks, all three watching me with puzzled expressions.

"Yes, sir," I said. "I guess I knew that. I don't know why I said she hadn't."

"You've been acting," Arturos said, "like she used a forget spell—a big one, too—on you."

"Indeed," the Warlock said. "That could explain why such a perceptive individual would fail to notice the signs of a glamour spell."

"A forget spell? She's not a witch. How could she use even one powerful spell, much less two?"

"By herself she could not, but an experienced witch or wizard can bind spells to an object—a scarf, say, or a brooch—for a mundane to use."

"Even then," the Earth Mother said, "a glamour spell has to be tailored to the individual, and she has to be taught how to use it." She frowned, and stared off into space, stirring her coffee mechanically. I watched the great emerald on her finger gleam and flash, and started when she addressed the two warlocks. "Both of you could see through the glamour spell. Did she need it?"

Arturos said, "Nope. She's gorgeous without it, and seemed to have a reasonably pleasant personality underneath."

The Warlock made a wry face. "I cannot comment on her personality, but she is indeed comely."

She said, "This story puzzles me a great deal. It's clear that she didn't belong here. I can see why you sent her home, Jean, and small blame to you.

"Please forgive me if I say things you already know, dear," she addressed to me, "but as you haven't been educated by one of the guilds I can't guess what you know and what you don't. Your supposition that Claire deserved a hearing because she used your help to get here is intriguing. I don't remember this situation ever arising before."

Arturos said, "There have been other cases where two supplicants came together. We don't let the stories get out. We'd rather not encourage it."

"None of the pairs I know about," she said, "included this type of magical coercion. In your case, it seems quite appropriate that you came to the Fire Guild, but a glamour spell spans my domain and that of the Air Guild. If it wouldn't let her go to the Water Guild, where she belongs, it should have driven her to one of us. Why did she come to the least suitable of the four?

"The other question, the one that disturbs me more, is who taught her to use those spells? Someone did it deliberately. Who, in God's name"—

she set her coffee cup down with a solid thump—"would teach an already pretty girl such a thing? Who? And why?"

She glared at the Warlock for a moment. He gazed back at her with furrowed brows.

She sighed. "That aspect of this story worries me. I don't like glamour spells in the first place. I wish I could wave my wand and make them all go away. If it was a member of the Earth Guild who taught her, they will regret it."

I asked, "Is there anything you can do for her?"

"Perhaps. This seems like a textbook example of Narcissism; a glamour spell gone bad, where the spell caster has become trapped and taken in by her own spell. Cures are not easy or quick, and not possible if she doesn't want the help. Nevertheless, I will see what can be done."

"Thank you, Your Wisdom," I said.

"Yes, thank you, Celeste," the Warlock added.

"You're quite welcome, Jean."

She glanced at me. "Yes, I know it's a ridiculous name for an Earth Mother. But my parents thought I would be an air witch, and I'm stuck with it."

We rose, and the two warlocks escorted her away down the corridor. Jean? Celeste? I gazed after them until they rounded the corner and disappeared from my view.

I had never heard the Warlock's baptismal name before. I had known only his war name, Quicksilver. Sometimes at night, I wondered about his life before he became the Warlock, but during the day I was so busy I never remembered to ask.

I encountered Mrs Cole on my way upstairs after supper, and I asked her as we rode up the moving staircases together. When I got to my room, I walked over to the bookshelf and stood beside it for a long time, looking at but not seeing the two histories that I had lugged all the way from my father's house. With no conscious urging, my finger traced the author's name stamped in gold leaf on the red leather: Jean Rehsavvy, Flame Mage, Lore Master, at twenty-seven among the youngest ever to assume the Office of The Fire Warlock, and now at one hundred forty-three, the longest serving, by more than half a century.

On Being a Witch

René said, "You have to be a fire witch. It doesn't make any sense that you aren't."

I'd had enough. I grabbed him by the collar and hauled him down the corridor towards the dining room, where I cornered our tutor. "Master Sven, can you tell when you meet somebody if he or she has magic talents?"

"Yes, of course, I—"

"How?"

"With my mind's eye. The combination of talents another witch or wizard displays is as distinctive as a face, and harder to change or camouflage. It takes practice to form the mental image, but it's a useful skill."

"Do I look like a witch?"

"No, not to me, but I—"

"See, René? You don't believe me, but he ought to know. I'm not a witch."

"Hold on," Master Sven said. "I can spot a witch who's level two or higher. Lots of level ones don't put out enough power for me to distinguish them from mundanes."

René said, "So Lucinda could be a level one and you wouldn't know?"

"Yes, but I assumed that if she was, His Wisdom would have sent her to work in the school in Blazes."

"You didn't ask him, did you?"

The dining room doors opened. Continuing this argument over dinner wouldn't improve my appetite. I snapped at René, "Go ask him yourself, since you won't listen to me."

He grabbed my arm, and Master Sven's, and towed us along at a run to grab the coveted seats at the head of the table. I protested that we were being rude, but to no avail, and soon the Warlock was looking at me with arched eyebrows and asking, "So, my fine young friends, what is on your minds today?"

René said, "Is Lucinda a witch?"

The Warlock didn't answer for a moment, looking first at René, then at me, and back at René.

I said, "Go ahead, Your Wisdom. Tell him I'm not one. He doesn't believe me."

"He does not believe you, my dear, because it is not true. You are a witch."

I dropped my fork on my plate with a loud clatter. Master Sven's eyes widened. René pounded on the table with his fist, and crowed, "I knew it. I knew it. I knew you were a witch." Scholars turned to look at us, and my cheeks burned.

I said, "But, Your Wisdom…"

He cocked an eyebrow at me. "Do you disagree with my assessment?"

I clutched at the tablecloth. "Yes, sir. I can't be a witch. If I were one, shouldn't I have known about it?"

"Not necessarily. The one talent that we are quite sure you have, baking, is often not considered a magic talent, because it is usually women's work, and therefore not taken seriously.

"Further, some talents are so weak or so camouflaged that their owner never gains conscious control over them. That seems to be the case with your other talent, which, as far as I can determine, is a minor variety of prescience. However, since you cannot control it, the two talents together place you only in the lowest tier, level one, along with thousands of other young women who can bake and do a few other minor things without ever coming to the notice of the guild."

"Two? That's it?" René said, looked disgusted.

"As talent goes, yes. The third and, in my opinion, most important factor that makes Lucinda a fire witch is not a magic talent. It is her burning curiosity. Several of our outstanding theoreticians have had little practical talent."

Master Sven said, "She does have the potential to be a fine scholar, Your Wisdom. The Scholar's Guild doesn't normally accept women, but they have made exceptions for witches. I hadn't realised she was one. If the Fire Guild would accept her, she might find a place in the Scholar's Guild."

The Warlock frowned. "You must not get your hopes up. The Guild Council and I do not agree on such matters, particularly when they involve women."

"It wouldn't hurt to ask, would it?"

Talk about my prospects with the guild flowed around me, but I sat silent, trembling. The Warlock knew more about witches than I did, but even he could be mistaken. Didn't he once say so himself?

He watched me with a slight pucker of his eyebrows. I bent my head and stared at my plate, looking up again only when the conversation moved away from me.

"You made it sound," René said, "like lots of people don't know they're witches and wizards."

"Why should they?" the Warlock said. "The majority of talents are minor, unnoticed by their owners or disparaged by the witches and wizards they go to for testing, who are usually only minor talents themselves."

"But then they miss out on going to the school."

"Yes, but that is just as well. If they all came, the school would be overwhelmed. Left alone, the level one talents will not do much damage. We must focus our attention on the ones who can. It is the responsibility of the licensed testers to entice, persuade, or coerce them into coming to us."

"I wanted to come here. Why would you have to coerce anybody?"

"What is the primary objective of the Fire Guild?"

"Training witches and wizards to use their magic?"

"Certainly not. Someone with enough raw talent can learn the rudiments without ever coming to the school. The Guild's primary objective is ensuring the safety and security of the kingdom, and that includes policing the behaviour of guild members. Many witches and wizards have tried to avoid that scrutiny, either out of a desire to use magic for unlawful ends, or out of fear of the demands on the guild during a war."

"What demands on the guild?" René asked. "Aren't you the only one who has to fight?"

The Warlock fixed René with a stern glare. "Remember this, my young friend. All members of the Fire Guild are tools at the Office's disposal, and it does not hesitate to use them. It has no conscience, and individual lives mean nothing to it. It will do whatever is necessary to protect Frankland, even if that means burning through every member of the guild.

"War is coming soon. When it does, your life as well as mine may be at risk."

Master Sven and René finished their dinners and rose to go. I stood too, but the Warlock signalled to me to sit down again. I couldn't pretend I hadn't seen him. I sat, and went back to staring at my uneaten dinner.

He said, "I am sorry I sprung the news you are a witch on you in such a fashion. Your talent for prescience is intriguing. I had hoped to understand it better before bringing it to your attention, but René took the initiative away from me. He had a serious motive for asking that question, and, for reasons related to his problems and not yours, I needed to give him a serious answer.

"But, my dear, most people, on finding out that they are a witch or wizard, are excited, even eager. Why does it upset you?"

"You just told us that the Office could burn through the entire guild. Shouldn't I be frightened?"

He sighed. "I exaggerated somewhat. In dire circumstances it could come to that, but it has not yet done so, and is not likely to in the near future. It is only the level fives—the warlocks—whose lives are always at risk. Lower level wizards and witches have lost their lives in the service of the Office, but it is uncommon, even for level three and four talents, and less likely the further down the ranks we go. For the lower levels, the benefits of being a guild member far outweigh the risks, and you have a stronger affinity for the Fire Guild than is common even in the middle ranks—"

"Don't say that, sir."

"Why does the prospect disturb you?"

"I don't know, Your Wisdom, but this talk of war scares me. The guards are saying the emperor is jealous of you, but that's always been the case. He wouldn't go to war just because of that, would he?"

"That is but one factor. Of more import to the ordinary citizens is that we block easy trade with the New World. Their ships must travel far to the north through treacherous seas to avoid us."

"Can't we let their ships through the channel?"

"And allow them to cut us in two? Never. You are evading my question. Given that past wars have burned whole cities off the map, a level one witch in the Fire Guild is no more at risk than any other citizen of Frankland. You know that. You were disturbed before the conversation went in that direction. Why?"

"I don't know, sir." My hands shook. I sat on them. "If I were to be in one of the guilds, the Fire Wizard's Guild is the one I would have chosen. I don't know why I'm terrified." What an awful word to choose. He would think I was a mouse.

He studied me in silence, his frown deepening the longer he watched me. I couldn't meet his eyes. He got up, saying, "I have other things I must attend to, but your behaviour concerns me. You are not easily frightened. If you have any further insights on this subject, I would like to hear them."

I fled back to the kitchen, feeling like a fool.

"You've been saying the same nonsense for a week now. I am not going to apply for membership in the Fire Guild, and that's final." I turned my back on Master Sven and walked away.

He followed me into the dining room and sat beside me. "You are being ridiculous. I might have to take back what I've said about you having a good mind. Refusing to ask for membership seems incredibly senseless."

"If you're trying to sweet-talk me into going, you're going to have to try harder."

"What? Oh." He flushed. "Sorry."

"What's it matter, anyway?" René said. "I don't care what the Guild Council says. I know she's a witch."

"She's got a better grasp already on the basics of theory than most graduates of the guild school. With more training, she could teach there. Joining the guild would guarantee her access to a library, too. She needs to read more widely to be a better conversationalist."

The boy sniffed. "How's that going to help? She's already more interesting to talk to than anybody else in the Fortress, except for Arturos and you and the Fire Warlock."

I gaped at him. He had been eager all week to talk about spellcraft. Somebody—not me—must have worked some magic on him.

Master Sven harped on the subject of guild membership all through dinner. On leaving the dining room, I went to the library instead of the classroom, and sat in a window seat far away from ancient history. I drew my knees up with my feet on the cushion and tugged at the heavy curtains to hide me from the view of anyone else in the library. It was a warm day in June, but I shivered.

A little while later, at the sound of a purposeful tread on the boards behind me, I pulled open a gap between the curtain and wall, and watched Master Sven walk through the library, scanning each alcove and bay of bookshelves as he passed by. He stopped at the librarian's desk; Master Thomas looked around and shook his head. I let the curtain fall closed, and shut my book. I'd not gotten past the title page, anyway.

The hand that swept back the curtain moments later was not the one bearing the brilliant ruby, but I knew him the instant the fabric twitched. Who else would know I was there? Or moved with no more sound than a drop of mercury sliding along a glass?

"I had expected you to be elated that Master Sven is at last giving you the attention you deserve. Tell me why this displeases you."

I turned my head and stared out the window, my throat tight. "I'm no more a witch today than I was last week, whatever you say, Your Wisdom. Why should it make a difference?"

"Would you have found Master Sven so appealing if I had not said he was determined to be a mage?"

"He wants to be a mage. I don't want to be a witch."

"Ah. An important distinction. Then go to the next council meeting, and put an end to his false hopes."

I looked at him over my shoulder. He stood with his arms crossed, frowning at me.

I said, "You're sure they won't take me?"

"Can you light a candle?"

"You know I can't."

"Then they will not accept you."

"And the Scholar's Guild won't take me either, without me officially being a witch?"

"There are, perhaps, other avenues. Is that your desire?"

I rested my forehead against the cool glass with my eyes closed. Talk about false hopes. No one would believe I belonged there. Would I believe it myself? And why would I want to spend the rest of my life chained to a desk?

"No, sir. I want to marry a scholar. I don't want to be one."

"But the prospect is not easy to dismiss, is it? You would be proud to be accepted. But your concerns are practical matters regarding the lives of ordinary people and the world they inhabit, not impressing other scholars with your erudition. In temperament you are closer to Arturos than to most scholars."

I turned and looked at him smiling at me. "Arturos?"

"He, too, is an avid reader with a burning curiosity. One might not suspect from his sometimes unpolished manner that he took a first at Oxford." His eyes twinkled. "Any more than one might guess an aproned girl with flour on her cheek would grasp the essentials of an obscure taxonomy."

I stretched my legs out full length on the cushions and leaned back with a sigh. The afternoon sun warmed me. I'd have to move soon, or get too hot.

"You are in good company, my dear," he said. "And you should go to the council meeting. I have been remiss in not sending you sooner."

"Can you light a candle, Miss Guillierre?"

"No, sir."

Four of the six warlocks glared at Master Sven. "Why did you bring her here, then?" Warlock Flint barked. "You're wasting our time."

Master Sven's nostrils flared, but his voice held only a hint of irritation. "Please let me explain…"

I studied the members of the Fire Guild Council while he made my case with more eloquence than I wanted. He had described them to me on our way to the Guild Hall in Blazes, "Warlock Nostradamus is eighty, the oldest after His Wisdom, and getting senile. Warlock Venturos is next, with a sound mind but bad heart. Warlock Sunbeam is in his sixties, always cheerful but a bit flighty. Then there's Warlock Flint in his late forties. They say he's never forgiven His Wisdom for naming him that, but it fits."

"And finally there's Warlock Arturos, the Practical Arts teacher, in his thirties. He's the youngest on the Council, and so carries the least weight— ironic, no?—even though he is, by far, the most sensible. And he's the last. Historically, they've always been able to rely on a steady stream of new candidates for the Office, as there would be at least one new warlock showing up every five to fifteen years or so. That means there ought to be someone in his twenties or late teens at the outside. The fact that there's no one after Arturos is causing a good deal of concern."

To my relief, only Arturos and the Fire Warlock voted for my admittance to the Fire Guild. The others scolded Master Sven, but if they were annoyed with me, they didn't show it.

"You're spending too much time with scholars, dear," Warlock Sunbeam said. "I'll introduce you to our unmarried wizards." He began scribbling a list of names that the other warlocks called out.

I thanked him. Master Sven scowled.

They dismissed me, and I explored the Guild Hall while waiting for Master Sven, who had other business with the Council. A young woman was setting tables. I went up to her and introduced myself.

"I'd heard about you. I'm Jenny McNamara. What did you want with the Guild Council?"

Explain that I wasn't a witch, even though the Fire Warlock said I was one? No. I said, "Master Sven said I should see if they would accept me in the guild since the Scholar's Guild doesn't accept women."

Her smile disappeared. "Why would they? You're not a witch."

"I never said I was. I don't want to be in the guild."

"That doesn't make sense. Why are you here if you don't want to be in the guild?"

"I'm only here because Master Sven insisted I should try."

Her eyes narrowed and her nostrils flared. "For somebody who's not a witch, you seem to have cast quite a spell."

Was this one of the witches with an eye on Master Sven? "Don't be silly. I couldn't steal Master Sven away from a real witch."

Her face turned bright red and she shouted at me. "Who do you think you are, telling me I'm not a real witch? You better keep your claws away from him or I'll give you more heat than you can handle."

I stammered, "That wasn't what I meant," but she wouldn't listen to my apology. When an older witch came over and added her voice to the din, I said, "You must not be much of a witch to be threatened by a nobody like me," and stalked away.

I retreated to the Guild library, in the room adjoining the council chamber, closing the door behind me. I sat in a wing chair by a window, without looking at the books. I had hoped to make friends with some of the fire witches. I'd made an enemy instead.

The warlocks in the next room were shouting at each other. Typical fire guild behaviour, wizards and witches alike. I had been lucky that witch hadn't flamed me.

Good God, I had insulted a fire witch. I should have been scared of her. What was wrong with me?

I pulled my feet up onto the chair and hunched over my knees, shaking. Was I that stupid? "I wish," I said, "that the next angry member of the Fire Guild wouldn't even notice me."

Behind me, the door to the council chamber flew open and banged against the doorstop. Someone stomped into the room, shouting. "That boy should be down here at the school." The voice belonged to Warlock Flint.

Master Sven, his voice also raised, followed him. "His Wisdom wants me to see to his education. He would be bored silly with the level of theory taught in the school, and the practical training needs are quite different."

"The traditional education has served us well for the guild's entire existence."

"Have you forgotten the Scorching Times? Quicksilver has been saying for decades they were the result of inadequate and improper training."

"Hogwash. The education is—"

"What do you know about education? Arturos and I are teachers, and we agree with him. If his time is running out, what is the Council doing to get a new one trained and ready?"

"You're not on the Council, Sven. Mind your own business." Flint stomped through the library and out the other door, slamming it behind him.

I scrambled to my feet and turned towards Master Sven. "I'm sorry, Master Sven. I didn't mean to eavesdrop."

He wheeled, and gawked at me. "Where did you come from? There wasn't anybody here."

I said, "You couldn't see me from the door."

"I should have with my mind's eye. I wouldn't have said... Flint wouldn't have said..." He waved a hand. "Never mind, I guess I was too angry to notice. Come on, let's go home before I lose my temper with any of the rest of them."

On the outskirts of the town, he asked what I had made out of what I overheard.

I said, "The guild school doesn't do a good job of preparing warlocks for the Office of the Fire Warlock?"

"Does it or doesn't it? What do you think?"

I thought about the Scorching Times, those horrible periods in our history when the Office had gone from one warlock to another in rapid succession, the countryside still showing the scars of the most recent period, ending a little more than a century ago.

"The Scorching Times are called that because each Warlock's reign ended with him making some ghastly mistake in how much fire power was needed, and burning out himself and everything else for miles around. If they had better training, they ought to last longer and not hurt as many people. Only a level five fire wizard can get to be the Warlock, so it would make sense for their training to concentrate on things that the lower levels wouldn't need, like estimating huge surges of power. I take it they all get the same training?"

The good-natured mage had cooled off. He grinned. "You have confirmed my hypothesis that a level one witch with a good intellect and some common sense is more useful than a level five warlock with a head like a stone. You are correct. That wasn't the case in the early days. The Warlock was a lecturer at the university before the Office came to him, and he's given more thought to the subject than most of them. He and Arturos have been trying to reform the school, but Warlock Flint will never budge.

"The Council is quite conservative—always has been—and most of the Council members disagree with him on every point out of spite and jealousy that he has hung on for so long and not given any of them a chance to be the Warlock. As if anyone should want the job. Idiots. Of course, the fact that a level five comes along only once a decade or so doesn't help matters, but as there's now a gap in the ranks it makes it that much more imperative that the training of the next one be better."

I said, "So that's why the Warlock is keeping René up at the castle instead of sending him to the school?"

"I didn't say that. I didn't hear you say that, either. I don't know anything about René's future. Whatever the Warlock knows or guesses he hasn't seen fit to tell me."

I didn't point out that the Warlock had already confirmed my suspicions on that account at dinner the day he said I was a witch. Did René know he would be a warlock? From his reactions to the lectures Arturos had been giving him about control, I suspected he did not.

We reached the Fortress gate, and I stepped into the shadows with my heart in my mouth. I dogged Master Sven's footsteps until we were safely inside the curtain wall.

The Warlock thought I didn't frighten easily? And he was supposed to be hard to fool.

I said, "What did you mean about his time running out? Did you mean the Warlock?"

We stepped onto the moving staircases. Master Sven looked out over the railing, away from me. "I don't want to see his reign end. I don't think any of the warlocks besides Arturos can handle the Office, and the prospect of another Scorching Time terrifies me. But what we want doesn't matter. There are rumours that seers have said he won't be the Warlock much longer. I don't know any more than that."

We rode up the mountainside in silence. I clutched at the rails with both hands, fighting dizziness. The holders of the other three Offices could retire, but the Fire Warlock couldn't. Nobody knew why, but the Office wouldn't let him. If he didn't make a fatal mistake and burn himself out, it chose when to replace him. When it wanted a new Warlock, it fried the old one to a cinder and moved on. That prediction, if true, was a death sentence.

The Christening

George said, "Did you hear the royal baby is a girl? The guards are saying the emperor wants the king to promise she'll marry his son."

I snorted. "Won't happen. The Warlock will never let us be sucked into an alliance with the Empire."

The guards had sent my old friend to the Fortress for more training, and he came up to the kitchen to see me as soon as he had a free morning. I fixed him some lemonade, and we swapped gossip while I worked.

He said, "The officers think the king is going to try anyway. So when His Wisdom overrules the king, the emperor will say we've insulted them, and declare war. The Empire gets what it wants either way."

The rumours that the Empire was looking for an excuse to invade Frankland had been growing for months. George's news coming hard on the heels of the prediction of the Warlock's imminent demise made my blood run cold.

George leaned back with his arms crossed and frowned. "The guards say the king would sell the whole country out to the Empire if he thought it'd give him an edge over His Wisdom. But I don't understand why."

I said, "It's the perennial power struggle. The partnership between king and Fire Warlock died with Charlemagne and Fortunatus, and they've been at odds ever since. Our kings see rulers in other countries doing things that the Warlock keeps them from doing, and they want that power."

"I can see that. But the king wouldn't be any better off under the emperor's thumb, would he?"

"Probably less so. A small group of warlocks holds all the power in the Empire. Everything I've heard or read says the emperor has less respect for mundanes than our king has for commoners. If we were absorbed into the Empire the royal family could only hope to become puppets, managed by a cabal of wizards. Maybe not even that."

"That's what I thought, too, and I'm a dumb country boy. The king's supposed to be educated—why can't he see it? The whole lot of them don't seem to have any more sense than a flock of sheep."

"I don't know. They weren't always like that. In the early days most of our great thinkers were nobles."

"So what happened to them?"

I shrugged. I'd wondered that, too. And why wouldn't the Warlock allow any alliances, not just ones with the Europan Empire?

I was taking a tray of meringues out of the oven when the Warlock walked in, dressed in the uniform of a captain of the guards. I came to attention and snapped off a salute. George twisted around and saluted in turn.

The Warlock returned our salutes with a smile. "Good morning, Lucinda. Good morning, George."

He reached around me for the meringues. He had said treat him as he was dressed, hadn't he? I flicked a tea towel at him. "Behave yourself. Those are for the scholars' dinner."

His head snapped around, brows drawn together, fire in his eyes. I froze. For three heartbeats we stared at each other, then his face relaxed. He said quietly, "I will not flame you for doing as I bid you. Breathe, girl."

I took a deep breath. "Yes, sir."

"Thank you for pointing out I still have a few things to learn about playing a role."

He picked up several of the meringues. I blurted, "Be careful, they're hot."

Once again, his head snapped around, but this time his eyebrows shot skyward. He walked out of the kitchen laughing to himself. I sat down at the table fanning my hot face and waiting for my racing pulse to slow down. Too bad I missed the chance to ask him about alliance marriages.

George didn't seem to have noticed anything amiss. He watched the Warlock walking down the corridor. "I thought I'd seen all the officers by now." He picked up his glass. "Who was that?"

"The Fire Warlock."

I handed him the tea towel and told him to mop up the lemonade he'd sprayed halfway across the table.

"Inbreeding."

I had encountered Arturos at the stairs, and asked him George's question, "Why aren't the nobles any smarter than a flock of sheep?"

"It's the same problem a shepherd has if he doesn't manage his flock properly. The noble class is dying from lack of new blood. The royals can't make alliance marriages, none of our neighbours will marry any of them without the properties and treaties that make an alliance, and they're too proud to marry commoners. So, they're all cousins several times over. They've been on a steady decline for centuries—in magic talent as well as intelligence—but it seems like it's gotten worse lately. It's not healthy for them. It's not healthy for the country, either."

I said, "How bad is it? We get along without them doing much, most of the time."

He shook his head. "It's bad. You just haven't seen it yet. The magic guilds have been picking up more and more of the governing that the nobles are supposed to do, because somebody's got to do it. The Water and Air guilds are suffering from the strain.

"Your village has gotten off easy because your baron and his buddies spend their time hunting and don't pay any attention to you. The fisher folk in the north where I come from have never had an easy life, and a rapacious earl has been making it hell for them lately.

"I'm afraid that within a few years some parts of the country will rise up in open rebellion. I dread what will happen then."

Neither of us said anything for a while. He scowled off into the distance as if he'd forgotten I was there.

I asked, "Will the guilds and the Offices side with the nobility or the commoners? There are witches and wizards from the nobility in all four guilds, aren't there?"

"There are, but there haven't been any level five talents from the nobility in any guild—Earth, Air, Fire, or Water—in nearly three hundred years, and there haven't been any new level fours in three generations. At the rate they're going, in another century there won't be any level threes, either."

"So then the guilds will side with the commoners? If the nobles are so inept then they won't stand a chance, will they?"

"By themselves, no. But the Offices protect and serve the nobles, and we can't change them, even if most of the guild membership sides with the commoners. If there's a civil war, with the guild members opposing the Offices, there'll be the devil to pay. There may not be anything left of Frankland when it's done."

He jammed his hat on his head and stepped onto the moving stairs. "And I'm afraid it's going to happen on my watch."

I stood by the stairs gazing after him, long after he was out of sight. When had the happiness I had experienced on coming to the Fortress begun to fade? When the Warlock said I was a witch? Or earlier, when Master Sven avoided me outside of the classroom?

He had shown real interest while he thought I might become a member of the Fire Guild. Since then, he confused me, warm one day, cool the next. If I pursued him, he would run at the sight of me. I didn't want to anyway—why did I have to be a witch to hold his interest? I still thought him the most handsome man I had ever met; if I hadn't, I might not have cared.

I'd met the most promising of the Fire Guild's other unmarried wizards—an uncouth lot, while the scholars were merely feckless. I wanted a man with a sense of humour and the ability to carry on a spirited conversation, and who knew the answers to my questions, or didn't mind admitting that he didn't know.

Master Sven needed a little more of a sense of humour.

Warlock Arturos fit the bill, but he said he wouldn't remarry.

I rubbed my hands together. Strange that I should be cold in July. Perhaps not so strange I got gooseflesh whenever I recalled my dreams. The ones of the glass cage and Storm King's shadow were increasing in frequency, interspersed with other equally disturbing dreams. Of blinding flashes of lightning. Of my clothes on fire, my skin burning. I would wake in a cold sweat, gasping for breath. Sometimes at odd moments, my pulse would race for no reason, and I would tremble on the edge of panic.

I called myself a fool for not telling the Warlock about my dreams. The next time he walked through the kitchen I stopped him.

"Your Wisdom, sir, do you have a moment?"

"Certainly, my dear. Tell me what is on your mind."

As I framed my question, the shadows thrown by the fire shifted. A looming blackness, the outline of Storm King, grew behind him.

"Sir, I've met both scholars and fire wizards…" I faltered. That wasn't what I meant to say.

"Go on," he said.

I gulped. Might as well. "Few of the scholars have any fire, and most of the fire wizards aren't scholars. I don't want to be greedy, but…"

"But you do not want to settle for second rate. I cannot blame you; I would not either. When you arrived here, I assumed you would easily find a scholar who suited you, but I had underestimated your affinity for the Fire Guild. I understand now that you desire a flame mage, or a scholar or wizard close to one, and such men are far too few. Master Sven is perhaps your best match, but he desires a witch, although he would prefer one with a good mind. Your mind and personality appeal to him, but your lack of talent makes him uncomfortable."

I nodded, my throat tight. I watched the magical rolling pin on its own levelling the piecrust to exactly the right thickness. Maybe being a fire witch—a nice, safe, non-threatening level two—wouldn't be so bad.

The Warlock said, "Master Sven is as constrained in his choice of a wife as you are in your choice of a husband. None of the young witches in the Fire Guild displays the interest in theory and history that you do. He may yet decide in your favour. I think he should. You would impress the men he aspires to be counted among more than Miss McNamara would, but he has not asked my advice."

I looked up to see him smiling at me. "Nor have you met all the country's unmarried scholars. Several of the University's best teachers will make visits here during the August recess. Do not give up hope yet."

"Yes, sir. Thank you, sir."

He strolled away, leaving me warm but not reassured. I was an ordinary woman, not a threat to anyone. The Office wouldn't harm me. I shoved the empty pie plates in the oven, and wondered why I was afraid to tell him about my dreams.

"The new princess is being christened this afternoon," Master Sven said over breakfast. "The galleries in the ballroom will be open to the public. Would you care to go? It should be quite a spectacle."

"I'd love to," I said. I wasn't sure which thrilled me more, the prospect of seeing the nobility in their finery or that he had asked me rather than Jenny McNamara.

"What about you, René?" he said. "Do you want to come?"

"Sure!"

I sighed. So much for that being a romantic overture.

Master Sven gave his other students the afternoon off, and the three of us set out after dinner. With gates at the foot of the mountain opening out to all the cities and many towns, it was a few easy steps to the royal palace.

We arrived as guards opened the palace gates and people began flooding into the palace grounds. By what combination of magic, persistence, luck, and rudeness we managed it, I do not know, but before long we were on the second-floor gallery, near the middle of the room, René and I in front at the railing, Master Sven behind us. A prime spot. I could see everything from the thrones on the dais at one end to the cavernous fireplace at the other. Below us stood row after row of chairs for the honoured guests—the nobles, dignitaries, priests, witches, and foreign visitors—who were trickling in, chatting and flaunting their fancy clothes on their way to their assigned places.

After an interminable wait while the main floor of the room filled, the royal family and their attendants paraded in.

Master Sven nudged me and pointed. "The Frost Maiden."

As if that wasn't obvious. The woman was young, blonde, and beautiful, with the Water Guild's emblem of rippling waves on her shoulder. Flashes of blue from a ring caught the eye and held it.

I rubbed my eyes, and looked for emerald green. "Where's the Earth Mother? Shouldn't she be in the procession, too?"

Master Sven frowned, and craned his neck to get a good look.

The attendants put the royal baby in a cradle on the dais. King Stephen, Queen Marguerite, and the crown prince sat, and the ceremony began. It was splendid to watch, but mind-numbing to listen to, with one sermon or speech after another by assorted priests and scholars, interspersed with arcane rituals and solemn music. The nine-year-old prince looked bored silly. The summer day had started out warm, and with hundreds, no, thousands, of people in the hall, it was soon quite hot. The Queen looked like she was melting.

I was in a linen dress, and I would rather have been in my shift. I would have felt sorry for those over-dressed people down there if they hadn't been nobles. They didn't have to wear all that satin and lace.

The baby princess woke up and cried. Several ladies-in-waiting fussed over her, then whisked her away. While she was attended to out of sight, jesters, jugglers, and livelier music entertained us. When the attendants brought the baby back, the ceremony picked up where it had left off.

While the ceremony was going on, we, and the rest of the public up in the galleries, were busy studying the privileged guests below us, whispering, fanning, and making so much noise it was difficult to hear the speeches even when they were interesting. Bits of conversation I overheard suggested I wasn't the only one who found Mother Celeste's absence troubling. Below us, the gathered witches were looking around, craning their necks, and whispering to one another. There were about three-dozen of them—the level four and five witches from all over the country.

One of the foreign dignitaries on the dais kept looking towards the outside door, as if he were expecting—and dreading—its opening.

"Is he a wizard?" I whispered to Master Sven, who nodded.

Where or when I had seen him before? Never. I told myself not to be silly, but the longer I watched the foreign wizard the more puzzled I became. "Who is he? What's he doing here?"

Master Sven shrugged and shook his head.

After an eternity, the speeches and sermons ended, and we got to the real heart of the ceremony, the actual christening. The baby made cooing noises and waved her little arms and legs, and was paraded around the room, looking adorable. And then we got on to the next most important part of the ceremony, the bestowing of blessings by the gathered witches. The buzz in the galleries had gotten much louder. The witches, too, were agitated, talking among themselves and turning searching faces in every direction.

The Frost Maiden rose to be the first offering a blessing. There was an audible intake of breath from the watching crowd, and the buzzing became a muted roar. We didn't like this, not at all.

René, trying to see everybody in the room, leaned so far out over the railing that I grabbed his shirt and hauled him back in. Master Sven shoved René aside and leaned over the railing himself.

The gathering of witches stood, and formed a line to take their turns offering their blessings. Master Sven straightened up and said, "I've got to tell His Wisdom that the Earth Mother is absent. Can't do it here, too noisy. I'll find you later." He disappeared into the crowd.

I strained my ears, but the muttering of the crowd was so loud I couldn't catch any of the blessings. A few minutes earlier I had wanted the ceremony to be over, and to get away from the heat and the press of people. Now I started praying, take your time; give the Earth Mother a chance to get here. When we were down to the next to last witch, the king and the foreign wizard were smiling broadly, looking relaxed. Queen Marguerite rocked in her seat and wrung her hands. Master Sven moved back into place behind me.

The next to last witch finished, and before the last one, a frightened-looking air witch, could step up, the Fire Warlock stepped out of the cold fireplace.

Power Struggle

When I first met the Warlock, he looked so ordinary that I could not have picked him out of a crowd, and on several occasions I had not been aware he had come into the kitchen until he spoke to me. But now, in a crowded ballroom filled with thousands of people, no one missed his arrival. In less than five seconds there was dead silence, except for his footsteps as he strolled up the aisle towards the dais. I held my breath. So did everyone else, except for the baby, and René, who opened his mouth and drew in breath. I elbowed him in the ribs. He closed his mouth and glowered.

The royal couple recovered enough to stand and pay their respects. The seated guests rose as a body. The noise they made lasted mere seconds, as no one wanted to miss the fireworks that were surely coming.

The Warlock was, as usual, clad all in black and silver. He wore a black tunic thickly embroidered with silver thread, black leggings and boots, the heavy silver and opal belt, and a matching band and bouquet of dancing flames on a black hat. The ruby in the Token of Office glowed and sparkled, sending red light flashing along the walls and floor. Despite the heat, he looked cool and comfortable, and amid all the pastels and bright summer colours, he stood out like a raven in a flock of canaries.

He looked quite debonair. His Satanic Majesty—he could have been Mephistopheles himself.

He reached the dais and said, "Your Highness," making a deep bow to the king. "Your Highness," bowing now to the Queen. He greeted the other guests, ending with a shallow bow and a wave of the hat to the galleries.

Good for him. That was more than we got from the king.

The Warlock said, "Please be seated." The nobles sat, and he waited for the noise to die away.

"Please forgive my late arrival, but my invitation must have gone astray. Perhaps it was in the same packet as the one for Her Wisdom, the Earth Mother. She sends her regrets, but says she cannot attend on such short notice."

He paused. The king and the foreign wizard seemed to relax. The crowd gave the faintest hint of a sigh. "Therefore I beg you to let me offer a blessing in her stead."

The king and the wizard both stiffened; the crowd breathed. After a slight hesitation, the king said, in a strained voice, "We would be honoured."

The Warlock turned towards the baby, and seemed to notice the waiting witch for the first time. He bowed his head towards her, and said, "After you." The relieved-looking little witch curtsied to him, then stepped up and gave her blessing—the gift of a pleasant singing voice—with a shaking wand.

The Warlock glanced around as if looking for anyone else waiting their turn, and motioned to someone I couldn't see behind one of the supporting pillars. The crowd strained to see. The witch behind the pillar seemed reluctant to come forward, and the Warlock made her a deeper bow, saying, "Please, I insist. After you."

Master Sven breathed in my ear, "That's why he came instead of her. Nobody will get a chance to go after him and defuse the blessing. They can't make that obvious a breach of protocol."

I breathed back, "A fat lot of good it would do anyway."

A woman came out from behind the column, and looked for help, not from the king, but from the foreign wizard. The flock of witches craned their necks as if they had never seen her before, and whispered to one another. The wizard shrugged his shoulders, and the witch stepped up and said something, so low that I couldn't hear it.

Then the Warlock stepped up onto the dais and next to the baby's cradle. He waved his wand over the princess, and speaking slowly and distinctly, so that everyone in the hall could hear, gave the Earth Mother's traditional blessing: "May you have a long and happy marriage to a man of your choosing."

I, and everyone else in the galleries, let out a sigh of relief. King Stephen glared. Queen Marguerite slumped in her throne and beamed at him.

We sucked in our breath again as the foreign wizard stood out of turn, and stepped to the front of the dais. The king glared at him, too, but didn't say anything. The wizard was a tall man, almost as tall as Warlock Arturos, though Arturos's shoulders were twice as broad. The wizard looked down his nose at the Warlock, but the Warlock was on his home ground.

The wizard said, "Your Wisdom—" Somehow the honorific sounded like You Dunce, and I snarled without sound.

"I am sure you intend to prevent an alliance between this princess and the emperor's son, but I am afraid you are too late. Your king has already signed and sealed an agreement, written on unburnable paper, that the princess will be given in marriage to Prince Sigismund when she reaches the age of twelve."

The crowd hissed. The Warlock didn't look surprised. "May I see that contract, Ambassador?"

The wizard looked smug. "No, I am afraid you may not. I have put it in safekeeping until I can deliver it to the emperor for him to sign."

"Then what is this?" A sheet of parchment appeared in the Fire Warlock's hand. The wizard looked shocked. The Warlock handed the parchment to the king. "Would you please confirm that this is the contract in question?" King Stephen looked sour, but nodded. The Warlock handed the paper to the wizard, and asked him the same question. The foreign wizard puffed his cheeks in and out a couple of times, then nodded.

The Warlock said, "Then shall we see if it is unburnable, as you say?"

The page became a sheet of flame, and the wizard jerked his hand away. It rose gently in the air, then broke apart into small scraps of ash that settled back towards the floor.

The Warlock said, "If the princess decides for herself, when she is old enough, that she wants to marry your prince, the Fire Office will not object to her doing so. But she would go as a mere wife, not as a princess with lands and honours to add to the Empire's."

His voice was like flames climbing up the columns and over the railings. He was not loud, but his voice resonated in my head. Many of the nobles clapped their hands over their ears.

"The Office of The Fire Warlock will not allow alliance marriages, most certainly not to our traditional enemies. Such marriages are a threat to the integrity and safety of this kingdom. The Great Coven made that decision a millennium ago.

"The king's domain is the governance of the people and trade with other states. The security of the kingdom is mine. The king may not, can not, make contracts that impinge on one of the four Officeholders without that power's consent."

The king and many of the nobles cringed. René, like many others in the gallery, cheered.

The Warlock stepped down from the dais. The foreign wizard, with a show of bravado, said, "You may not allow them, but your days as Fire Warlock are numbered. Your long reign is at an end. I have seen it."

The Warlock answered him with a mocking, "Thank you for your concern," and bowed. He bowed as before, to king, queen, and other guests. He ended with a wave of his hat to the gallery.

We applauded, despite looks like daggers thrown from nobles on the floor, as the Warlock sauntered down the aisle. When he reached the fireplace, tongues of flame shot out of it, sending nearby nobles scattering. He stepped into the fire, then he and the flames vanished.

Whatever was left of the ceremony was forgotten. The crowd roared and surged for the doors. The nobles shot to their feet. King Stephen shouted at the wizard and his court, then swept out in a fury. Queen Marguerite and her ladies gathered up the baby and beat a hasty retreat out the rear. I put my hands over my ears to protect them from the noise.

The three of us fought our way through the crowd, the mass of people taking eons to push through the doors and out into the fresh air. By the time we made it out my head hurt and we were all soaked through, our hair plastered to our heads, lines of sweat trickling down our backs and legs.

We met Warlock Arturos at the outer gates of the palace grounds. He was dressed in full fire wizard regalia and leaning nonchalantly against one of the columns supporting the gates, to the obvious discomfort of the guards. I wouldn't have dared tell him to move, either. Most of the people flooding through bowed or curtsied to him, with some of them saying things like, "Tell the Warlock we thank him" or "Our blessings on the Fire Guild, sir."

As we came up to him he said, "We can walk back together. I figured you three would want to talk."

René and I started in with questions, but he waved us off, saying,

"Later, after we reach our gate." The hordes of people surrounding us moved aside to let us through, but watched us avidly, not bothering to hide their curiosity. When we reached the Warlock's gate the guards saluted Arturos and let us through. I was relieved to be away from the staring eyes, and back in the blessed coolness of the plateau on which Blazes stood.

We talked about the pros and cons of alliance marriages, and why the Great Coven had forbidden them, until we reached the foot of the moving staircases. I stepped on first and turned to look at the big wizard. He was the last on, and we were now eye-to-eye. "Wasn't there any way the Warlock could have voided the contract without insulting the empire?"

Arturos shrugged. "Maybe. But war is coming sooner or later. He'd rather have it sooner. Problems don't get any better by pushing them off."

I shivered from dismay and because my wet dress felt clammy in the cool, dry air of the plateau. It stuck to me as if it were another layer of skin. Arturos stared, his eyes narrowed.

What nerve. I was—well, I should have been offended. I should—oh, my clothes were dry. "Thank you, sir," I said, feeling foolish.

"Besides," he said, "The king and his noble cronies are an even more ignoble lot than usual, and have been trying the Warlock's patience rather badly, so the four Officeholders conferred and agreed it was high time the Warlock should flex a little muscle."

"Oh," I said, "You mean the Frost Maiden knew what was coming?"

He shrugged. "Of course. In a contest between the Fire Warlock and the king, she'll support the Fire Office, no doubt about it—not that she has much choice. The Water Office would force her to, even though she hates the Warlock himself."

The Warlock was waiting at the tier with the wide courtyard. I wondered again if he ever wore anything beside black or dark grey. Mrs Cole had said they were practical, considering how much time he spent in and out of fireplaces.

He greeted us as we stepped off the stairs. "Thank you, Master Sven, for informing me that the christening was proceeding without the Earth Mother's presence."

Master Sven beamed. "Of course I should have realised you would already know, Your Wisdom."

"I did today, but I may not always. With war coming, all guild members

113

have a duty to report problems." He repeated one of his favourite adages, "It is better to repeat oneself—"

"—than to let something important go unsaid," all four of us chanted in unison.

"Oh no, have I been repeating myself that often?" He smiled, but his eyes looked unusually sombre. "I suppose I have. I find it hard sometimes to remember which of you children I have said something to.

"So what did you think of today's events?"

I said, "It was another round in the power struggle that's been going on between Fire Warlock and king for centuries. You won this round, but…"

He shook his head. "No, my dear. There is no power struggle between me and the king."

I goggled at him.

René said, "What?"

The Warlock's smile was bleak. "Does a boulder believe itself to be in a struggle with a mouse, whose claws scratch at the rock as he scrabbles over it? This is, of course, a matter of perspective. The king sees a power struggle that he is forever losing, against an obstinate and vindictive competitor. He believes he is David fighting Goliath, and will someday win if he can find my soft spot.

"I see an untalented and unintelligent man doing more damage to himself than to the rock he throws himself against. His true foe is the Office of the Western Gate, not the Warlock who temporarily holds the Office. He cannot wrest from me power that is not mine to give."

I said, "But… You're saying it's the Office that forbids alliance marriages, not you personally?"

They all stared at me. The Warlock looked disconcerted. That was impossible. My stomach did a flip-flop and I backed away from him.

Arturos grabbed my arm. "Don't fall down the stairs."

The Warlock said, "Why, yes. I thought that was common knowledge."

I was sweating again, but it was too late to take back my question. "It is. But just because everybody says something's so doesn't make it so. I assumed it had to be a stricture enforced by individual Fire Warlocks, not by the Office. Otherwise how could the contracts that were made have been allowed to stand?"

Flames crackled in the Warlock's voice. "What do you know about those?"

Gibson's *History*

The Fire Warlock, angry with me? I would have gone backwards down the stairs if Arturos hadn't still had a grip on my arm.

René bounced on the balls of his feet, brimming with questions but not saying anything.

Master Sven's gaze flicked between the Warlock and me. "Is she right? There have been contracts?"

The Warlock nodded without looking at Master Sven. His eyes, showing no hint of amusement, were intent on my face.

I said, "I read about them in Gibson's *History of the Office of the Fire Warlock*."

The Warlock gaped at me. He recovered and let out a bark of laughter. In his usual courteous voice he said, "Oh, my. Well, my dear, you continue to astound me. I commend you on your persistence."

I leaned against Arturos and whimpered.

"I hope you will forgive me for frightening you."

"Yes, sir," I bleated.

"How Gibson took such stirring events and reduced them to a soporific doorstop is beyond me. That book has never been a standard text at the universities. The histories that are, are less complete and sometimes misleading, which is why you, Master Sven, were unaware of these little details."

The Warlock laughed again. "She may know the political history of the Office better than you do."

Master Sven glared at him.

Arturos's torso shook. Startled, I looked up. He winked at me. He was laughing? I was making a spectacle of myself. I scuttled, crablike, away from him, and away from the stairs.

The Warlock sobered. "Lucinda, do you know what happened to those contracted marriages?"

What had it said? I couldn't recall any details. "No, sir."

"Very well then. I would rather not address this question, but with the curiosity you three exhibit, you will be more dangerous if you do not understand than if you do.

His voice, no longer quite so courteous, held the crisp snap of command. "Lucinda, René, Master Sven, the three of you will take a break from magical theory and research this historical question instead. The details are not all in Gibson; you will have to consult several other texts.

"This is Fire Guild business. You are not to talk about what you find with anyone other than the five of us here now. Master Sven, René, you are bound by your oaths as members of the Fire Guild."

The two of them exchanged wide-eyed glances.

"Lucinda, I must put a spell on you so that you cannot talk to the wrong ears. I am sorry, as a scholar I do not want to forbid another scholar from talking about his or her research, but this is for your own safety."

A spell? I didn't care. He wasn't going to hurt me. And he had called me another scholar, as if I were his equal. I melted into a warm, happy puddle.

"There have been nine attempted alliances. Come and talk to me when you have found them all. Now you must excuse us. Arturos and I have business to attend to."

The two warlocks rode off up the stairs, leaving Master Sven and René staring at me.

René said, "He made it sound like we're going to uncover some deep, dark secret."

Master Sven looked worried. "I think we are."

At supper that night, I told Mrs Cole about the christening. She wanted to know all the details, so we sat over our coffee for a long time, talking. On the way back to our rooms, I asked her about the Frost Maiden.

She said, "Why don't they get along? I don't know. I just know that they never have. There are some hair-raising stories about fights centuries ago between the two Officeholders. Conferences involving the current pair can be quite uncomfortable, I hear. They behave better than some of their predecessors, but can hardly stand to be in the same room together. Comes from having been lovers once, I suppose."

The Fire Warlock and the Frost Maiden? Lovers? Impossible. Wasn't it? Please, wasn't it?

She sighed. "I'm sorry. Of course, you didn't know. That was a long time ago, back before they were the Warlock and Frost Maiden. They're about the same age, you know, and both came into their offices during the last war with the Empire."

She sighed again, and said, "I feel for the poor dear. He must get awfully lonely, trapped up there all alone for more than a century. Such a virile young man, too, but after what happened to Nicole and Terésa, he doesn't have any choice, does he?"

We parted, and I brooded in my bedroom's window seat, pondering the events of the day. How much foreknowledge did the Warlock have of his own death? Would it be soon?

What had become of the Warlocks who had loved Nicole and Terésa, after their lovers' deaths? I had always before thought of them only as dirty old men. Now, having seen the Warlock as flesh and blood, not just the Office, I felt only one emotion, one that I had never before imagined that the Warlock deserved: pity.

"So what have you found?" the Warlock asked.

We were in an alcove in the library, where we had waylaid him. After he cast a spell blocking listening ears, Master Sven read down the list of attempted marriages and their outcomes. It had taken us several days, even with Master Sven's spellcraft and help from Master Thomas, to track all down all nine. It was a distressing list. Sometimes the Warlock had stepped in and forbidden the alliance, but in several cases that had not happened. Even so, the weddings had never taken place. One child died of a fall, another of a fever, and in the case that had come the closest to succeeding, the ship taking the princess to her wedding had foundered, and everyone on board drowned.

René said, "It doesn't seem right that they all died. Lots of people die young, but the royal family has an earth witch on duty all the time, right? And the Frost Maiden and Air Enchanter protect ships. They'd be keeping a tight watch on a ship carrying a princess, wouldn't they?"

The Warlock said, "They would. They did. But the Office of The Fire

Warlock is more powerful than either of those Offices, and when the fifty-seventh Warlock met the demands of the Fire Office by sinking the ship and murdering everyone on board, the other Officeholders had no choice but to go along."

Was he joking? His expression showed no trace of amusement. He had become so familiar that it was easy to forget how old he was. Not now. He looked ancient—not grey and wrinkled, but timeless, like a Greek statue. Even his normally vivid eyes were cold and hard.

Master Sven cleared his throat. "Do you know that for a fact, or could it be merely an unfortunate coincidence?"

"His private writings left no doubt; that is an historical fact. It was his last opportunity to deal with the problem. If he had not sunk the ship the Office would have killed him, and moved on to another warlock, and another, until it found one who would stop the marriage from taking place.

"He was, I dare say, the most evil-minded criminal who has ever held the Office. A responsible Warlock would have dealt with the problem much earlier. The conflicts between the Fire Guild and the other guilds are not one-sided. That goes for the tensions between the Fire Guild and the royal family as well. It would be good for you to remember that."

My heart was pounding, my hands trembling. "But, Your Wisdom, I don't understand. I thought when innocent people died it was because the Fire Warlock made a mess of things. The Fire Office protects the people of Frankland, particularly innocent children."

He shook his head. "No, my dear. That is what the Great Coven wanted the citizens of the country to believe. The true purpose of the Fire Office was to consolidate and hold the territory King Charles the Great conquered. When he died, Frankland consisted of an unhappy coalition of warring tribes—Franks, Saxons, Celts, Britons—those are but a few. By all rights, we should have splintered into dozens of petty fiefdoms to be swallowed up, one by one, by other conquerors. Only the four offices held us together.

"It has taken centuries to meld us into a cohesive country, but the role of the Fire Office has not changed with the decline of internal strife. It will, at all costs, ensure the integrity of the state of Frankland. A small, semantic difference, perhaps, from the publicised purpose, but a vital one to the lives of many people."

René said, "Doesn't it have to protect the state to protect the people?"

"Perhaps, but it has no judgement in doing so. In creating the Fire Office under King Charles's orders, the Great Coven gave the Office a set of mandates it must follow. The primary mandate is the preservation of the physical boundaries of the country against threat of invasion, political negotiation, or civil war. The Office may respond to the lesser mandates only after the greater mandates are satisfied. The mandate to protect innocent lives is rather far down the list, I regret to say.

"Consider a situation where we are at war, and all our harbours blockaded. If our crops failed, and our people were dying of famine, it would be only humane to surrender before the people of Frankland ceased to exist. But the Office will never allow surrender. Every last man, woman, and child in Frankland would die of starvation and the Office would still not allow another state to absorb the barren shell that remained."

We stared at him in shocked silence. He paused and looked at each of us in turn, making sure he had our full attention.

"This is the secret that I cannot allow you to talk about. Only the other Officeholders and a few members of the Fire Guild understand this.

"The lives and personalities of individual people mean nothing to the Office. Anyone who comes in conflict with one of its mandates will die a violent death. It has killed innocent people in the past, and will undoubtedly kill more in the future.

"If Charles the Great had understood that to follow this mandate the Office could and would kill even members of the royal family he would have had the members of the Great Coven executed for treason. That was why the myth was sown that the purpose of the Office was to protect innocent lives."

We sat for a while without talking, digesting what he had said.

Finally, René said, "Why were you angry that Lucinda knew about the marriage contracts?"

The Warlock smiled—a thin-lipped smile with no amusement in his eyes. "I was shocked, because I have, against all my instincts as an historian, been trying to suppress that information."

I gasped. He looked at me, and his eyes sparkled for the first time since we sat down.

He said, "I did not think that anyone living other than I had read all the way through Gibson's opus. Congratulations, my dear. That feat alone, and your grasp of the implications of what you read, would earn you a place in the Scholars' Guild, if I dared tell them. I regret that I cannot."

His praise—reward enough—went to my head like strong ale. "It doesn't matter, sir."

René said, "I still don't understand. Why do you want to suppress it?"

"Because I do want to protect the lives of innocent children. The Office will not let me tell the king the penalty for disobedience—that an alliance marriage would doom his daughter to a certain death at a young age. If he learns about those contracts, he will think, as Lucinda did, that it is just the Warlock being obstinate, and will keep trying to evade me. I would much rather he believed the Office forbade the contracts being made in the first place, and that it is futile to attempt them."

He looked at Master Sven, the tension in his face ebbing. "You should read Gibson's *History*. It is the definitive text on the Fire Guild's dealings with the nobility."

Master Sven groaned and muttered something under his breath. The Warlock laughed.

Other things I had read in Gibson's *History* had puzzled me. Were there other mandates the Office required the Fire Warlock to fulfil, even if it meant the Warlock looked like an obstinate jerk or incompetent bastard? Perhaps I should reread it. I was not going to ask the Warlock that question.

René said, "Were there other—Ow!" Master Sven and I had both elbowed him sharply in the ribs.

The Warlock's eyes twinkled. "Yes, alliance marriages are not the only such mandate. You are already bound not to disclose the secret; you need not fear to discuss what else you find amongst yourselves, or with me."

Need not fear? My mouth was dry and my pulse raced. I already knew which dream would come that night, the one of the shadow of the Office looming over me, poised to blot me out. And I no longer had the false comfort of believing that because I was harmless, the Office would not harm me.

I woke in terror three nights in a row from the dream of Storm King's looming shadow. Even during the daylight hours, my hands shook and I gasped for breath. I'd forgotten something—something important—long ago.

I lied to Mrs Cole when she asked what was wrong, saying I'd had word of a death in Lesser Campton. I needed help, but she would have told the

Warlock. I ducked out of sight whenever he appeared.

When Arturos came for dinner, I sobbed with relief. He and René sat talking with a couple of scholars long after everyone else had gone. I bit my fingernails down to the quick waiting for him to leave the table.

I pounced on him as he walked out of the dining room. "Sir, do you know anything about locks?"

Unlocking

Arturos looked baffled. "Locks? I know a little. Not much. Why?"

We walked towards the kitchen, René following. I asked, "How do they work?"

"A lock has a metal cylinder with pins in it, and when you put the key in—"

"No, no. I meant the magical kind. Lock spells."

"Oh, sorry. I don't know much more about them than I know about the mundane kind. Locks are barricades to protect something. That usually has the side effect of hiding whatever it is you're trying to protect, but not always. Most spells are about making things happen. Locks keep things from happening, and it takes a different way of thinking to get them to work than most witches and wizards can deal with, so the guild schools don't teach them.

"About the only other thing I know about them is that a good lock takes more energy to release—or break—than it took to set the lock in the first place."

We sat down at the table in the quiet kitchen. I sat on my shaking hands. "Have you ever used one?"

"No, can't say that I have. I tried one once when I was a student, but it didn't work. Well, it wasn't really a lock, just a bit of doggerel from an old children's story. I didn't really expect it would work, couldn't believe it was as simple as that, and I'd've been up a creek if it had."

The world stood still, waiting. I croaked, "Doggerel, sir?"

"From *Jack and Julie and the Three Witches*. 'Hide from witches my witchery. Send them away, and let me be.' Have you heard that story?"

123

A long-forgotten memory surfaced of my mother telling me bedtime stories. I nodded.

René said, "I don't know that one."

Arturos said, "Once upon a time…"

The verse he had just spoken appeared in my mind's eye. The letters hung in front of me, as clear as text on a page. I imagined a flame tracing out each letter, starting with the last and running backwards. What was I doing? I wasn't a witch. I couldn't unravel a spell. The flame sizzled through the letters, finished, and with a little 'pop,' the door to the glass cage flew open.

Arturos leapt to his feet, sending his chair crashing backwards onto the floor. His coffee cup smashed into pieces on the flagstones, the coffee splashing across the kitchen. He shouted, "What did you just do?"

The lines of text reappeared in my mind's eye, the flame racing through them. The door in my mind slammed shut again.

The fire roared. The Warlock charged out, scattering sparks and embers before him. I screamed. He scowled, and raised his wand, poised to strike. The massive ruby throbbed like a heartbeat, the light as painful to the eyes as looking into the sun. He came to a stop in front of us, balanced on the balls of his feet, his eyes darting around the room, taking in everything, scowling at me as if I were a total stranger.

Good God, he looked wicked. I jammed my fist against my mouth and whimpered.

Arturos held up a hand, then waved at me.

The Warlock asked, "Is there a threat here?"

Arturos chewed the end of his moustache. "Probably not."

The Fire Warlock relaxed a little, sinking back down and lowering his arms, but he still scowled. René opened his mouth and Arturos hissed, "Shhh."

The Warlock walked in a circle around us, making sweeping motions with his wand. On a second circuit, he paused at every step, tapping things—the table, the chairs, me, René—with a feather's touch of his wand. When he finished, he flicked his wand at the floor. The coffee and pieces of broken cup flew through the air into the fire.

He said, "It is not safe to talk here." He looked at Arturos. "I will go to the aerie with René and set the wards. You come with Miss Guillierre as soon as they are set." Arturos nodded. The Warlock motioned to René, and they vanished together into the fire.

I hunched over, hiding my face in my hands. My heartbeat pounded in my ears. "Arturos, I—"

"Be quiet," he barked.

We waited without speaking for several minutes. The only sounds in the quiet kitchen were the bubbling soup, the crackling of the small fire, and my rasping breath. I peeked through my fingers at Arturos. He glowered at me, looking as ferocious as his little pet.

I would rather have faced the lion.

"It's time." Arturos rose and started towards the fireplace, motioning for me to come.

I followed him to the hearth, but my feet wouldn't obey my order to go further.

He put his arm around my shoulders. "Close your eyes if that will help." I closed my eyes and let him guide me into the flames.

The Aerie

We took three steps and Arturos's arm dropped from my shoulders. I opened my eyes, and was disoriented. What was I seeing? Oh, my God. I screamed and clutched at Arturos. We stood in the open air on top of the highest peak of Storm King. Outside of a small flat circle, the ground dropped vertically on all sides, the vast caldera yawning at my feet, the long drop to the plains at my back.

I yammered, "Falling, falling…"

Walls and a ceiling appeared, closing us in. My vertigo disappeared; the other terrors resumed.

The Warlock said, "My apologies. I forget how this appears to visitors, I rarely have them here."

Couches appeared, arranged in a square around a central fire pit. The pulsating ruby lit the room. A small fire in the fire pit gave it no competition.

"Please, sit," he said. "We may be here a while." We sat. He paced. "Each of you in turn will describe what just took place, starting with René."

René said, in an unsteady, high voice, "I didn't do anything this time. Honest, Your Wisdom."

The Warlock, no longer scowling, but with his eyes hooded and face unreadable, said to René, "I did not mean to suggest that you did. I asked what you experienced, that is all. Tell me."

René said, "We were sitting at the kitchen table. Arturos was telling a story, when all of a sudden he jumped out of his chair and yelled at Lucinda. She did something, but I don't know what. And then you came. I don't know anything else."

"Thank you, René. Your turn, Miss Guillierre."

Miss Guillierre? I felt as if he'd stabbed me through the heart. What happened to 'my dear'? I clenched my hands together in my lap, and stammered a barely coherent explanation of my dreams, the conversation about locks, and unravelling the spell. "And then Arturos yelled at me, and before I had even had time to think, I had read the spell and the door slammed shut again. And then you came charging out of the fireplace. And that's it."

They stared at me, Arturos with an expression of disbelief on his face. I couldn't read the Warlock's expression. Did I dare say, may I go now? No.

There was a long silence. The Warlock resumed pacing, his hands together behind his back, the wand twitching. The pulsing of the ruby slowed, but the light was still bright enough to hurt. I couldn't look at it. Or at him.

He said, "You are telling me then, that you, as a small child, with no training, took a bit of doggerel from a child's story, and created a lock from it—a lock so powerful it hid an important talent from view for more than a decade. You held the lock for so long because you forgot its existence, and when reminded, could not remember the words of the spell. Is that a correct summation?"

What could I say? I looked at Arturos and René, but got no help from either. "I don't know, sir."

The Warlock paced another circuit of the room. "Your turn, Arturos."

Arturos said, "It's pretty much as René said. Lucinda asked about locks and I told her what I knew. I was starting to tell the story when I was shocked by the appearance of a…an apparently high-level magical talent that I didn't recognise, emanating, as far as I could tell, from the young woman across the table from me. I shouted at her—I don't remember what—and the high-level talent vanished. Like a door had slammed shut, just as she said. As far as I could tell from that brief glimpse, it seemed to be at least a level four, maybe even a level five talent."

René stared at me with eyes and mouth both wide open. "Are you a level five witch?"

I shook my head. The Warlock continued to pace, frowning at me. He said, "A good question. I also was shocked by the sudden appearance of what seemed to be a level five talent, one that I, too, did not recognise, shining like a beacon from inside the Fortress. I assumed that the Fortress was under attack by one of the Europan Empire's warlocks. I located the source in the kitchen, but it winked out before I got there.

"Miss Guillierre, I do not know how much you know about the castle's defences—I hope neither you nor René know much—but such a thing should not happen. Ever. Having known you now for several months, I would like to believe your story, and trust that you are not one of the Empire's spies. But as I had not seen any indication of talent from you greater than level one, this sudden jump to level five is extremely disturbing. Not just to me, but to the Fire Office. Even more so to the Office, which has little regard for personalities or the lives of individual people. Let me remind you that the primary purpose of the Office of The Warlock of the Western Gate is the defence of this country. Everything else connected with the Office—the library, quests, the lives of the people holding the Office, everything—is secondary."

He sank down on the couch across the fire from me, and looked at me sombrely. "I am afraid that we are going to have to make a test to see if your story is true, and to assess the full nature of your talent."

I said, "Do you want me to run the spell backwards again?" I brought up the mental image of the lines of text. Both warlocks shot to their feet shouting, "No, no, no," and waving their hands at me to stop.

I cringed, and blinked away the image. The Fire Warlock crashed back down onto the couch and raked a hand through his hair until it stood on end, the monstrous ruby throbbing like a heartbeat.

He said, "Good God, girl, you have no idea what you do to me. I do not know who is more terrified, you, because you do not know what will happen next, or I, because I do. Yes, soon I will want you to drop your lock—assuming that is what it is—but please do it when and where I tell you, or we risk the Office assuming the worst."

He got up and went back to pacing. He had always seemed to me to be the calmest person I had ever met. His pacing terrified me as much as his words. "Please keep in mind that while I have some discretion in guiding the Office in how best to achieve its goals, if it perceives that I am at odds with it, it will have no compunction about reducing me to a cinder and choosing a new Warlock. It has done such things many times already, and surely will again."

He smiled wanly. "And while I am not completely averse to sacrificing myself if it would improve the overall outcome, doing so simply because I am at odds with the Office serves no useful purpose. It would choose another Warlock, and another, until it found one who would satisfy it. No other candidate can perform the necessary test as gently as I can, so putting two lives rather than one at risk does not seem wise.

"I am holding back the demands of the Office as best I can, to give us breathing space to find out what the situation is, but the Office is pressing me quite hard to do something I would rather not have to do. It demands a full probe, and I cannot hold it off much longer.

"We will go down into the caldera, where the volcano will protect us on all sides from prying eyes, and there I will ask you to release your lock. Then Arturos and I will each, in turn, probe your mind and heart for all possible magical talents, and for whether you are an agent, or the dupe of an agent, of one of our country's enemies."

Arturos growled, "Hold on, why do you need me to do it, too? If she is a level five with a special talent for locks, then you'll find that out and you'll come back up here and we'll drink a toast to her health and the discovery of a new witch."

"You are not thinking this through. If she snapped that lock back on so quickly after you shouted at her, then we risk her shutting it back down reflexively in response to the probe. If she does so while I am probing her, that will have dire consequences." Arturos's face went white. "If you go first, she will know what to expect when I probe her, and is less likely to come to grief."

Arturos nodded slowly, looking sick. "I suppose that makes sense. But I don't have to like it."

The Warlock gripped the big wizard on the shoulder. "If you did, you would not be my friend." Then to me, "It is not a pleasant experience, and if done by a hostile wizard, or with a subject who fights the probe, it can cause permanent scarring. But Arturos and I have both experienced it first-hand, as a necessary part of our induction into the ranks of potential Officeholders. We suffered no lasting damage. I assure you we will probe you with as light a hand as possible while still getting the job done."

I nodded. I couldn't speak.

The Warlock looked from me to Arturos and back. "Then let us go before we have any more time to scare ourselves. It is too dangerous to use the fire to get down into the heart of the volcano. Instead, we will fly."

He offered me a hand, and helped me up. "Put your arm on my shoulder."
He put one arm around my waist, and the other around Arturos. One wall
of the room disappeared, and he led us out into the empty air.

The Probe

We floated downward into the volcano as if we were autumn leaves drifting towards the ground. The enormous crater, miles across, into which we descended looked like nothing I had ever seen or even imagined before. There was no grass, no trees, nothing green or living anywhere in that vast expanse. It looked like Hell.

Why was I not afraid of falling, when I had been so dizzy on my own with both feet planted firmly on the ground? Was it because I trusted the Warlock? If things went bad, he couldn't save me from the Office. Maybe I was so terrified of what would happen when we landed, that nothing more could scare me.

As we sank, the Warlock said, "As best I can describe it, the test we will be using feels like someone rummaging around in your mind, watching your most embarrassing memories. It is a galling invasion of privacy, but it feels slightly different for everyone who has gone through it. I experienced it as quite rude pushing and shoving, and I came out flaming the warlock who performed it on me. Celeste described her experience as being groped by a drunken soldier.

"The probe is a specialised form of mind-reading, but it looks strictly for magical talent, or traitorous intent. We are not interested in the boy you kissed at age fifteen under the apple tree."

I was sixteen, and it was behind the church. My cheeks burned before I realised he was making an educated guess.

"Or the petty sins you confessed to your pastor. If, however, those experiences involved any magical talent, we will see them. It will also stir up a number of old memories, some bad but some good, and you will have nightmares for several weeks afterwards."

The nightmares I was already having weren't bad enough?

Farther down, he sucked in his breath. "I forgot about René. I should have sent him back down to the Fortress after hearing his version of the event. He should not have had to hear all that."

On the other side, Arturos rumbled, "Maybe not so bad. You've giving him a first-hand demonstration of the need for control. Might do him more good than all my lecturing."

We landed, and the Warlock led us into a narrow tunnel. "A lava tube," he said. "Do not touch the sides; the rocks will cut like broken glass."

A few yards in, the tunnel opened out a bit wider, and the Warlock motioned for me to stand in the middle of the wide spot. There was no air movement. I tugged at the neckline of my dress. Five minutes in there and Arturos would have to dry me off for the third time.

Arturos stood in front of me, hefting his wand and blowing out through his moustache for a bit, before nodding and saying, "I guess I'm ready." He reached down and tapped on the floor of the tunnel. Cracks opened and a fiery pentagram surrounded my feet.

The Warlock said, "While the pentagram is there, Miss Guillierre, do not attempt to step out of it. Remember, the less you fight the probe, the easier it will be. Remember also, you must not reset the lock until we are done. Release it when you are ready."

I blinked back tears, and brought up the words of the spell in my mind's eye. I tried to trace backwards with the flame, but it wouldn't move. This was what the lock was for, to protect me from tormenting wizards. I struggled and shoved, and finally forced the flame to creep backwards. Tears cascaded down my cheeks. When the flame reached the beginning of the spell, I once again heard the little 'pop' in my head. The glass door of the cage flew open.

Arturos raised his wand, tapped me on the forehead and the temples, and began.

Memories—things I hadn't thought about in years—went flickering by. He dredged up everything I'd ever done that was embarrassing, awkward, rude, or sinful. What right did he have to see any of that?

The probe hurt, too, as if Arturos was manhandling me and stomping on my toes. A hard jolt, as if he had poked me in the ribs with an elbow, made me flinch. The lock spell flashed into my mind's eye. The flame raced through the letters. I caught and stopped it, even as the Warlock barked, "Stop!" Painfully, letter by letter, I forced the flame backwards to the beginning of the spell.

After that happened several times, I gritted my teeth and held the flame in place. Better to have it before me and stopped rather than risk it snapping all the way through before I could react.

How long would this go on? How long had it been? Fifteen minutes? Half an hour?

Arturos dropped his wand and the feeling of shoving vanished. The pentagram disappeared. I let the flame go, and as the lock snapped back into place, I stepped forward and slapped him as hard as I could. We both stammered out, "I'm sorry, I'm sorry." His arms came around me, holding me tight, stroking my hair. I sobbed into his tunic.

The Warlock gave me a few minutes to recover before saying, gently, "It is time, my dear."

If I didn't obey, the Office would have no mercy on me. I pulled away from the comfort of Arturos's arms and moved back into the middle of the tunnel. "It might be easier to ensure I don't use the lock again if I'm already holding it and concentrating on not letting it go."

"You have a point. If you would prefer to do that, you may."

He tapped on the floor and the pentagram reappeared, then he stood in front of me for a moment with his eyes closed, turned slightly away from me so that with his right arm raised and his left hand tucked into the small of his back, he looked like a fencer waiting for a challenge. He opened his eyes and looked at me. "Release your lock when you are ready."

There were tears in his eyes.

A strange calm settled over me. I was still close to a violent death, but Warlock Arturos had already seen that I was not a spy. The Fire Warlock must have thought that he, too, would see that I was a true daughter of Frankland—he had gone back to 'my dear' instead of 'Miss Guillierre.'

The conversations Arturos had had with René about power and control reassured me. Of all the Warlocks I had ever heard of, past or present, Warlock Quicksilver would be the most gentle.

Again I struggled with opening the lock, and then I held the lines of the spell in my mind's eye, with the flame poised at the beginning but not moving, and said, "I'm ready, sir."

He closed his eyes. Without looking at me, he touched me lightly with his wand and began to probe.

Vivid memories, good as well as bad, flashed past. The pressure was more like my father's firm hand on my shoulder when I was a child than lustful groping or bruising violence. I grew angry, as before, but at the Office for subjecting me to this indignity, rather than at the Warlock.

He had been wise in having Arturos go first. Having been prepared by clumsier handling, I did not often flinch. The flame quavered and pulsed, sparked and jumped, flared and danced, but I held it at the beginning.

And held it. For twice as long as Arturos had probed. What had been easy when it started became harder with every minute. I ground my teeth, breathing shallowly. Rivulets of sweat trickled down back, chest, legs, arms. I closed my eyes to keep the sweat out of them. The flame seemed mere inches from my eyes, burning them. My right foot was at a slant on the rough rock, straining the knee, but I couldn't see the pentagram, and didn't dare move. Locks of hair wet with sweat came loose and slithered down my back.

After it had gone on more than three times as long as Arturos had probed, I was in agony. I shook as with a fever, and my right knee throbbed. I flinched at a mild jolt that would not have bothered me at the start, and the flame slipped away from me. I caught it halfway through, and forced it back.

If it happened again, I wasn't sure I could catch it. How quickly would I die if I couldn't?

The Warlock said, "Done." The pressure vanished.

I gasped and let the flame go. The lock snapped back into place. I opened my eyes. The pentagram had disappeared.

I took a step towards the Warlock, my tortured knee gave way, and I pitched forward, falling towards the rough floor.

The Missing Warlock

I did not fall far. The Warlock caught me, and staggered with my weight. For a moment we clung together, sodden dress against wet tunic, fighting for balance. Then Arturos pulled me upright, away from the Warlock.

He stood with his head lowered, eyes closed, cheek turned towards me, expecting me to hit him, and willing to let me.

I said, "Thank you."

His head snapped up, and he stared at me with red-rimmed eyes.

Arturos growled, "Let's get out of this hellhole." He picked me up with as much ceremony as he would have given a sack of flour, and carried me at a trot towards the tunnel mouth.

As soon as we were clear the Warlock grabbed Arturos and we shot into the air, soaring upwards as fast as a striking falcon dives. The wind whipped the rest of my hair loose, and it streamed out behind like a banner. The vast bowl, so hideous before, now seemed imbued with majesty, but I had no time to contemplate its beauty as we rocketed up towards the pinnacle. René, with frightened eyes and a pale face, waited in the space of the aerie's missing wall. We were on him and he scrambled away as we tumbled in, staggering as we landed and collapsing on the couches.

The wall snapped back into place and shut out the sight of the caldera. A tray appeared, with glasses and a bottle of spirits. The Warlock reached out to pour, appeared to think better of it, and asked René to do it. I used both hands to hold the glass steady. I took big gulps, and choked and gagged, but forced it down, the awful, wonderful stuff burning my throat and spreading heat all the way down, like a lava flow of my own in the pit of my stomach.

Arturos was also shaking, sloshing the spirits out of his glass, but both men drained their glasses in one long, steady draught.

I finished my glass, and lay down on the couch to wait for the trembling to stop.

Where was I? I raised my head and looked around. I was in a room with four sofas around a small fire. A red-haired giant sprawled on his back on one sofa with arms and legs too big to fit splayed out in all directions. Another man, more compact, lay turned away from me, face down on another sofa. He looked like a lazy black cat. A boy sat with his arms around his knees, staring from one to another with wide eyes.

What in the world? Disconnected memories flashed past, none explaining why I was here—wherever here was. I sat up, and had to grab the back of the sofa to keep from falling off. Why did I feel drunk? Had I fallen victim to the lascivious men Mother Janet always warned me about? Everything hurt. I inspected my arms and found bruises.

The memory of the probe came back, and I recoiled. I slid back into a prone position, and reviewed the recent torture.

I was alive. I had used a lock spell. I was a witch?

My whole body ached. A drunken orgy might not have been much worse than the beating Arturos had given me, but it was a small price to pay for surviving. He hadn't wanted to hurt me. He'd done the best he could, and I'd repaid him by slapping him.

I hit a warlock? My God.

"Arturos, I—"

"Not Arturos." He turned his head without moving anything else and looked at me. "Beorn. After what we've been through, we must be the closest of friends or the worst of enemies. I'd rather have you as a friend."

"Thank you, Beorn," I said, trying out his name shyly.

The Warlock rolled over on his couch, exposing his ring. The ruby had gone back to its usual hypnotic flashes and deep red glow. He eased himself upright, wincing, but his voice was steady. "Quite right. You must call me Jean."

Jean? "I can't do that, sir."

"Why not? Am I not deserving of friends, too?"

My protest that of course he was, died, half-formed. He was teasing me.

"Of course, you should continue to call us by our *noms de guerre* in public, but it is inappropriate to make such distinctions of rank between warlocks in private."

I jerked upright, facing him. "What do you mean, between warlocks?"

His eyebrows arched upward. "My dear, if you can address me in that tone of voice, surely you can manage to call me by my name."

My cheeks burned. He was teasing me again. Damn the man—he made me blush entirely too often. And what did he mean, between warlocks? I was a witch.

Oh God, I was a witch.

He said, "As you are still here—praise be—you may surmise that I, Beorn, and the Fire Office are all satisfied that you are not a threat to Frankland. The Office therefore has little interest in you. Beorn and I, on the other hand, are finding you to be a very, very interesting young woman."

Arturos said, "I always said she was interesting."

The Warlock said, "Had I argued? I meant in terms of magical talent. My flippant analysis turned out to be almost correct, much closer than I would have thought possible. That is, at the age of six, you displayed a precocious talent for the specialised subcategory of spells known as locks. And so, on some occasion, when an adult you did not like probed too hard, you created a simple but quite effective lock."

"Who was it, Your Wisdom?"

He waved his hand. "A stranger you are unlikely to remember. Your lock hid your magical talents from his probing eyes. You did not know how to undo the lock, and its presence made no difference to your life at the time, other than having the desired effect of getting rid of nosy strangers, so the lock stayed in place and you forgot about it. Hiding your talents from the outside world did, however, have the side effect of hiding them from yourself as well, and you arrived at adulthood with no training in how to use your talents, and not even aware that they existed.

"As far as your talents go, the range is such that for the most part you are an ordinary level three fire witch—"

"Is that all?" René said. He looked disappointed. The Warlock eyed him but didn't respond.

I was a witch. After what they said earlier about level four or five, level three was a relief. Maybe I could handle that. And Master Sven would be pleased.

The Fire Warlock said, "The sole talent that you have developed unconsciously is prescience, attuned to a strong sense of self-preservation. You were wise in not telling me about your dreams."

His eyes were quite sombre. "If the Office had divined that you were hiding a magical talent under a lock before you knew how to release it… Steady, girl."

Arturos sat down beside me and put his arm around my shoulders. The Warlock poured me another glass of spirits and waited for my shaking to subside before continuing his analysis.

"What sets you apart from the ordinary are three things." He ticked them off on his fingers. "One: your burning curiosity, manifested in a love of scholarship. What you lack in practice, you are making up for in theory. In the past five months, you have blazed through the basic texts on magical theory. You and René are working at the university level. You can read a recipe, and with tutoring in the practical arts, you should someday be able to work almost any spell you put your mind to."

René's eyes glowed. I looked away from his eager face.

"Two: power and control. You have both of those as well. You need training in using them, but the fact that you could create that solid a lock at a breathtakingly early age indicates you already have an intuitive grasp."

Training? Did that mean the school, and not Master Sven?

"Three: your talent for locks. Most spells make something happen. Locks are about prevention. Most witches and wizards spend their lives mastering the art of agency. Few study locks. Those that do may find they cannot adjust mentally so as to make them work. Perhaps the fact that you had no training in spellcraft is what allowed you to create that simple and elegant lock. I do not know, I can only speculate. There have been few natural locksmiths in our history, and we know little about them, but you appear to be the most powerful one since the Warlock Locksmith of the Great Coven a thousand years ago."

René crowed, "I knew it, I knew it. I knew she was good."

When did the Warlock start speaking gibberish?

"And so, taken together, that adds up to a level five talent."

Level five? Hadn't he just said I was level three? I raved at him. "What do you mean, level five? Are you crazy? That's impossible! I've never done anything…I couldn't possibly…"

The Warlock was on his feet, towering over me, his black hair standing on end like an angry cat's, sparks flying from his eyes. "Be quiet and listen," he thundered. Arturos and Rene scrambled to their feet, looking stunned.

I said, "Yes, sir," and shut up.

The Warlock turned to Arturos and said in a normal voice, "Just trying to get her attention." Arturos grunted and fell back onto the couch.

René looked at the Warlock as if he was a cat the boy wasn't sure would purr or scratch. "How did you do that with the sparks?"

The Warlock grinned and said, "Nice parlour trick, eh? Some day I will teach you, but not today." He staggered a little sitting back down.

I said, "I'm sorry, sir."

He sighed. "I suppose it is upsetting to find oneself a level five witch with no warning. It must be as shocking to you as it is to me to find out that you fooled me, and the Office, for so long. I feel rather like getting hysterical myself."

He poured another round, and proposed a toast. "To the Fire Guild's newest warlock."

"But, sir—" I said.

"Jean," he corrected.

"Yes, sir, Jean, sir, I mean." His dark eyes danced. "Why are you calling me a warlock?"

"Ah, I beg your pardon. I assumed you would have heard about this little linguistic anomaly. Silly of me. We have our basic wizards and witches, male and female. The upper echelons of the other guilds have their male and female counterparts—sorcerers and sorceresses, enchanters and enchantresses, mothers and fathers—but there is no female equivalent to warlock. So by courtesy all the level five fire witches are called warlocks."

"Good gracious. I had no idea. Do you mean that of the seventy-three Fire Warlocks, some of them have been women?"

"Yes, of course. During the Scorching Times, with Warlocks dying right and left, there would not have been enough level five talent available to hold the Office if it had not been willing to use women, but the historical records are not clear. Most of the Warlocks had beards, or wives, or some other feature indicating that they were men, but at least three were clearly women. There are more than a dozen where I cannot tell which they were."

René eyes were round. "Does that mean Lucinda could end up being the Fire Warlock?"

I don't know how the men reacted to this idea. I did what any sensible person would have done under the circumstances. I fainted.

They made me lie with my feet up on the sofa until we were sure I wasn't going to faint again. Nobody had much to say; neither warlock ventured to answer René's question. I didn't want to hear an answer anyway. I watched Warlock Quicksilver. He and Arturos—Beorn—stared into the fire as if trying to read the answers to the world's problems there. His clothes were rumpled and his hair stuck out in all directions. I had never before seen him look dishevelled.

Why had I ever thought his looks ordinary? His face, with its expressive eyes and rapid mood changes, fascinated me. I could have gone on watching him for hours.

He looked up, and saw me studying him. He smiled, but it was a bleak smile, as if the weight of all those centuries of history were resting on his shoulders.

I asked, "What are you going to do with me now?"

He considered my question a while before answering. "You need intensive tutoring in the practical arts, and for several reasons it makes more sense in the Fortress rather than down in the town. There is an unused practice room with a shield to minimise the noise; we can use that. Keep your lock in place to hide your abilities whenever you are not in the practice room with your tutor. Beorn, you will move up into the Fortress and take over that aspect of her education."

Beorn drew in a long, deep breath, held it for several seconds, then let it out again. He nodded, and glanced at René, then looked a question at the Warlock, who said, "It will be easier for Lucinda if she has a partner. René, you may study the practical arts under Arturos's tutelage also. I will set the shield so that the geas on you will be lifted whenever you are in the practice room with Arturos."

René's eyes glowed, and he barraged the two warlocks with questions that they answered in a distracted manner. I watched the two of them exchanging looks over the boy's head.

René didn't get it. They weren't telling us everything, and they were worried.

Practical Arts

I said, "I don't care where you go. Just get out of here. Now!"

René's face fell and he shuffled out of the kitchen. I felt as guilty as if I'd kicked a puppy. Mrs Cole cast a questioning glance at me, but I didn't explain.

I'd had a wretched night, tossing and turning for hours, and when I did sleep, I woke in a cold sweat.

I was a witch? Not just a witch—a warlock. God Almighty. No wonder I'd hidden my talents.

I came down to the kitchen with a pounding headache. René bounced in early, eager to get started on the practical arts, and making so much racket I wanted to scream. I encouraged him to go to the library, the classroom, or anywhere else. When he didn't take the hint, I lost patience and ordered him out.

As we went in to dinner, I braced myself. The Warlock was going to stroll in looking cool and calm. Why didn't he ever have a bad night?

The doors opened, and he walked in looking frazzled and worried. There were bags under his eyes. My appetite vanished. Several of the scholars cast questioning looks in his direction and whispered among themselves.

May God forgive me for wishing he'd have a bad night.

After dinner, the Warlock asked Mrs Cole and me to come with him, and led us into one of the cave-like storerooms ranged on the mountain-facing side of the kitchen. On approaching the stone wall at the back, he told me to put out a hand and push. I did, and a section of stone swung open like a door.

He bowed us in, and we walked through a short tunnel into a room big enough to swallow the town hall in Rubierre. Two rows of small skylights cast a dim light. He flicked his wand and small flames dancing on air appeared in brackets spaced between the skylights. A fireplace large enough to roast an ox dominated one end of the room; a large table with several chairs stood halfway along the opposite wall.

Mrs Cole looked around with wide eyes. She said, "Well, La-di-dah! I'd heard the castle had some secret rooms, but all these years I'd had no idea one was right off the kitchen."

The Warlock said, "It is not right off the kitchen. The tunnel between the two rooms did not exist until this morning, but—"

I said, "How did you do that? Isn't that earth magic?"

"It is, but an earth witch performed a favour for me. We do favours for the Earth Guild, too. That is not new. There are several of these shortcuts around, including a few that exit the castle completely."

Aha. "Like one that comes out in that big cave of a fireplace in the royal palace?"

He smiled. "Yes, but please do not ever tell the king about that one. We are digressing. Rose, I wanted a way for Lucinda to come and go unnoticed. I need your help in this, but I am going to repay you by taking your assistant away. I offer you my apologies, but I am afraid it is necessary."

Mrs Cole stared at him. "Take her away? Why, what is she going to do?"

"Arturos will be tutoring her and René in practical witchcraft, starting this afternoon. Tomorrow they will be practicing with Arturos in the morning and continuing with their studies in theory in the afternoon." He gave Mrs Cole a condensed, matter-of-fact version of the previous day's events, leaving out the high drama. He did not give any information about levels, just stating that I was a more powerful witch than he had suspected.

Mrs Cole's head swivelled back and forth between the Warlock and me as he talked. She stared at him a bit longer, and said, "I can see there's more here than you're telling me, but don't worry, I'll keep my eyes open and my mouth shut."

He bowed to her, saying, "Thank you, my dear, I knew I could count on you."

On her way out, she whispered to me, "If you need a hug or a shoulder you know where to find me." She patted my hand and scurried away.

The Warlock told me to wait, and left by a different door.

I walked across the room to the marble table, and sat in one of the metal chairs, scuffing my toes on the flagstone floor. My nearly empty stomach growled. How angry would he be if I ran away? Not that I would. If I was a witch, I was going to be a scorcher of a good one.

The Warlock returned with Master Sven, René, and Arturos. Arturos and René went to inspect the contents of the boxes on the metal shelves at the far end of the room while he related the same story to Master Sven.

The tutor looked startled but delighted, and offered to help with our training in any way he could. "Should René and Lucinda continue as they have been in general theory, or should we focus on specific areas, to reinforce what they will be doing in the practical arts?"

The Warlock said, "Yes, indeed, I was coming to that. I do want a change of focus. The three of you will learn what you can about locks."

Master Sven looked taken aback. "Er, Your Wisdom, I know next to nothing about locks. I don't even know where to begin."

The Warlock flicked his wand at the table and two piles of books appeared, a short stack of about half a dozen, and a much larger pile.

"You will begin here. These are all the books I have found in the past century that address locks, and as you can see there are few. This stack," he tapped a book on top of the big pile with the butt of his wand, "reduces to this, if you eliminate the repetitions and plagiarisms." There were now three where there had been three dozen. "In a few months' time, you will all be world experts on locks. Is that a fair trade for keeping their studies a secret for the present?"

Master Sven said, "Why do…" and then a most extraordinary set of expressions flitted across his fair face—surprise, comprehension, shock, horror, before settling into resolution. "Yes, Your Wisdom, quite fair. I will do my best, sir."

I turned away. Sven was not helping me calm down.

René and Arturos came towards us carrying a box of candles. The three wizards and René discussed how to begin, and Master Sven left to go back to his other students.

The Warlock said, "Most of what you need to learn, Arturos will teach you, but there is one area neither of us knows much about. Lucinda, I want you to teach René your lock."

"I don't know what I did, sir. How can I teach it to someone else?"

"Attempting to explain it to René may help you clarify it in your own mind."

"Yes, sir. I'll try."

"Thank you, my dear." Then, leading me out of earshot, he said, "I want a private chat with you later. Come up to my study when Beorn is through with you here."

"Yes, sir."

"Good girl," he said, and left.

"Yesterday, you proved beyond a doubt to Jean and me that you are a fire witch," Beorn said. "Today, you're going to prove it to yourself." He set a candle in a candlestick on the table in front of me. "You are going to light a candle."

I backed away as if it had fangs. "How do I do that?"

"You combine your ability to create mental models of physical objects and real events with your innate ability—commonly referred to as magical talents—to apply the changes you make to the models in your mind back into the real world. The making and reshaping of mental models is the first and most fundamental of the four magics. All humans have that ability to a greater or lesser extent."

I rolled my eyes. "Yes, sir. I know, that's basic theory."

I knew that manipulating the mental models does not always go hand in hand with magical talent. Some mundanes—scholars, inventors, craftsmen, mathematicians among them—manipulate the mental models. Some witches and wizards—the annoying troublemakers the guilds have to spend too much time policing—direct the energy without understanding what they are doing.

The witches and wizards that are most valued are those adept with both the mental models and the flow of energy in the physical world. I had the mental capacity, but I would have to practice to become proficient at using my talent. The Fire Guild Council would never let an untrained warlock run loose, and I didn't want to spend the rest of my life with them breathing down my neck.

I said, "I meant—how do I get started? I've never done this before."

Beorn scratched his chin. "Oh. Interesting question. Most youngsters arriving here have been making nuisances of themselves, like René, by setting fires right and left without meaning to. I can tell you what I do, but the form of the mental models varies from person to person, and the key to tapping the energy also varies. What works for me may not work for you…"

"Go on. What do you do?"

"I'm tactile. The key for me when I was first starting out was rubbing my fingers together, feeling the energy between them. Now I do it in my head, but it still feels like flames are dancing on my fingertips."

I shuddered. I'd burnt my fingers too many times in the kitchen. "What about you, René?"

"The first time I used magic I was cold and wanted a fire. I pretended I was listening to the sound of the fire burning in the fireplace. Then I thought I wanted to hear that same sound coming from right in front of me, and there it was."

"Yes, that simple," Beorn said. "What happened when you created your lock?"

"I imagined the writing in my mind's eye, and saw a bright flame dancing along the lines."

"Your mental models seem to be textual and visual. Perhaps you should try imagining the sight of a flame on the candle."

Nothing happened.

He grinned. "Maybe you should unlock first."

Feeling sheepish, I released the lock and tried again. Still nothing happened.

"Hmmm, maybe not just a flame. How about the flame you were using on the text?"

I brought up the mental image again, and blinked away the written words, leaving just the flickering flame. I moved the flame so that it danced on the candle. Still nothing. I glared at it. *Light the candle, drat you!*

René jumped backwards three feet as the candle exploded in a foot-long column of burning wax. My jaw dropped open. Beorn's laugh echoed through the big room. "Ha, ha, knew you could do it, ha, ha, just a little problem of control, ha, ha, ha."

"I did that?"

"You betcha. Now you see why there's no burnable furniture in this room." He put another candle in the candlestick. "Try it again, more gently this time."

I imagined the flame shrinking until it was a mere spark. Again, nothing happened until I ordered it to light the candle. A red glow that lasted a few seconds appeared on the wick, then went out with a thin trail of smoke.

"Much better. What did you do to make it work?"

I told him about both the images and the words.

"Interesting. What happens if you think at it, without the image of the flame there, too?"

Nothing happened. I was soon convinced that I needed both the visual image and the words.

He said, "A little unusual, but we already knew you were that. Not that it matters. The important thing is finding out what works for you. Now both of you practice lighting candles until you can get the size of flame you want."

We practiced for the better part of an hour. I judged the amount of energy needed better than René, despite his already having used magic for some time. As we worked, something wound up tight inside me let go, and I began to enjoy myself. I picked up a bunch of candles with both hands, and lit them all, one after another, with flames all the same size. I grinned at Beorn. "I'm a fire witch. I am a fire witch."

He grinned back, and winked. "You're going to have to work hard, René, or you won't be able to hold a candle to her."

Later, Beorn set us to lighting other small things such as paper, wood chips, and pieces of kindling. When we started, lighting the candle seemed one of the easiest things I had ever done. After three hours, I ached, and the flame seemed like a real flame burning my eyes. René looked exhausted. He might have given up much earlier if he'd been willing to admit a girl could get the better of him.

Arturos let us stop when I lost control, and scorched entire sheets of paper instead of lighting corners.

The Warlock had said to come see him when we were done. I put my head down on the marble table and cried.

An Argument with the Warlock

The Fire Warlock wanted to talk about the prospect of me someday becoming the Fire Warlock. Why else would he want to talk to me alone, in his study? And what was he going to say when I broached a subject both he and Master Sven have warned me away from?

My body trudged on its own accord towards the stairs. My head pounded, stomach growled, muscles ached, and eyes burned. I would rather go to bed. I would rather go back to Lesser Campton. I would rather go just about anywhere else.

The Fortress, as a rule, was never a noisy place, but down on the level of the library there were the small sounds of scholars and staff moving about and talking in low voices, and the kitchen with its fire and bubbling pots of soup was never quiet. The silent stairs carried me away from those whispers. In the stillness, my own breathing seemed raucous. It was cold, too, even in August.

Mrs Cole had directed me to take the middle set of stairs (there was a set at each end of the Fortress, plus a grand one in the centre) and go to the first door on the right in the uppermost level. As the last flight of stairs rose, my heart sank. The double doors of carved mahogany, more than twice my height, were as intimidating as the entrance to the Fortress from Blazes. I couldn't knock on that.

He opened the door as I stepped off the stairs, and ushered me in.

Floor-to-ceiling windows marched along the outer wall. He gestured towards chairs by a window, and I waded across a carpet the size of the Rubierre town square. The carpet glowed in reds, yellows, and oranges against dark carved panelling on the other three walls.

I sat in an armchair upholstered in dark red. The chair fit as if it had been made for me. I ran my hands over the chair arms and marvelled at the softness of the leather. How many calves died to upholster this room? They didn't get this off of Old Bessie.

Under my skirt, I slipped my feet out of my shoes and dug my toes into the rich pile. My feet could be comfortable, even if my head wasn't.

The Warlock took a chair facing me. We studied each other for a few moments. He looked weary and out of sorts, and cleared his throat twice. He didn't want to talk to me, either. My stomach fluttered.

He said, "I am sorry you had a bad night. There are sleeping draughts you may take if you wish, although I would not advise taking them often. You will have to ride out the nightmares sooner or later."

"Yes, sir. Thank you, but I knew that. That's not what I'm concerned about." I took a deep breath, then said in a rush, "Your Wisdom, does René know he's a level five?"

He sat with his arms folded, his eyes guarded, a slight frown on his face. "No, because he is not one."

"Not yet, but you think he will be, otherwise why would you be spending so much effort on his education?"

"Yes. He came here already a level three, and most people do not display that level of talent until well into puberty. A good thing, too. Can you imagine what the world would be like if we had to deal with four-year-old warlocks throwing temper tantrums? The human race would not have survived this long."

"Yes, sir, but about René?"

"His talent outstripped his emotional maturity, and he was causing problems for everyone, including himself. I put a geas on him to prevent him using his magic until he had a better understanding of what he was doing, and the possible consequences."

"So why have you changed your mind? Why now, and why so much secrecy? Are you going to tell him? I think you should."

His frown deepened; the black brows drew together and his eyes grew even more guarded. He took a deep breath, and seemed to be choosing his words with care.

I said, more sharply than I had intended, "Don't lie to me, sir."

"Of course not," he snapped. "Surely your parents told you, never, ever lie to a warlock."

"Of course they did, sir. So?"

"Fool girl, are you forgetting you are a warlock? It applies to me, too. If I lied to you it would come back to bite me."

Maybe there was something to be said for being a warlock. "Aren't you lying to René?"

"I most certainly am not." The glower got even deeper. "I have not told him everything I know. That is not the same thing."

"It's close enough, if it misleads him."

"I am not misleading him. I am not burdening him with information he is not yet mature enough to handle. You did not like the suggestion he made yesterday that you might someday be the Warlock; you fainted. How well do you think a twelve-year-old will deal with that news? He might either be so scared by the idea that he would cower under the bed—"

"Not René."

"No, probably not. Or he might be so thrilled that he swaggers about and lords it over everyone else who is not level five."

"Or it might make him think and start to settle down to deal with consequences and control issues. That's what you want, isn't it? Beorn has been trying to make him appreciate the value of control, but he's not likely to understand if he doesn't see that that it applies to him."

"Enough. I did not invite you here to argue about René."

I glared at him with my arms crossed. He sat with his fingers steepled, eyes closed. After a bit, he went on in milder, almost placating, tones, "You may indeed be right about René. It has not been clear to me how I should handle him. I do not promise that I will tell him, but I will give your argument serious thought. I trust you will be content with that."

The Fire Warlock backing down? Miracles still happened. The throbbing in my head diminished. "Yes, sir."

He rubbed his eyes, and appeared to stifle a yawn. "Part of my concern about telling him is that he would have difficulty in keeping the secret, even with magic protecting it. Both he and you need breathing room in which to come to grips with your own powers before having to face the world with them. You are unusual in exhibiting strong talents without having developed defences at lower levels. There are forces in the outer world that would seize this opportunity and strike down an emerging warlock. We must keep your talents secret as long as possible, so that neither of you attract attention from our enemies until you can defend yourselves."

"I'm sorry, Your Wisdom. I should have known you would have good reasons."

"You need not apologise. It is good for me to have you take me to task. There are far too few people who are willing to do so."

He was thanking me for arguing with him? I stared at him.

"For someone who is usually so mild," he said, with his ghost of a smile, "you can put up a good fight."

"Do I, sir? I don't mean to. I mean I…"

He chuckled, dark eyes dancing. "You mean you would rather not fight if you did not have to. Correct?" I nodded. "But you have the intelligence, backbone, and other characteristics needed to put up a good fight if you feel you must protect someone you care about, like René, or your stepsister Claire.

"I know you rather well. If not before yesterday," he said drily, "certainly now. If the Office ever lands on your reluctant shoulders, you will carry it with more grace and wit than some of the more ambitious but less sensible warlocks who have coveted it."

The throb in my head came back, fiercer than before. "That's what you wanted to talk to me about, wasn't it, sir? About being a warlock?"

"Actually, no." He acknowledged my surprise with a small smile. "I would rather not talk about that, but I suppose I must." There was no trace of laughter about his eyes now. "Let me reassure you it is improbable you will ever be the Fire Warlock, nor is it likely to happen for many years, if it ever comes to that. I am not a seer, I cannot predict the future with any certainty, but I can say that I and all the other male warlocks will do our best to prevent that from ever happening."

"But how can you prevent it? Doesn't it always go to the oldest warlock? Won't it be my turn someday?"

"Certainly not. That is an old wives' tale told by people who do not understand how the Office works."

"But I thought…"

"No, the original texts left by the Great Coven confirm they never intended for the Office to choose the Warlock. That was a back-up plan, in case the recently deceased Warlock had failed in his responsibility of anointing his successor. The Office has some discretion; it will not choose either Warlock Nostradamus, whose mind is not up to the task, or Warlock Venturos, whose body is not. Further, it will choose a woman only if there are no competent male warlocks left. You look too happy, girl—you make me nervous."

I couldn't help it. The icy fear that had gripped my heart for the past day was melting away, my headache easing. He was teasing, anyway. No one could make the Fire Warlock nervous.

"But then why does everyone think that the Office always goes to the oldest available warlock?"

He sighed. "Laziness, neglect, irascibility, and all the other sins have taken their toll on the knowledge of the Office. For the first two hundred years, the Fire Office did go from appointed warlock to appointed warlock in orderly succession. We Warlocks have all been mere humans, not demigods, as popular opinion seems to hold. Far too few have been scholars, and few of us have ever wanted to admit that the end of our reign is just around the corner, so this important bit of information was lost in the mists of history. I did not know it when the Office landed on me, but since then I have read texts no one else has seen for hundreds of years. I am a font of trivia about all things relating to the Office, some of it even occasionally useful."

This last came out in a surprisingly bitter tone. I don't think he'd wanted me to hear that; he hurried on. "And while I encourage women to be scholars and mages if they have the intellect, I confess that I am old-fashioned enough to find the idea of a woman holding this Office appalling. The Office is here to protect women, not to put one where she will die a violent death."

"What? But you said…"

He smiled wryly. "I beg your pardon. Old habits are hard to break. Rather, I feel it is my duty to protect women and children."

I sat up straight. "Yes, sir. Thank you. Have you anointed…."

"Yes, Beorn is to be my successor, and he knows what to do to anoint René." I winced, and he said gently, "As I said, I am not a seer, but others are. We have reason to believe René will not be called on to be the Fire Warlock for years, perhaps not for decades."

"But someone has seen him as the Fire Warlock?" He nodded. "As an adult?" He nodded again.

I leaned back in the chair, relieved about René. My fears for Warlock Quicksilver were not relieved at all.

He said, "It is unlikely that you will become the Fire Warlock, but I cannot promise you will not. Despite our precautions and the Office's own safeguards, it may come about that you have to hold the Office between Beorn and René, or after René. I simply do not know. That is why, for your own protection, Beorn and I intend to give you the same training that we are giving René. Will you go along with this plan?"

I nodded slowly. He sighed. "Thank you, my dear."

"Sir, how does the Office transfer to a new Warlock? I mean, how does he know?"

"The Token of Office—the ring—goes to the successor. I was sitting at my desk in my study at the university when the ring dropped onto the page I was writing, setting the papers and nearly the whole study on fire. I had not expected the Office to come to me so soon. There were two other warlocks in age between my predecessor and me, so it was quite a shock. I have since come to believe that my predecessor—my teacher and a good friend—somehow stumbled on the key phrase used for anointing a successor."

"What if you didn't want it? Could you just, say, pick it up with tongs and hand it on to the next warlock?"

The Warlock looked dumbstruck. He blinked at me, before saying, "Ah... I have no idea. No one has ever attempted that. You must understand that, even with the inherent difficulties that come with the Office, the allure of power is strong, as is the sense of duty. I had not thought I wanted it, but when it was there, I did not hesitate to accept. It never occurred to me not to."

He considered this idea for several minutes. I think for a while he forgot I was there, because he came to with a start. "I beg your pardon. I want to talk to you about a different subject entirely." He paused, and rubbed the back of his neck. A muscle under his eye twitched.

What could be worse than talking about being the Warlock?

"It concerns your natural talent for locks. The Warlock Locksmith of the Great Coven played a large role in the creation of the interconnected spells and locks that make up the four Offices. Our enemies have had no success in breaking the Offices largely because there simply has not been anyone, in this country or elsewhere, for a thousand years, who has had the talent to understand what he did.

"There has been speculation for at least two centuries that we were due to have another locksmith arise. I have been searching high and low for most of my reign, hoping to find such a person. That is what most of my little jaunts outside the Fortress have been about—inspecting adolescents who have been rumoured to display unusual talents." He gave me a rueful smile. "And here you were, under my nose, for months." He paused, and rubbed the back of his neck again. "My dear Lucinda, I need your help."

"That's why you told us to become experts in locks, isn't it? But what do you want me to do?"

His voice was steady, but he had a white-knuckled grip on the chair arms. "I want you to help me break the Office of the Fire Warlock."

The Warlock's Plea

I held my breath, waiting for lightning to strike. Had Warlock Quicksilver gone mad? Break the Office? If he had said he was handing Frankland over to the Empire I would not have been more shocked. The ruby in the Token of Office glowed and sparkled in its normal glittering dance, not at all like the previous day's angry throbbing. I breathed again.

"I'm sorry, sir. I must have misunderstood. I thought you said you wanted me to help you break the Office of the Fire Warlock."

He gave me a rather tight-lipped smile and let go of the chair arms. "That is what I said. I am afraid I exaggerated to make sure I had your attention. I do not intend to abolish the Office. I want to fine-tune it to better meet the needs of the country, but in order to do so we need to take it apart and rebuild it."

That sounded saner, but only a little. "But, but…"

"But what? How? Or why? Let us start with why. The Office is far too rigid. I think you are aware of that. I ascribe many of the problems we have, from the uselessness of the noble class to the scorched circles on the landscape, to the inflexibility of the four offices. The world outside has changed, and we have not. Things that worked well for us during the first five hundred years, when the rest of Europa was in chaos, do not work well anymore. Our merchants and craftsmen are not keeping up with innovations in other countries. Our brightest scholars are going to universities elsewhere rather than foreign scholars flocking here. That is galling—my own personal bias. Three hundred years ago, our universities were the best in the world.

"The Office has one reason for existence and one only, the safety and security of the kingdom. The grave danger is that the Office's rigidity will become the most significant threat to our security. Whether the Office itself will recognise that it has become a menace—and what will happen if it does—is an open question. I do not know which I fear more: that the Office never changes and the country slowly chokes to death in its embrace, or the Office recognises the threat and destroys itself. If that happens, chaos will reign, and we will be swallowed by the Empire."

He paused and studied me again. "Have I frightened you enough?"

"Yes, sir. Would you please stop? I'm tired of being scared."

"I am sorry, my dear. I would no more frighten you deliberately than I would set a kitten on fire."

"Yes, sir."

"You may know that the Fire Office is not the only one with problems. The Water Office is broken—the Frost Maiden spends less energy using her office than in opposing it. It dispenses a nobles-are-presumed-innocent, common-people-be-damned variety of justice that is no longer appropriate. But she would not welcome my suggestions about fixing the Water Office."

"Yes, sir. That's obvious."

"As to how…" He went to a bookcase standing next to a large desk, and took three large bundles of papers off the shelves. "I have been working on that for more than a century." He hefted the bundles of papers, and then dropped them, one by one, onto the desk with a thud. "This is my life's work. When the Office came to me, and I perceived the problems it caused, I undertook the task of puzzling out the spells that had gone into creating it. At the time I thought a few adjustments would make things run more smoothly. What I found was an interconnected tangle that may not function if one piece is out of place.

"I spent more than seventy years researching and studying, and planning what needed to change. I got this far," he said, resting his hand on the pile of papers. "And then I ran into a wall. After twenty years—twenty years!—on the problem, I gave up. There is, at the core of the spells making up the Office, at least one lock, possibly more, that completely baffles me. I recognise that there is a lock, and that is the extent of it. I cannot make changes to any of the spells while that lock is in place. Even if I were able to, until I know what else is hidden I cannot risk making changes for fear of the whole thing crashing down like a house of cards."

He walked back to the chair and sat down. "I am the most powerful and capable wizard in the known world, but I have been defeated by a single lock."

We sat in silence while I struggled to make sense of all he had said. An orange tabby emerged from under the desk, walked over to us, and rubbed up against the Warlock's legs.

"Ah, Lucinda, may I introduce Cassandra? Cassandra, Lucinda." The cat jumped into his lap, and he scratched her under the chin. "She is my sole concession to female companionship, and is quite spoiled, I am afraid."

The cat settled down on his lap and he stroked her head and back. I imagined him doing that to me. I cursed myself as hot blood flooded my cheeks. He looked down at the purring cat, and didn't seem to notice. I had my treacherous face under control by the time he looked up.

"Sir, why hasn't the Office blasted us out of existence for talking like this?"

"That is a good question. For many years, I lived in terror that it would do so. When I began this project, I did not dare talk to anyone or even write down what I found. As time passed, I started making notes. The only other people I have talked to about this are Beorn, his father, and grandfather, and Mother Celeste. I broached the subject with Beorn's grandfather only after I ran into the wall about the lock.

"The Office is not a living thing. It does not have a mind of its own, and yet sometimes it acts as if it does. It is, as far as I know, the most complex entity ever created by magic. I sometimes wonder if the whole is greater than the sum of the parts, and that the Great Coven created something that even they did not fully understand. Can mere humans create something with a mind of its own, or even something that simply acts that way? And if we could, how would we ever determine which it is?"

He smiled at my bafflement. "I am sorry, that is a theoretical question for another day. Neither of us is in prime shape to tackle that one now. Back to the question at hand. Sometimes I have the oddest feeling, as if there were something aware, or almost aware, looking over my shoulder and approving of the work I have done, as if the Office itself recognises that it is too rigid and needs to be repaired.

"But that is most likely sheer nonsense," he went on briskly. "More likely either the Great Coven never considered the Warlock himself would be a threat, or whatever the Office is, it is supremely confident, knowing that my puny efforts will come to naught, and feeling no need to waste any effort protecting itself.

"Maybe none of those explanations make sense to you. The only things I know for sure are that the Office has never applied any pressure to make me stop trying to remould it, and that it does not now see you as a threat. That does not mean I may not yet trigger something that causes it to blast me into a charred lump."

"And me along with you?" I asked.

"That is indeed possible." He took a deep breath and let it out with a long sigh. "Given your sense of self-preservation, that might explain your reluctance to be recognised as a witch."

It was too late to go back into hiding. I chewed on my lip. I'd rather help the Warlock than do anything else with my life. If the Fire Office killed me for it, I would have a clear conscience, and it was better than drowning.

"At least it will be a swift end. Is there anything I should do now besides read those texts with Master Sven and René?"

He looked startled. "My dear, I assumed you would tell me to go jump in a lake—a dreadful thing to say to a fire wizard, by the way. I am honoured you are willing to help me. The only suggestion I have for now is that you should change the lock hiding your magical talent to one that hides it from everyone else, but not from you. I could suggest wording changes, but it will be better if you work something out on your own."

"Yes, sir, I'll try."

"Any other questions?"

"Yes, sir. Do I need to spend all my time with Beorn and Master Sven? I enjoy baking; I'd like to still help Mrs Cole in the kitchen."

His eyebrows rose, and he smiled. "That was not what I expected, but if you find it relaxing, then certainly you may, and not just because I enjoy the results. All work and no play makes Jill a dull girl, and all that. Just be clear in your own mind that the baking is secondary to your studies.

"One more thing. All of the four Officeholders are required to introduce a new level five talent to the others. This is something we cannot avoid, but I can postpone it for another week, perhaps. I am not worried about the other Officeholders; there is no danger of any of them talking where they should not. The members of the Fire Guild Council are more likely to talk without thinking, but we can delay introducing you to them for longer, perhaps even several months.

"Now you should go back downstairs, eat an early supper, and go to bed."

He rose, making the cat jump to the floor. She ran and hid under the desk. At the door, he paused, as if he wanted to say something but couldn't find the words. With his hand on my shoulder, he said, "Thank you. Sleep well," and let me go.

The Warlock needed my help. I floated down the stairs, happier than I had any right to be after agreeing to take on a task that might end in the Fire Office blasting me off the face of the planet. Further, I had stood my ground over René and he had backed down. I could have taken on Storm King itself.

In bed that night, my mood was not so sanguine. Rumours and speculation about the Warlock's time being about up were running rife in the Fortress and Blazes. I had bolted from the table when the scholars around me began laying odds on how long his successors would last. Considering a future without him in it made me feel as if I were back in the aerie, my head spinning with vertigo, a great void yawning at my feet.

How could I learn enough about locks to be useful in a short time if he had worked on the problem for decades and gotten nowhere? Even if I did figure them out someday, how could Beorn or René hope to repair the Office if he wasn't there to guide us?

Mrs Cole gave me a sleeping draught, and suggested I read something dull while waiting for it to work. Without enthusiasm I picked up the first book that came to hand on my bookshelf. I didn't look at it until I settled under the sheet, and then I flung it as hard as I could against the far wall.

Contrite over my mistreatment of a precious book, I got up and put it on the table by the door. I would take it back to the library tomorrow. Having *Nicole and the Warlock* in my room would not do anything for my peace of mind.

Preparations for War

The next morning the dining room was abuzz with gossip over the Warlock's actions the day before. Mrs Cole filled me in as I kneaded dough.

"He went to see Mrs Johnson—she's a housewife down in Blazes—and was with her for a long time, then the two of them together went to the school, where he pulled Warlock Arturos out of his class, and left Mrs Johnson there. Then he and Arturos went to the Guild Hall where he laid down the law, finally, to the rest of the Guild Council. He said he was out of patience, that Arturos was going to be spending all his time now at the Fortress getting ready to be the next Warlock, and that Mrs Johnson was taking over for Arturos. They of course got all huffy. Flint did most of the talking. He said that was ridiculous, Mrs Johnson was only a level three, Arturos wasn't next in line, and that kind of training wasn't needed anyway. He—Himself, that is, not Flint—said Mrs Johnson was an excellent teacher, Arturos was next in line because he said he was, and in the early years the Warlock had an apprenticeship of ten years or more. If Flint didn't like it, he could go jump in a lake. And on the way out, he turned back and said—and the clerk in the Guild Hall swears these are the exact words—'You, Flint, should thank me, because, God knows, if another Scorching Time comes, you will not last three weeks.'

"He's set the Council on its ear, that's for certain. They're pissed off, but the rest of us, we're scared. He's been the Warlock longer than even most of our grandparents could remember, and what it will be like without him…I don't even want to think about it." She wiped her eyes with her apron. "Of course, after what happened at the christening…" Her voice trailed away.

I understood. He was getting ready for war.

Beorn started the day's session by asking, "What are the three ways to stop a fire?"

René said, "Cool it off, or smother it."

I said, "Remove the fuel."

René smacked himself on the head, "I knew that!"

Beorn asked, "Now, which of those methods is available to the Fire Guild?"

René said, "Cool it off, I think."

"Right. Removing the fuel works sometimes for someone who is telekinetic, but neither of you are, and that isn't specific to fire wizards anyway. An air wizard could blow it out, and a water wizard could pour water on it, but we can't, and we don't generally have any means of smothering it, so for a fire wizard, that leaves sucking the heat out of it. How does that compare with starting a fire?"

"It's harder." We both knew that.

"Why?"

"Because once it's burning the fuel, it's hotter than the little spark needed to set it going," René said.

I added, "And you have to have somewhere else to transfer the energy to that won't burn."

"Correct on both counts. There's the further point that you are trying to gain control of something, rather than using energy you already control. You can absorb some of the energy yourself, but you nearly always have to have somewhere to dissipate some of it. Generally this means either the ground—rocks, boulders, sand, those are all good—water, or straight up into the air. That is what we are going to be practicing today, and since it's harder than starting a fire, you are going to spend a lot more time practicing this skill."

René and I both groaned.

"What? Do I sense a certain lack of enthusiasm? You have no idea how impressive it can be to instantly snuff out a raging bonfire. Let me demonstrate."

He piled up wood in the big fireplace, and set it ablaze. He let it burn long enough that we could feel the heat and see the wood start to char, and then snuffed it out. The heat was gone instantly; the charred places were as cold as the stone floor.

I said, "I have to admit, that's impressive."

"Good. Your turn."

I gulped, and eyed the big pile of wood with misgivings.

Beorn grinned. "But let's not start there. Start with a piece of straw."

"Yes, sir." My relief lasted only until we sat at the table, which held a sheaf of straw and a stack of iron bars. There was a box on the floor beside the table. I lifted the lid and saw rolls of fabric and jars of ointment—the Earth Guild's burn medicines. I looked up to see Beorn grinning.

"Glad you peeked?"

"No."

"Things happen." He shrugged. "The best way to guarantee that something will happen is to be unprepared for it."

Things did happen; we both suffered several burns—painful but quickly mended. All that heat had to go somewhere. It was supposed to go into the iron bars, but remembering to be a conduit does not come naturally. It took more power, too. By dinnertime, I was famished. When Beorn let us go, René hurtled for the door.

I lingered, despite my own hunger pangs. "Beorn, do you believe the rumours? The seers who say the Warlock's time is about up—are they credible?"

He combed his beard with his fingers before answering. "Lucinda, I'm one of those seers."

My stomach lurched. "Oh."

"Right. I know I'm going to be the Warlock. So, yes, I believe his time is about up. I read what was already written, but I feel guilty, as if it's my fault somehow."

I sat with my hands pressed tight between my knees. "It doesn't seem fair that the other Officeholders can retire and the Warlock can't."

"Scorching right it's not fair." He sighed. "It's especially not fair to Jean, given how well he's handled it. I wish I knew why the Great Coven made it impossible to retire. Maybe they still believed in Valhalla when the Offices were forged. I wonder if they thought all warlocks should die like warriors, so we would be there to fight for the gods when Ragnarök, the end times, come. Sometimes I wish I believed in the old gods; it would make the Office easier to bear, maybe."

"Did you say it wouldn't be fair for you to marry again because you know you're going to be the Warlock?"

"You betcha. I've read what Warlock Alchemio wrote after Terésa died in his arms. Heartbreaking…"

"What's the matter with the Fire Office? Plenty of fire wizards marry mundanes without burning them to death. It happens all the time, doesn't it?"

"Sure, but the Fire Warlock is different. Having the power of the volcano at your fingertips all the time is too scorching dangerous…I wish I could marry again. I don't want to live the rest of my life like a monk. It's been torture for Jean. At least I won't last as long, but could you imagine killing your own wife? Compared to that, knowing I'm going to die a fiery death myself isn't so bad."

Cold chills ran down my spine. "Just because you know you're going to be the Warlock doesn't mean it has to be soon."

The look on his face was so bleak that my spirits, already low, slid right down onto the cold, hard floor.

He said, "No dice. I've seen myself as Warlock with no more grey in my beard than I have now. There's no way around it. He's not going to last to the end of this war."

The memories that had been disturbed by the probe continued to surface at random intervals. I threw fits of temper at the least provocation, and burst into tears several times a day. My erratic behaviour didn't seem to bother either Beorn or Master Sven—one or the other was at my elbow every meal, making excuses for me and deflecting questions.

When a memory surfaced during the day, I would lose concentration, with unfortunate results. I suffered far more burns than René did. Beorn wouldn't let René tease me, but he wouldn't let me slack off, either. He made us practice snuffing fires over and over and over again, and wouldn't let us move on to anything else until we could extinguish the straw instantly and coldly. By the end of the week, we were both heartily sick of burning straw, but Beorn gave us no respite. We left our morning sessions physically exhausted, ravenous, and drenched with sweat.

The afternoon sessions with Master Sven left us mentally exhausted. He was even more focused and serious than usual, and he left his other students to fend for themselves while the three of us sat with our heads together over the texts on locks. They were as dense and obscure as Father's law books. When René complained, Master Sven said, "Remember that these aren't textbooks for students; these are scholarly texts written by scholars and mages for each other. The mages, especially, were trying to impress the other mages and scholars with the depth of their scholarship while still holding back a few little secrets, so some of it was written with the intent of being obscure. You have to read this stuff in the right frame of mind, which is that if it says 'individuals not yet having reached the age of maturity should be processed by the visual organs rather than perceived by the auditory system' it means 'children should be seen and not heard'."

That advice helped. I read each sentence with a critical eye, to see how it could be unravelled into something simpler, and soon it began to make more sense. Towards the end of the second afternoon Master Sven looked up from his book and said, "It appears to me that 'lock' is a bit of a misnomer—at least they aren't locks in the physical sense where a lock is only part of the protective structure, and fits onto a door or box lid or something like that. It's useless to put a sturdy lock on a flimsy box, as you can still get to whatever the lock protects by breaking the container. These magical locks, on the other hand, are the complete container, and there isn't any other weak point. You have to either break or release the lock to get to the contents."

"So how do you do that?" René asked.

"I wish I knew," he said glumly, and went back to reading.

I revised my lock to say, 'Hide from witches my witchery, all save me, still let me see.'

The glass cage enclosed me, but I could still light a fire. I no longer felt as if I were suffocating. It felt comforting, like a shield, so I kept it on all the time, both in and out of the practice room, as neither Beorn nor I wanted me to risk forgetting and going out without it.

After a week, I made it through a morning's session without losing my concentration, or getting burned, once. I began to relax. In two more days, the Warlock would introduce me to the other three Officeholders, and then the worst would be over.

Or so I thought. I was in the classroom when a memory flashed through my mind's eye.

Why hadn't the Office killed me? It might yet.

I came to, and found Master Sven and René staring as if I'd been speaking gibberish. How long had I been lost in a flood of bad memories? I wiped damp palms on my skirt and stood up, leaning on the table for support. "Master Sven, I have to see the Fire Warlock. Right now."

The Chessmaster

Master Sven said, "Are you ill? Why do you need to see the Warlock?"
"He said to tell him if I ever figured out why I didn't want to be a witch. I—"

"Then by all means, go. Would you like one of us to come with you?" He looked worried. I couldn't blame him; I knew I looked haggard.

I assured him I was fine, and ran for the door. What would I do if Warlock Quicksilver wasn't in his study? I ascended the stairs with my heart in my mouth.

He opened his study door and greeted me as I stepped off the stairs. "To what do I owe the honour of this visit?" He ushered me in, and gestured towards a couch in front of the fireplace at the back of the room. "A social call? I think not. Not with such a woeful expression. What is the matter, my dear? Out with it."

We sat down side-by-side on the couch, facing the fireplace. The warmth of the fire was welcome, and I leaned forwards, hoping I could stop shivering. "I've just remembered something, Your Wisdom, and it's dreadful."

He didn't move. "I am listening. Pray continue."

"It's about the Empire's wizard—the one we saw at the christening, who said your reign was almost over. I thought I'd seen him before, but I didn't know when. Now I remember. He's the wizard who upset me so much when I was six that I created that lock."

His unruffled expression didn't change. "Yes, I know."

"You know? But…"

"My dear, did you not think we would examine that episode when we probed your mind? I am surprised you remember him, that first event happened so long ago. But yes, I recognised him."

He paused, studying the fire, frowning slightly. I watched him, twisting my hands together in my lap, the nails digging into the palms so hard they hurt. When he turned towards me, it was with a sombre expression.

"You have taken me to task for holding back information from René. I suppose I shall have to make a clean breast of it and tell you all I know about your own part in this story."

"What did he want with me?"

The Warlock held up a hand. "Please, you may call me a patronising old fool if you wish, but I felt you had had as much as you could take this past week. Are you sure you want to hear more?"

"Yes, sir." My voice trembled despite my best efforts to hold it steady. "If it's bad news, putting it off won't make anything any easier."

"Very well. The Earth Guild exposed some fragments after they began making enquiries about your stepsister's glamour spell, and the rest we have uncovered this past week. Watch," he said, pointing to the fire.

I looked into the burning embers, and they seemed to expand to fill my entire field of vision. I saw the Empire's wizard in the embers, and then the embers and the sound of the burning faded away, and I watched the foreign wizard walk towards the village of Lesser Campton, where I was born.

He was dressed in neither a wizard's robes nor the outlandish fashions of the Empire, but in a simple scholar's robe. He had sounded foreign at the christening but there was no trace of an accent when he stopped the first person he met in the village square.

"Could you please direct me to Scholar Guillierre's house?"

The butcher's wife, surprisingly young-looking, said, "Yes, sir. Follow that lane on the other side of the mill. Their house is the first one past the end of the rock wall."

Once out of sight of the village square, he took an instrument like a compass out of his pocket, and nodded when he saw it pointed towards our house. He walked past the gate and further down the lane, where he stopped and checked the compass again. Satisfied, he came back and knocked on our door. Although by now I expected it, I caught my breath when my mother answered the door. He introduced himself as a scholar on an errand to my father, and she led him to my father's study. My eyes stung when Mother left; I struggled to keep my mind focused on the wizard.

The scene blurred. Family and guest were eating dinner. My father sat at the head of the table and mother at the foot, the foreign wizard and a small girl sitting opposite each other. Oh, dear. No wonder Mother was always after me to scrub my face. The wizard argued some historical point with Father a bit absentmindedly, but neither Father nor Mother seemed to notice his rapt attention on the girl across the table. My younger self noticed, and didn't like it. I squirmed, glared, and stuck out my tongue.

"Lucinda, stop that," my mother chided.

I sulked. When she turned her back to reach for a pitcher, I stuck out my tongue again.

"Lucinda, I've had enough." She grabbed me and hauled me away upstairs, leaving Father apologising for my bad behaviour and the wizard chuckling.

After dinner Father, who was not in good health, went upstairs to take a nap, leaving the wizard reading in the study. The wizard listened until he heard Father's door close, then took out the compass and checked it once again. He raised a wand and summoned me to come to him. I came unwillingly and tried to hide behind the door.

He said, "Ah, my dear Lucinda. Are you fond of stories about the Fire Guild?"

I didn't answer. A look of concentration came over my younger face, as I set my lock.

"Would you like to meet the Fire Warlock some day? I could help you do so."

I crossed my arms and glared at him. He had other questions but I wouldn't answer any of them. It didn't matter, the longer the wizard studied me the happier he looked. He took other instruments out of his pocket and pointed them at me. When he let me go he was gloating.

The scene blurred and shifted, and the wizard was now in another scholar's study, a dim and dusty little hole of a room, the man occupying it clad in a threadbare and badly mended robe. Hadn't I seen him before, too? He quivered as the wizard counted out gold coins into three stacks in front of him.

The wizard said, "You know the scholar Guillierre who lives in the village of Lesser Campton?" The shabby scholar nodded. The wizard continued, "He has a small daughter who is destined for great things. I am interested in this child's welfare. For this sum you will do three things: one, send me a report yearly on her health and condition. Two, poison her father's relationship with the Scholars' Guild"—the scholar's head came up at this and his eyes widened; I clenched my hands into fists—"so that he does not bring her to the yearly meetings—she must not marry a scholar. Three, this girl will be a low-level witch, but talented enough to use a glamour spell. When she is old enough, hire an earth witch or air witch to teach her how to use one. I will give you a third of this gold now; the other two stacks will be yours on completion of the second and third items. Do you agree to do this?"

The scholar looked uneasy, but eyed the money. The wizard pushed one stack towards him, and he nodded slowly.

I was back in the Warlock's study, clenching my hands together in my lap. I glared at the Warlock. The black eyebrows lifted in question.

"Your Wisdom, I knew nothing of any of this. I did not and do not want to be this wizard's minion."

"Very well then, you should not start."

"Of course not! I…er, what?"

"You have not been before now, I think you should continue that way."

The smile in his eyes was back. I unclenched my fists and held my cold hands out towards the fire.

He said, "I have watched that wizard all his life. He styles himself the Chessmaster, and he has grand plans and Byzantine schemes involving dozens or hundreds of people that he thinks to move around as on a great chessboard. He never sees other forces at work that use him as he seeks to use others, or that his pawns pick themselves up and move around on their own when his back is turned. It is especially dangerous to treat a warlock as a pawn."

The Warlock paused, and reaching out, put his hand under my chin and turned my face so I had to look him square in the eye.

"You are a queen, my dear. You command the whole board. If not yet, then soon. Never forget that."

He pulled back his hand. "I do not mean to imply that he is not dangerous. He is. He is an enchanter with a well-developed talent for the magic of illusion. If you encounter him again, be wary. But he sought to use you based on prognostication without understanding your talents, so you have had the advantage. Even while you were not aware of your talents they have clearly been at work."

He gestured at the fire. Looking in, I watched Claire fasten a bracelet on her arm. The magnificent creation in gold and lapis lazuli was the perfect complement to her golden hair and blue eyes.

I pulled back from the fire. "This vision can't be real. I've never seen that bracelet before, and we couldn't afford anything like it anyway."

"Claire has worn that bracelet every day for the past five years."

I gaped at him.

He said, "That bracelet is enchanted with a forget spell, and a glamour spell that Mother Celeste says is one of the most powerful she has ever seen—one most members of the Fire Guild have no natural defence for. The Fire Office shields me, and Beorn, as my apprentice. If we did not have earth magic woven into the Fire Office…" He shrugged.

"You have seen the glamour spell was intended for you. The Chessmaster must have thought you would need it to get close to me. More fool him. A witch came to your home with the instructions to enchant a piece of jewellery for the level one witch of a certain age. With your lock in place, she saw Claire and never noticed you. It is just as well—you are more appealing as you are. If you had tried to use a glamour spell on me I would have banished you to Blazes, and the odds of your having survived last week's encounter with the Fire Office would have been slim."

I licked dry lips. "Why is he so interested in me?"

He stared at the fire for a moment, then sighed. "I would rather not show you this, but you will not be any better off not knowing. Some day there will be rumours about this, and you should be fore-warned. Watch the fire again."

Deep in the fire, the wizard reappeared, seated with our king in a private chamber.

"Your Majesty," he said, "your dynasty's long search for a solution to the problem of the Fire Warlock's usurpation of your powers is nearly at an end." Usurpation, my foot—I wanted to flame him. The king leaned forward eagerly. The wizard's portentous manner seemed to impress the king, but it made my hackles rise. And what was King Stephen doing conspiring with a foreign wizard against our own Fire Warlock?

The wizard went on, "I have read the signs and studied the omens, and I have seen a girl, a young woman of low birth, claim a place in the Warlock's lustful heart. Her destiny is written in the stars; she will wrest from him the hidden secrets at the heart of his Office, and bring about the accursed Warlock's downfall!"

I lurched backwards, my gut hurting as if the foreign wizard had punched me. I stared, speechless, at the Warlock, who unhurriedly flicked his wand. Another log dropped on the fire.

"Relax. If you were a serious threat to the Office do you think you would be sitting here?"

"No, sir."

I pulled my feet up onto the couch and hugged my knees to my chest, trying to still the hammering of my heart. It would have been impossible to keep the quaver out of my voice—I didn't try. "Was that a false prophecy, then, Your Wisdom?"

"Not…necessarily. Please remember that prophecies and oracles, even the ones that seem the most straightforward, are always ambiguous. Always. You have been over the theory with Master Sven. How does one cope with a prophecy one does not like?"

I gave the stock answer. "You invoke the fourth magic, the magic of the self-fulfilling prophecy, by finding an interpretation you can live with and working towards that."

"Exactly. There are other prophecies in play besides this one, some in apparent contradiction to it. There is a long-standing one that says a second warlock locksmith will refine the work the first one started. There are the visions Beorn has had that show first him and then René as the Warlock. The Chessmaster's prophecy does not indicate you will destroy the Office. Not at all. That is what he would like to believe, but it is wishful thinking on his part."

He reached over and squeezed my shoulder. "The interpretation that I have come up with—that I want to make happen—is that there is no threat to the Office. That you will unlock the secret at its heart—you cannot wrest it from me since I do not know it—and in doing so learn how to fix it. That Beorn and René, with your help, will recast the spells and locks that need fixing so the Office is stronger and Frankland healthier than ever.

"Now is that a bad outcome?"

I sat with my face on my knees, not looking at him, considering what he'd said. The interpretation he'd given was possible, and in the grand scheme of things, no, not a bad outcome. That's what my head said. The icy claw around my heart said something else entirely.

Still with my face turned away, I whispered, "How can it be a good outcome without you?"

Silence. Cassandra appeared and jumped up on the couch between us. I turned my head and looked at the Warlock; he was leaning forward, elbows on knees, staring into the fire. Was he seeing things there, or was he lost in his own thoughts? He glanced at me, and schooled his face into a neutral expression, but I had glimpsed bleak despair.

The cat butted him with her head; he ignored her. Still staring into the fire, he said, "People die. Those left grieve but continue with their lives. I am not so arrogant I think the world will fall to pieces without me, or that you will be wearing sackcloth and ashes ten years after I am gone. You will recover. You will marry and be happy. That is the way it should be."

"How can I be happy if I'm responsible for...for..."

I stalked over to a window, and stood with my arms folded tightly across my chest, looking out at but not seeing the barren lava fields stretching out to the southwest. How dare the Chessmaster use me like this! "What in God's name does he think I am going to do anyway?"

I didn't hear the Warlock move, but he spoke from right behind me. "I have not the faintest idea. It seems more probable I should be your downfall than you mine. For a few hours last week on Storm King, I believed both of us faced immediate death, but that did not fit with the prophecies either."

He paced down the row of windows, and then back. He stopped beside me, gazing out the window. "It seems far more likely I will die in battle the same way so many of my predecessors have, by becoming so drained I can no longer maintain control. And war is upon us. The Empire is already making the first moves—they are harassing our merchants, trying to strangle us. I can do little about that, but the Air and Water Officeholders will make the harassment expensive for the Empire, and they will soon have to bring the fight here or back down. But I do not see what part you could play in that confrontation.

"I have faced battle and the prospect of dying before. The risk of disaster is always there whenever I draw on Storm King, no matter how ordinary the task. I am not afraid of death, but I am not resigned to it either. A year ago I would have welcomed it. I had failed at the task I had set out to do, and I was heartily sick of the Office." He resumed pacing. "But now—now I have both a renewed interest in living, and the knowledge that my time is running out."

For a brief moment, hope flared. I said, "Isn't there any way you can leave the Office? Retire, I mean. Wasn't there one whose wife got fed up, and one day said to him, 'Oh for God's sake, Harry, I wish you weren't the damned Warlock anymore,' and with that he wasn't?"

He turned to look at me with raised eyebrows. "Where did you—oh, yes, from Gibson's *History*. That story was about the seventeenth Warlock, one of many who were married when the Office came to them. As far as I can tell, the story is apocryphal. Gibson wrote his tome hundreds of years later, and I can find no earlier written record confirming it. I have wondered about that story many times—in everything else Gibson appears meticulously factual.

"If wishing were enough to get one out of it, it would have left me a long time ago, nor would I have been the only one. The fifty-seventh in particular loathed being the Warlock, and tried everything possible to get out of it."

There was a gleam of humour in his eye. "Just as well perhaps; he was quite a lecherous old goat, whose appetites caused a good deal of harm before the Office descended upon him. Being unable to touch a woman for twenty-odd years was a fine comeuppance." The humour faded. "No, I cannot see a way out, and I cannot afford to waste any more time looking for one."

He leaned on the window frame, looking more like a mere forlorn mortal than the powerful Warlock. I had to leave before I did something foolish. I laid a hand on his shoulder, said, "Jean, I'm sorry," and walked out.

Master Sven was waiting for me at the foot of the stairs on the kitchen level. His worried expression deepened as I got closer. I did not try to hide the tears on my cheeks. Without a word, he held out his arms to me, and I think I astonished him by accepting his embrace, and sobbing into his shoulder.

Fire and Frost

"It's beautiful, Mrs Cole, but I can't wear that." The gown she held out was a superb creation in burgundy velvet and satin. I made no move to take it. "That's much too grand. It must be worth more than all the clothes I've ever had, put together. If I wear it, I'll ruin it. Spill something on it, or tear it, or—"

She clucked at me. "Rubbish. You'll be fine. The dress you're wearing won't do for meeting the other three Officeholders."

I plucked at my linen work dress. "But I'm a supplicant. You said I should dress like one."

"You're representing the Fire Guild today, honey, and that's more important. You don't want to let Himself down, do you?"

My ears burned. "No, ma'am. Since you put it like that—"

"Good. Come along." She scurried down the corridor. I had to trot to keep up with her.

"Where are we going?"

"To the ballroom. There are full-length mirrors there, you can see for yourself how it looks."

Sitting in front of the mirrors while she fussed with my hair, I gaped at the stranger gawking back at me. I raised my chin and looked down my nose. There was no doubt about it—that woman was a fire witch.

"Mrs Cole, are you sure you're not a fairy godmother?"

She snorted. "I've been called a few choice things before, but not that. No, I'm not one, and you're not going to a ball to meet Prince Charming, either. You keep your chin up, your back straight, and look that old icicle straight in the eye. Show her what a jewel a fire witch can be."

My stomach turned a somersault. "You think I'm going to change her opinion of fire witches? Not likely."

"Maybe not, but don't worry about making it any worse. It's already as low as it can go."

How would the scholars react when they saw me in this dress? Did I have time to go the classroom and show off for Master Sven? No, I had spent too much time practicing curtseying in front of the mirrors. Just as well, I could go there after we got back, and not feel rushed.

I stopped for one final look, smoothing down the heavy skirts with my hands. Funny no one had ever said so, but my figure was better than Claire's. Or was it the gown?

Claire thought I didn't care about clothes. She should see me now.

I left the ballroom and took the stairs with butterflies in my stomach. If the Warlock wants to keep my talents a secret, looking like a witch wasn't going to help. Maybe I should turn around and change back into my usual dress.

Too late. Scholar Andreas came out of the library with his nose in a book as I reached the landing.

I said, "Good afternoon."

He looked up, nodded at me, and went back to his book. Two guards came down the stairs—one I knew would flirt with anything in a skirt. I waved at them. They went past without acknowledging me.

I watched them go with my shoulders sagging. This gown was real, wasn't it?

Beorn was waiting at the next landing. "Hiya, gorgeous," he boomed, and looked me over with the kind of grin Mother Janet would have insisted I slap him for.

My cheeks got hot, but I grinned back, and pirouetted for him, enjoying the billowing skirt. "Are you coming, too?"

"Yep. Jean thought they would want to hear my version of the story, and what I discovered in the probe."

"Why are we going to the Earth Mother's if the Warlock is the one with news? Shouldn't they come here?"

"The Warren is neutral territory. So is the Hall of the Winds. If things get out of hand, we can leave. It wouldn't do for Jean to throw her out."

"Why does she hate the Fire Guild? My stepsister has an affinity for the Water Guild, and we used to be good friends."

He growled, "Drowned if I know. Anybody who's not in the Fire Guild says the Frost Maiden is a friendly and pleasant person. Couldn't prove it by me…What I do know is that she'll watch you like a hawk with her mind's eye, and nothing gets past her. Lies, half-truths, evasions, omissions—she'll catch them all. She may look like she's not paying attention, but if you let that fool you, you can get into serious trouble."

We met Warlock Quicksilver at the top of the stairs. He liked how I looked. A girl can tell. A little shiver ran down my spine, and my cheeks, just cooling off, got hot again.

"My dear," he said, "you are enchanting, and far too conspicuous. We do not, at present, need a bevy of courtship-minded earth wizards coming to call, so I took the liberty of putting a spell—the antithesis of a glamour spell—on you. This afternoon only Beorn, I, and the other three Officeholders will be aware of you. I trust you will not mind."

At least I wouldn't have to blush for anyone else, but what was the point of having a fabulous dress if no one noticed? I'd be better off with Master Sven ogling me than these two. It wasn't fair. "Your Wisdom, how long will we need to keep my talent secret?"

He cocked an eyebrow. "You were the one holding the lock."

I glared at him. "That was because I didn't understand what I was or what I had done. Now…"

"I apologise. I should not have teased you. You are a forthright individual who does not enjoy keeping secrets. Unfortunately, I do not know how long it will be. There are two factors in play. First of all, you must be capable of defending yourself."

I would like to laugh in Jenny McNamara's face if she threatened me again. "No argument there, sir."

Beorn said, "You're going to get so good at setting a shield you could do it in ten feet of water—"

"Good grief. Of all the—"

"—or in the instant between when Flint flames you and the flames hit."

The butterflies in my stomach turned into vultures. "Flint?"

The two men exchanged a long look. Quicksilver said, "You will have a seat on the Guild Council. Unless you agree with Flint on every matter—an unlikely prospect—he will flame you. Being a woman will not save you."

"You're going to learn to fight back, too." Beorn grinned. "I hope I'm there to watch when you flame him."

Quicksilver said, "If you do not fight back, he will be contemptuous of you and bully you the more. You will begin fighter training as soon as we are satisfied you have mastered the basics. Now let us go to the Warren."

He offered me an arm. I didn't move. "You said there were two factors."

"Ah, yes, I did." He frowned, looking off into the distance beyond me. "The other is the Chessmaster's prediction. Your actions, whatever they are, may be the turning point of the war."

"Mine?" I squawked.

"Yes, yours, my dear. He still believes you are not a witch, and we must not let him learn you are. You have an advantage over him only as long as the element of surprise is on your side. Whatever you do, remember he is dangerous. Do not put yourself at risk."

He drew a deep breath, and focused on me. "I do not expect to survive this war—" Beorn and I both flinched, and he shook his head at us. "You are warlocks. A warlock must face facts, however unpleasant they may be. But you, my dear," his tone lightened, but there was no smile in his eyes. "You must live long enough to unlock the Office. That is an order. Understand?"

We walked in mute gloom through a short tunnel in the side of the mountain, coming out in the Earth Mother's sprawling home. The Warren had grown around a series of courtyards and fountains, but all I noticed were walls of warm red sandstone rather than the grey granite prevalent in the Fortress. Everyone we met paid their respects to the two warlocks, but looked away from me after the briefest of glances.

We skirted the Great Hall, the octagonal room rumoured to be large enough to hold the members of all four Guilds at once, with room left over. I caught glimpses of balconies, tapestries, carved woodwork, but they could not compete for my attention with the unsettled state of my stomach. Mrs Cole was wrong. I would drive the Frost Maiden's opinion of fire witches even lower if I vomited on her.

Quicksilver said, "On our return, if you wish, you may take time to explore the hall."

I looked at the carved woodwork with a spark of interest. That would be nice. Maybe by then I could appreciate what I was seeing.

We reached the Earth Mother's parlour, and I nearly threw myself into her arms when she greeted me as warmly as she greeted the two wizards. How would Quicksilver like it if people ignored him?

She studied me for a moment with both hands on my shoulders, then gave me a warm hug. My stomach and pulse settled down, and I felt better than I had in weeks.

"Thank you," I said.

Mother Celeste smiled. "Isn't that what healers are for?"

She directed us into an antechamber where the Air Enchanter was waiting. Although the newest in his office, having held it for fifteen years, he was physically the oldest. His predecessor had held onto the Air Office a good ten years after his Guild Council had suggested he retire, much to their consternation and his successor's discomfort. He was clad in white, gold, and diamonds, in contrast to the Warlock's black, silver, and opals. With his grey beard and grey eyes and stern, if somewhat humourless, face he looked every inch a king, and far more imposing than King Stephen.

He greeted me gravely, and I made him a deep reverence; a far better one than I had managed on my first meeting with Warlock Quicksilver. From the wink he gave me behind the enchanter's back he seemed to recall that too. After exchanging pleasantries with the Enchanter, we moved on into the inner room, which Quicksilver lit by tossing little balls of flame into the air. They scattered into the corners and along the ceiling, lighting the whole room, warm yellow light reflecting off the honey-collared walls. There were no windows, and thin sheets of amber covered the walls, ceiling, floor, and even the doors. With the doors closed, the room was an amber box.

"You look amazed, Miss Guillierre," the Enchanter said. "And you should be. I know of no other room like this anywhere in the world. The amber serves as magical shielding. We may talk freely here in complete confidence that no one will overhear."

Quicksilver added, "The shield is as good as, perhaps better than, the one on the practice room. You may release your lock here and none but the four Officeholders will be any wiser."

The Frost Maiden glided in a few minutes later. I did a double take, she so strongly reminded me of Claire on first glance.

That was silly—Claire was gold, this woman was silver. Claire was small and delicate; this woman was…small and delicate. But not helpless.

No one would ever offer to protect her. She was dangerous enough to make my skin crawl. I backed away from her, my hands and face cold.

Her acknowledgement of the Fire Warlock was cold but well mannered. She was cordial to Mother Celeste, and bantered with the Air Enchanter. With her perfect features and regal carriage, she seemed a fitting queen to his noble king. Her pearls glowed; sapphires sparkled. When she moved, her blue silk shimmered like water. The burgundy velvet I was so proud of seemed dowdy, fit only for a gawky tomboy. I backed up another step.

I could understand how she had charmed Quicksilver. That didn't mean I had to like it. Deep in my chest, something burned.

Mother Celeste turned to introduce me, and I stepped forward with my chin up and back straight. I made a deep reverence the Frost Maiden didn't respond to. She studied me with flared nostrils, not a trace of warmth in her blue eyes, nor, when she spoke, in her voice.

"So, you are the missing warlock, hiding your talents under a lock all this time. What is your *nom de guerre*?"

I should have thought of that. My cheeks burned. "I don't have one yet, Your Wisdom."

"I assume you will have one; all members of your tribe do."

"Yes, ma'am." I laced my fingers together behind my back so they wouldn't curl into fists.

The Enchanter said, "Perhaps the Second Locksmith? There is some precedence for that."

She said, "Or perhaps the Lesser Locksmith?"

Burn the woman—I did not want to be the same colour as my dress. The fire in my chest got hotter

He said, "Now really, Lorraine—"

"I have met few female warlocks. Witches outnumber the wizards on the Water and Earth Guild Councils, but the Fire Guild Council is the domain of angry and overbearing men. Do you have a temper to match that of the Warlock of the Western Gate, child?"

I had seen little evidence of the Warlock's temper, except when he was dealing with proven fools, and if I spent much time in the same room as this witch, I was going to need a war name. I chose my words with care. "I do have a temper. Whether it matches his, I don't know, Your Wisdom."

She shrugged and turned away. I glanced at the Warlock, and found him displaying exceptional evidence of his own temper—scowling, and responding to the Earth Mother's hand signals to cool down with a set jaw and hard eyes. Behind him, Beorn whistled soundlessly and rolled his eyes at the ceiling.

The Enchanter coughed, shooting a sideways glance at the Frost Maiden's back. "Shall we get started then? If everyone will please be seated…" He gestured for me to sit next to him. The Warlock and Frost Maiden took seats at the opposite ends of the room, not facing each other, as if out of long habit.

The Warlock described what had happened the day I released my lock, what they had found in the probe, and the training I had received since then. I watched the flashing of the Frost Maiden's great sapphire out of the corner of my eye, without looking directly at her. The stones in the three other rings also glowed, sparked, and flashed in their own colours and tempos. I was spellbound, and for a few minutes forgot why I was there.

Then the Enchanter and the Earth Mother turned to me and asked questions. I answered with care—I didn't dare give any misleading or evasive answers. The Frost Maiden said little, and looked bored, but after Beorn's warning, I did not take that at face value. They had me unlock and relock several times; the first time brought a gratifyingly wide-eyed reaction from the Enchanter and Mother Celeste.

They sent me to wait in the antechamber while they questioned Beorn. He came out not long after, and we waited while the four of them talked. And waited. An hour crawled by, then two. I was glad Quicksilver had warned me to bring a book, but I couldn't concentrate.

"Beorn, what's taking so long?"

"This isn't a good place to talk. Later."

I returned to my book. I read five pages without having any idea what they said.

They talked for two and a half hours before they called us back in. I clasped my hands together behind my back again, to forestall wiping sweaty palms on my velvet skirt.

The Enchanter looked grave, and the Earth Mother looked troubled. The Frost Maiden still looked bored. Quicksilver's face looked calm enough, but his eyes had a smouldering, angry look to them and he paced while the Enchanter interrogated first Beorn and then me again.

His questions covered no new ground. After a few minutes, he thanked me, and they all rose. The Warlock and I were nearest the door; the Frost Maiden, by protocol the first to leave, had to pass us both on the way.

She stopped in front of me, scrutinised my face for a moment, then stood there a bit longer, her glance flashing back and forth between him and me. Her lips curled into—what? A smile? A sneer? She turned to face him, and he stiffened.

"I expect your plans will come to naught for other reasons." Her voice oozed honey. "You will make it a trio, won't you? First Nicole, then Terésa, now Lucinda. How sad."

I reeled backwards, slamming into the wall. Quicksilver's face went livid, and he started to retort, but bit it off after a glance at me. Turning on heel, he stalked through the door and slammed it in her face, hard enough that I felt the jolt through the wall.

Mother Celeste said, "Lorraine, how could you!" She sounded like she was scolding a naughty six-year-old.

The Frost Maiden shrugged, and continued out the door with no display of emotion. The Earth Mother and the Enchanter both talked at once; I have no idea what they said.

Beorn put an arm around my shoulders. "Let go of the wall. We're going home."

The next thing I knew he was pushing me into a chair. A moment later, he shoved a glass in my hand.

I pushed it away. "I don't want—"

"It's not booze. It's an Earth Guild concoction to get your blood flowing again after a shock."

I gulped it down, and looked around. We were back in the Fortress, in the Warlock's study. Did we walk here or jump through the fire? If we walked through the Warren's Great Hall, I didn't see it.

Beorn dropped into one of the armchairs and stared out the window. "They were talking about what Jean wants to do to the Office, and Paul, the Enchanter, didn't like it. Understandably. He's got his own problems with his Office, but it hasn't worn him down yet the way it has the others, and this was the first time he'd heard about Jean's ideas." His voice was so low I strained to hear him. "Jean decided that now was the time to tell them, so they wouldn't hear it first from me, when I become the junior member."

The rumble of thunder in the distance echoed the throbbing in my head. "Where is he now?"

He jerked a thumb upwards. "On the rim of the caldera, blasting boulders into gravel. I wouldn't expect him back down here for hours."

I put my face down in my hands. "I forgot my manners. I didn't take proper leave of the other two Officeholders."

He snorted. "Don't worry about that. Mother Celeste cares more about people than protocol, and I think Paul was as shocked as you were. I've heard the Frost Maiden say some nasty things to Jean before, but this is the first time I've ever seen her attack somebody else at the same time. Maybe you should take it as a compliment she thinks you're that important."

That was not a comforting thought. Even less comforting was the question, what could I say to Warlock Quicksilver the next time I saw him?

Lessons in Self-defence

I tossed and turned that night, shivering from cold, despite the August heat. When the Warlock appeared in the kitchen the next morning, I stiffened. I glanced at him, and looked away. He looked like he hadn't slept either.

He came over to where I was kneading dough, but didn't allude to either Nicole or Terésa, merely saying, "I am sorry I had to subject you to that unpleasantness yesterday."

I kept my head down, looking at the dough. "Yes, sir. It's not your fault, sir. I'm sorry I gave her something to attack you with."

He stood by the table for a moment. I didn't relax until he turned on heel and stalked out of the kitchen.

I avoided him for several days, ducking into the pantry when he came into the kitchen, and hiding behind the curtains in the library. It was silly, perhaps—he had already shown I couldn't hide from him—but I could not pretend, even to myself, that I was thinking clearly.

When he came into the practice room to inspect our progress, I concentrated on the burning straw and avoided looking at him. He seemed pleased with our progress, and agreed when Beorn suggested it was time to go on to the next step. He beckoned to René, and they left the practice room together, leaving me alone with Beorn.

"The next step?" I said. "You mean, training to fight?"

"Yeah." Beorn fingered his beard for a moment. "This is one of the areas where the guild school really fails warlocks, and we were thinking... Look, what happens if the Fire Warlock throws a bolt of lightning where another warlock is standing?"

"He kills him?"

"No, he misses."

"Wait. What?"

"The other warlock has jumped through the fire—he isn't there anymore. You've got to throw an attack to follow a warlock magically. Throwing an attack directly at him is easier, and it works against the lesser talents, so that's what the school teaches."

"So that's one of the ways the school fails warlocks?"

"Yep. I picked up a lot of bad habits before I started trying to fight like a warlock, and I'm still having trouble breaking them. We don't want you and René picking them up in the first place."

"Can you teach us, if you've got those bad habits yourself?"

"Don't know. We'd been talking about Jean taking over that bit, but with you two avoiding each other—"

"What? He doesn't want to talk to me, either?"

Beorn grinned. "Looks that way. I've been wondering if I should give him grief about not facing facts." His grin vanished. "I think you're both worrying too much about what that old crone said. If her prediction was true, we wouldn't have anything to worry about from the Chessmaster, would we?"

The Chessmaster's prediction echoed in my head: I have seen a girl claim a place in the Warlock's lustful heart. Did he think the Fire Warlock and I were lovers? Did he understand so little of our history that he believed that was even possible? Did the Frost Maiden think either of us was that dense or irresponsible?

I had been asking for trouble, just by thinking of him as Warlock Quicksilver. As if we could ever be equals.

Beorn thumped me on the shoulder on his way out. "Think about it. You can't hide from him forever, you know."

I sat in the dim light in the practice room with a piece of kindling I pretended was the Frost Maiden, and practiced setting it on fire, snuffing it out, setting it on fire, snuffing it out. After a while I got up and walked out, heading for the stairs.

I was on the uppermost flight when René passed me on his way down. He appeared lost in a brown study and didn't seem to notice me. At the landing I turned around, watching him dwindle below me.

In the silence of the upper tier, the sound of any movement carried clearly. Were the soft footfalls behind me a cat's?

"I took your advice," the Fire Warlock said.

"Mine, Your Wisdom?"

"My dear, do you not remember? I informed René he will be a warlock."

I turned and looked at him. "Why?"

"Because of the need to train you both in self-defence. The techniques I intend to teach you will be dangerous to him if he does not understand their purpose."

"Are you going to teach us yourself, then?"

"Yes. There is too much at stake for me not to."

"Yes, sir. That's good." I swallowed around a sudden tightness in my throat. "We'd be foolish not to learn all we can from you while you're here."

His unruffled expression didn't change. "And you are not a fool."

"Thank you, Your Wisdom."

"Jean," he said.

"No, sir, I can't call you that."

Lines around his mouth and eyes tightened, and he turned a little away from me. "Do I frighten you that much?"

"No, sir, Jean Rehsavvy doesn't." His glance, touching me and away, felt like a lightning bolt. My eyes stung. "But I am afraid of the Fire Warlock, Your Wisdom."

"I see." He paced to the edge of the landing, and stood with his hands on the railing, looking out. "As you wish. Even though the honorific feels ludicrous. Perhaps I should take lessons from you. At the moment you seem the wiser of the two of us."

"Sir?"

"I, too, fear the Fire Warlock."

"Sir?"

He had a smile on his lips, none in his eyes. "My dear Locksmith—"

I winced, and he flicked me another lightning glance.

He said, "I will teach you to defend yourself, so that you may survive long enough to unlock the Fire Office. That is my duty to you. Let us not, either one, forget that."

We shifted into a new routine, focused on self-defence and locks, and skipping all the nonessential spellcraft taught at the school.

I rose early, starting the day's bread and desserts before breakfast. Mrs

Cole used magic to do the rest. She could have made the bread with magic, but it turned out better if I did a little kneading by hand to check that the dough felt right, and pretending the ball of dough was the Empire's Chessmaster or the Office let me work off some nervous tension.

Mrs Cole would fill me in on the latest gossip while we worked on breakfast. The rumours of war grew, with news of attacks on ships and easily repulsed feints against ports.

She said, "The townsfolk are getting nervous, and wondering if they should start moving up into the Fortress."

"Well, shouldn't they?"

"I think so, but the Guild Council has been telling everybody to stay put. They don't think the Empire will launch a full-scale attack until next spring. I don't think they know what they're talking about. Himself has the other supplicants hard at work laying in stores as if there's going to be a long siege, starting soon. I hope it doesn't come to that." Under her breath she added, "I'm not looking forward to a flock of hotheads trying to run my kitchen, either."

After breakfast, I headed towards the practice room. All five of us— the Warlock, Beorn, Master Sven, René, and I—spent our mornings there. Aside from a break mid-morning to work on locks, our focus in the morning was on control. The Warlock gave us all exercises—simple ones for René, harder ones for me, and difficult ones for Arturos and Master Sven. Master Sven, a level four wizard, made up for in control what he lacked in power, and I never tired of watching the Warlock drill our two tutors as unmercifully as they drilled me.

The Warlock's talk with René about his future had the intended effect. René was unusually quiet and serious for three days, then bounced back to his normal exuberant self, but it was clear he understood the implications of being a warlock. He dogged Arturos's every move, demanding explanations for every detail of the exercises the Warlock assigned the big wizard, until I was as amazed by the two warlocks' patience as by René's persistence.

After dinner, René and I went back to the practice room, where we practiced setting and quenching fires under Arturos's watchful eye. He also taught us the low-level shield against fire, the one used as an everyday safeguard by every fire witch and wizard level two and above, and the more powerful shield against the heat of a blacksmith's forge, only usable by level threes and above. We practiced both shields until they were as easy as snapping our fingers.

We then had only a couple of hours in the late afternoon with Master Sven on theory, where we sometimes went to sleep with our faces in the books. After a quick supper, Beorn and I would spend an hour or so with the Warlock in his study, going over his notes on the spells making up the Office.

We all learned from each other, and with such intense tutoring René and I crammed into a few months what would have taken years to learn at the school. We ate like field hands, without putting on weight. I was too busy, and too tired, to waste time worrying about either the Frost Maiden or the Chessmaster.

The dreams about the glass cage or the looming shadow of Storm King vanished after I unlocked my talents, and I was very happy to have them go. The nightmares triggered by bad memories stirred up by the probe also diminished, but I dreamt of blinding flashes of lightning, or my clothes and skin burning. I slept enough that I could function, but never enough to feel well rested.

Mrs Cole covered for me well enough that the scholars didn't seem to notice my absence from the kitchen, but some did notice the bags under my eyes. I was the subject of speculation and jealous skirmishes, and I worried that if I had many sleepless nights my reputation could end up in tatters. If the knowledge the Warlock was by necessity chaste hadn't been so firmly ingrained in everyone's mind, gossip might have connected the two of us, as we had shown up at breakfast on more than one morning looking like neither of us had slept.

Instead, I gathered that rumours linked Arturos's name with mine. It didn't help that I sometimes forgot and called him Beorn in public. If that rumour had been true, I wouldn't have minded as much.

Master Sven often sat with me at dinner, growling at any scholar who captured my attention for too long, but he was far more circumspect about what he said. He treated me with respect and talked freely about theory and history, but the light chitchat dried up, and I didn't know what to make of it.

We worked our way through the theoretical writings on locks—the most useful, unsurprisingly, an unpublished manuscript by

Jean Rehsavvy. We learned there were different locks for hiding physical objects, living creatures, energy, and ideas, and the more abstract the thing you were trying to hide the more difficult the lock was.

At our first session on locks, we sat around the table with unlit candles in front of us, attempting to use a lock that would hide the candle. The Warlock and I were the only ones who had executed a lock before. Mine disappeared immediately, drawing "ahs" from the wizards. The Warlock's disappeared a moment later. Master Sven scowled at his, the scowl deepening the longer the candle refused to disappear.

I patted his hand, "You're trying too hard, ease up."

He looked at me, and the candle disappeared. "I don't think I'm ever going to get this to work."

"You just did."

"I did? I did. What did I do?"

Arturos struggled the longest, but, after much groaning and cursing, even he hid his candle. Reversing the lock has harder. The Warlock made René stop and rest after he became so angry he began unwittingly scorching everything at hand, but René was adamant that if Master Sven could do it, so would he. After a night's sleep, he succeeded on the first try.

After practicing hiding objects, we moved on to hiding crickets, and the next day a cageful of white mice. After several days, we moved on to hiding candle flames. That was easy for the Warlock and me, but the others struggled.

None of them—Beorn, René, Master Sven, or the Warlock—could duplicate my feat of hiding my magical talents. We decided that perhaps it was due to the lucky chance of my trying locks before I started doing any other magic, and that it was too late for the rest of them, except possibly René, to make the mental shifts needed to get it to work. René tried gamely, off and on for several weeks, but never succeeded.

The Warlock brought me objects with existing locks that over the years he'd found scattered around the Fortress. I practiced on those while the others grappled with the basic mechanism.

Each spell unfolded before me in a distinct handwriting, and I learned to identify the handiwork of the few witches and wizards who had set the existing locks. A witch from four hundred years ago wrote in a fine, spidery hand. A wizard a century before her had a fondness for red ink.

The Warlock Locksmith of the Great Coven, who had set most of the locks still in existence, was most distinctive, writing in a big, bold black hand words that always seemed to have an angry undertone to them.

The Warlock one day handed me a book with blank pages and asked me what I could make of it. I sensed the work of the Locksmith, but could not read the spell. Theory said that in creating a lock a witch or wizard could work into the spell any number of conditions restricting who could read it, and when. Most of the existing locks had no conditions; others had conditions that depended on the frame of mind, and the text of the spell would only appear when you were in the right emotional state. I tried for an angry frame of mind, but that didn't do it. I puzzled over it for several days, until one morning I sat glaring at it, wanting to burn it.

"Easy, easy," the Warlock breathed in my ear. "Do not break it."

I turned to him, trying to shake the anger and change my frame of mind. "Why is the text hidden? What's it about?"

"Black magic—poisons, simulacra, and the like."

"Eww!" I drew back from the book, and the text of the lock unscrolled in front of me.

Elation shot through me, and the words disappeared. I looked at the Warlock sheepishly.

His eyes twinkled. "Poisons, simulacra, black magic," he prompted.

When I regained the feeling of revulsion that had swept over me, the words once again appeared, and I released the lock as quickly as I could. I flipped through several pages before handing it back to him. "I don't want it."

He snapped the lock back in place, and the pages blanked out. "Nor should you. The exercise, however, was good for you. You may need to run the full gamut of emotions—jealousy, joy, disgust, contentment, who knows—before you find the right one. Do not be surprised if you encounter more of this kind of rot as you become more familiar with the Locksmith's handiwork. He seems to have had a rather twisted mind."

"But the histories and stories all make the members of the Great Coven seem to be such flawless heroes."

"They were not perfect, not by any means. They were as human as the rest of us. Several of them did not like each other. I do not mean to belittle their work—they put aside their differences and worked together long enough to create something truly marvellous, but after it was done they went their separate ways. The Locksmith seems to have spent the rest of his life in a state of bitter anger. I am sure you have noticed."

"What was he angry about?"

"That is not clear. He may have expected to be the first Officeholder, and was disgruntled when it went to Warlock Fortunatus. The records also hint at jealousy and bad blood between the two over some woman. Whatever it was, they seem never to have spoken another word to each other after the Forging was done, communicating through servants and letters even though they were both living here in the Fortress."

"I had no idea, sir."

He shrugged. "The early writers were more hagiographers than historians." He smiled. "Let us hope they do a better job on me."

After we became adept at setting shields, the Warlock started a new exercise. He drew a circle of flame on the floor in the practice room, big enough to touch the walls. He told Arturos to stand in the centre, blindfolded, and flame him while he moved around the circle. He lectured us all the while he strolled about, appearing and disappearing at random spots, sending jets of fire at Arturos.

"You must learn to sense an attack coming from any direction, and to direct your return strike to follow the attacker rather than aiming. Your shields can absorb the attack, but it is less tiring to deflect it. It is more effective, also, to mirror it straight back to the attacker. We will each take a turn in the centre. When you are not there, walk about the room attacking from random spots."

His movements were as fluid as the Frost Maiden's, every action elegant and efficient. I was spellbound, watching him. Did he walk with such feline grace in his youth, or was it hard-won from a century and a half of life?

"Aren't you getting dizzy?" I asked.

He shook his head. "No. As far as I am concerned, I am walking in a straight line, and I am not looking at the people and walls shifting around me. I do not need to know your physical location to respond to you."

We spent many days going through this exercise for an hour or so, with each of us getting our turn as the target in the circle. With five people throwing flame, the room would fill with smoke, and become quite hot.

When it was my turn and René's, we began by throwing flame at the others moving around, and then practiced deflection while they attacked us. The deflection was easy, but my attacks were feeble, and I could not do them together. René picked both up quickly. When he scored a direct hit on Master Sven after only a week of practice, the Warlock was delighted.

When was I going to earn his congratulations? He was polite, of course, but he was frustrated at my inability to handle this exercise. Arturos pointed out that I was reluctant to attack my friends, and René suggested I pretend they were people I didn't like, such as the king or the Frost Maiden.

The Warlock's stern response shocked me. "Absolutely not. The Office does not have a sense of humour, and it will not abide even the pretence of an attack by a warlock on the king or any of the other Officeholders."

My mouth went dry and my heartbeat thudded in my ears. Thank God I never mentioned to anyone the piece of kindling I'd pretended was the Frost Maiden.

"Even if the Office did not care," he continued, "I will not countenance anything that increases the friction between the two guilds. We have more than enough problems working together, as it is." In a milder voice, he said, "Pretend one of us is the Empire's Chessmaster, if that will help. But not the Frost Maiden, please."

October arrived, and with it my twentieth birthday. I reflected on everything that had happened in the past year as I brushed my hair before bed. I had gotten so many things I wanted, and other things I didn't even know I needed. Gladys, the old fire witch from Lesser Campton, had been right—I was better off as a witch. Once the Fire Guild accepted me as a warlock, I would be able to support myself, and no one could deny me access to the Fortress's library. I would have power and prestige, especially if I could unlock and help fix the Office.

I had even had adventure. More than I could stomach, really, and it was not over yet. Be careful what you wish for, for you will surely get it, Mother had often said. I should have listened.

What I did not have was a husband, but the economic necessity to marry well was no longer an issue. I felt nothing but relief on that score. I could afford that great luxury—marrying for love. But who could I marry? Master Sven?

I stared at my reflection, open-mouthed, hairbrush in mid-air. Master

Sven should have listened to my mother. He had wished for a witch with a good mind, and had found one. But he had not been careful. He had gotten a witch more powerful than himself, and he was too cautious to forget the old adage: never, ever, lie to a warlock.

I put the hairbrush down and studied myself in the mirror. "Face the facts. Master Sven is scared of you, and he's the only fire mage available. All your scholar beaux are going to run away in terror when they find out you're a warlock. Beorn isn't afraid of you, but he's going to be married to the Office. You're an old maid, and you're going to stay that way."

I glared at my hair. My best feature, is it? When had it ever done me any good?

"I wish," I said to the mirror, "I wish a wizard who knows and appreciates what I am would show me he loves me. I'd even cut off my hair for that."

After three months of practice, René and I were both handling fire better than many witches and wizards who had practiced for years. We could light candles in the kitchen from the practice room, light a dozen torches spaced around the room in a single motion, send great spouts of flame shooting all the way across the cavernous room, and hold little dancing balls of flame in the palm of our hands. We could also quench any of those fires in a snap of the fingers, and stand in the flames unscathed.

Beorn said, "You two have been doing well. Very well. It's time for a break. We're going to have fun tomorrow."

I slumped in one of the hard metal chairs, exhausted after lighting and relighting a bonfire with water-soaked wood. I could use some fun. I couldn't even lift my head to look at him.

He said, "Be sure to eat a good breakfast. After breakfast, go to the Warlock's study. Wear layers of clothes so that you're ready for either very hot or very cold weather."

René asked, "What are we going to do?"

"Launch an invasion."

Hooknose Ridge

Launch an invasion? I jerked upright and stared at the big wizard. He grinned at me. This was his idea of fun?

Neither René nor I could get him to say anything else. I stomped off to confront the Warlock. René hurried to keep up with me. He wanted to know what was going on, too, but he was excited. I was furious.

The Warlock said, "The issue is control."

René said, "I know you've been making us work on control in all our exercises, but what does control have to do with launching an invasion?"

The Warlock laid a hand on René's shoulder. "Control of magical power is only one form, my young friend. The Fire Warlock must deal with control in all its forms: political control, control of the battlefield, and control of one's own temper and desires, among others.

"This war will be waged on my terms, not the Empire's. They do not want to launch a full-scale invasion until the spring. It is advantageous to us to fight during the winter, and if we can persuade them to invade before they are ready, so much the better.

"That is the point of tomorrow's exercise; to provoke them to attack on my timetable, not theirs."

Sensible, my head said. My heart said, No, no, hold the war off. Every day matters.

I croaked, "What are we going to do tomorrow?"

His eyes sparkled. "You will see soon enough, and I want to enjoy my surprise. It will be fun."

I shook my head. His hand moved to my shoulder, and he leaned his head towards me. The tenderness in his expression made my heart bound.

"My dear," he said, "you have lived in fear far too much of late. Life is too short. We must make the most of what little time we have, and live with a light heart even in the face of catastrophe.

"Relax. Enjoy yourself tomorrow. For my sake if not your own."

Perhaps he worked some magic with his hand on my shoulder. I slept without dreams that night, and woke feeling rested and excited about the day's adventure. René and I would have raced through breakfast if Beorn hadn't warned us not to. We were ready and waiting at the Warlock's door ten minutes before he and Beorn made their leisurely way up the stairs.

René said, "Are they being sluggards just to torture us?"

I glared down the stairs and tapped my foot on the floor. "Patience is a virtue. Develop some."

When the two wizards arrived, the Warlock inspected the clothes we were carrying, then sent us both back downstairs; René to get a warmer hat and gloves from Mrs Cole, me to put on my lightest summer dress under the heavier dress I was wearing. When we were dressed to the Warlock's satisfaction—he and Beorn dressed in or carrying as many layers as René and I—he led us through the tunnel to the Earth Mother's great hall in the eastern mountains.

Mother Celeste and the Air Enchanter were waiting for us. She greeted us with a cheery, "Welcome, friends. May I come with you and watch the show?"

René and I exchanged glances. What show?

Enchanter Paul said, "I'd like to see it, too, provided you don't mind if I tag along."

The Warlock said, "Not at all. The more the merrier."

Mother Celeste led us to a tunnel, and soon we stood at the mouth of a cave leading out into a clearing high on the side of a mountain. It was late autumn, but the air was bitter cold, and several feet of snow covered the ground. I pulled my cloak tighter. Why did I need the summer dress?

Mother Celeste cleared the snow from a group of boulders in the clearing, and the Warlock told us to find seats on the rocks and make ourselves comfortable. "As comfortable as one can on a rock, and a cold one at that."

Mother Celeste laughed. "I, for one, am always quite comfortable on rocks." She seated herself on one of the larger boulders with as much aplomb as if it were a royal throne. Enchanter Paul looked askance at the rocks, and remained standing. I sat. Sitting got me out of the wind, but the rock sucked heat out of me. I shivered.

Beorn sprawled beside me and winked. "You'll get warm, soon enough."

I sniffed, and pulled my hat farther down on my ears.

The Warlock gestured towards the forested slopes on the other side of the narrow valley. "Today we will be starting, and stopping, forest fires."

That did sound like fun. René whooped.

The Warlock said, "I appealed to the Earth Guild Council's generosity and sense of patriotism. They agreed to let us burn the side of Hooknose Ridge, and cleared all the wildlife from this section of forest.

"You have been practicing so far using the energy you each have from your own physical reserves, but as potential officeholders you each need to experience a greater flow and to practice estimating the power needed for bigger tasks. Today you are going to use me as a conduit to draw on Storm King, to work with more power than you have had available before. I will channel the energy, and step it down so that you will not risk burning yourselves out by over-estimating and getting a surge you cannot handle.

"With enough power, and the right mental models, either of you can set this entire mountain ablaze, and then put it out. With practice, you may someday exercise enough control to burn a horizontal slice five feet high, twenty feet off the ground." Behind him, fire roared across the mountainside, a small section of trunk on each tree ablaze. An instant later the fires were extinguished.

"Or burn every fifth tree." Again the fire roared, individual trees burning, their neighbours untouched. He didn't even turn his head to confirm his description.

I gaped, stunned by such a casual display of immense power and control. The magical noise this created would be tremendous.

Mother Celeste and Enchanter Paul applauded. Beside me, Beorn mumbled, "Show off."

The Warlock's eyes widened in mock innocence. "I demonstrated what is possible, that is all. I have been through this exercise once, more than a decade ago, with Beorn. He needs a refresher, so he will be doing this also. Who would like to begin?"

René leapt to his feet. The Warlock held out his hand. "Set as much of the forest as you can control on fire, then put it out. Draw less power than you need, and feel your way up to the right amount. Do not overdo it. Ready?"

René nodded, and took the Warlock's hand.

Even the weakest witches and wizards for miles around would notice this. I scrambled to my feet. "Wait, wait."

They all turned to look at me. I shivered from head to foot, and from more than the cold. "Your Wisdom, isn't this dangerous?"

His eyebrows rose. "My dear, I explained that I will control the amount of power—"

"I meant, we've been trying to keep my talents secret, but won't the Empire's spies see this? And René, you didn't want anyone knowing about him, either."

"Ah, I beg your pardon. You and René catch on so quickly that sometimes I forget what you do not know. I am remiss in not explaining that we have taken precautions to ensure neither you nor René will be identified."

Panic relaxed its hold on me, and I felt giddy. I leaned on Beorn so I wouldn't topple over.

Enchanter Paul reached over and patted my shoulder. "That's why I am here today, Miss Guillierre. I am lending the support of the Air Office to this endeavour. Between your lock and the spells cast by three Officeholders, your secret will be quite safe."

I sat down and hugged myself to stop shivering. "Thank you, Your Wisdom."

The Warlock said, "Even if the Empire's spies determine you are here, which is unlikely, they will not see you take any part in this exercise. They will think you are here as... For other reasons."

René said, "But they will see that something's going on?"

"Indeed, if they do not I will be sorely disappointed. I want them to see that I am training other warlocks to draw on Storm King's power. They are already afraid of facing me alone. If they believe they may soon face other warlocks as powerful as I, they will panic, and attack prematurely. Now do you understand?"

René and I both nodded. I said, "I'm sorry, Your Wisdom."

"You need not apologise. I would rather you questioned everything I did than allow me to make a mistake through carelessness. Now, René?"

The boy studied the mountain for several seconds, then a small section directly across from us burst into flame. Another larger section of forest followed. We applauded.

The Warlock said, "Put out, each time, what you just set afire. That will give you more practice where you need it most."

René groaned, but obeyed. After a dozen more tries, he started a blaze in a gush of flame so strong we felt the heat all the way across the valley. He then had considerable difficulty in putting it all out. When he finished, he stripped off his hat and unbuttoned his coat, saying, "Gosh, I'm getting hot!"

The Warlock said, "Of course. You must use your own energy to manage the power you are drawing from Storm King. What you have used is a minute fraction of what is available. Now perhaps you begin to see why Warlocks who misjudge do not survive."

The boy looked up at him and nodded. The Warlock ruffled his hair. "You did well for a first try. Now, Lucinda."

I stood up and took a deep breath. If I couldn't do as well as René, I had no business being here. I took the Warlock's hand, and called up an image of my flame covering the forest in front of me.

"Now," I whispered. A surge of heat coursed through me like spirits burning my throat and warming my stomach. The mountainside lit up. I gaped at it.

Mother Celeste said "Oh, how lovely." My audience applauded.

The Warlock laughed. "Excellent control, my dear, but you need to be a bit more forceful."

I had not started a small forest fire, as René had done. I had started a large swathe of small fires. A section of the mountainside was aglow, each tree holding a small ball of flame in its centre.

"Now put it out," he ordered. After some struggle, all the fires were out. After several more tries, each time with a larger surge of energy, I managed to create a respectable blaze, and to put it out again. My head swelled, and I laughed out loud.

"Well done," the Warlock said, giving my hand a squeeze. My treacherous hand didn't want to let go.

"Your turn, Beorn." The big warlock spewed a torrent of flame in one long sweeping arc, getting a blaze covering most of the mountain on the first try. On his second try, he over-estimated and burned part of the forest on our side of the valley as well. His third try was perfect. After that the Warlock had him doing variations and patterns—a ring of burning trees one time, stripes across the mountainside another—to work on control.

After many long hours cooped up in the practice room, being out in the open air was exhilarating. Within an hour we were all sweating, the bitter air no match for the heat we were producing. René and I threw snowballs at each other to cool off. The Warlock dived into a snow bank and rolled around in the snow. He came up grinning at the astonishment on my face.

"Did you think I was not getting hot, too? I have been working the whole time, while you have worked only a third of it. This is one of the reasons I prefer to fight wars during the winter."

By late afternoon we had reduced the vegetation on the mountainside to smouldering ash. We reeked of smoke and were drenched in sweat and melted snow. I had shed all but my lightest dress; the men were down to their singlets.

Mother Celeste said, "What now, Jean? Are you going to teach them to call down the lightning?"

He pursed his lips for a moment. Were they mad? Beorn rolled his eyes; René edged towards the cover of the boulders.

The Warlock said, "It is far too dangerous for Lucinda and René. It is dangerous for Beorn, but it would be a useful experience. We may not get another chance. Very well, let us do it. The rest of you, retreat to the tunnel and cover your ears. Now, Beorn, I am going to call the lightning first, and I want you to feel the energy flowing through me so you have a better idea what to expect."

CRASH!

A bolt of lightning shot out of the clear sky and hit a boulder on the far mountainside, sending shards of rock flying and echoes of thunder rolling across the valley. René and I both flinched, and Mother Celeste put her comforting arms around us. The Warlock did it twice more, and then told Beorn to do it. Beorn looked as eager as I would have been to touch a live viper, but closed his eyes, concentrated, and sent a bolt crashing onto the mountaintop.

"Good. Now work on better direction," the Warlock said.

Three more blasts, and then Beorn pulled away from the Warlock. "That's it. I'm drained. If I try it again I'm likely to fry *us*."

The Warlock let him go. "Well done, class. Time to go home."

He offered me his arm. "Did you enjoy today's exercise?"

"Yes, sir. Very much."

"Good. Using power well is exhilarating, and being a warlock is all about taking control and turning one's dreams into reality."

"Taking control? Unlocking turned my life topsy-turvy. Between you and Beorn and the Office, all I've done for months is take someone else's orders."

"You underestimate yourself, my dear. Orders to another level five talent are effective only if he or she is willing to accept them. Whether you are aware or not, your own magic is at work, trying to bring about your own desires."

"Is it? I wish…" What did I want? If not even the Fire Warlock could avoid a war, my wishing it would go away wasn't likely to accomplish much.

"Be careful what you wish for," he said, "for you will surely get it. It is well to know one's own heart. The unacknowledged desires cause the most trouble."

"I wish that you can get what you want," I said, and the hairs on the back of my neck stood on end.

The Fortress Besieged

The Fire Warlock gave me a shocked stare. "What I want? My dear, that is…" I had never heard his voice shake before. He took a deep breath, and after a bit went on in a steady voice. "That is exceedingly generous of you. I want an orderly succession of Fire Warlocks, and for you and them to rebuild the Fire Office to meet the changing times. I hope neither will give you cause to regret your wish."

I was already regretting it. My God, what did I do? His list of wants didn't hold anything I hadn't heard before. I thought there must be something more.

He hadn't said he wanted war, but we'd just made sure it was coming. That must have been it. What a horrifying thing to wish for.

The next day at dinner, the Warlock made the announcement I was now expecting. "If I may have your attention, please. I regret to inform you that an attack by the Empire is imminent."

Heads jerked up. There was a flurry of nervous movement and chatter all around.

He held up a hand for silence. "I cannot say how soon it will come. It may be tomorrow, it may not be for several weeks, but we should be prepared. This afternoon I will invite the townsfolk to move into the Fortress."

How would Mrs Cole's comfortable kitchen fare with a swarm of temperamental fire witches invading it? She didn't look a bit happy.

The Warlock said, "Conditions here will be more crowded and chaotic, but that is necessary. I hope to keep disruptions to your studies to a minimum, but we cannot avoid some distractions. I beg your patience while this state of affairs lasts."

A querulous voice demanded, "Keep noisy children out of the library. I have serious work to do."

Another scholar hissed, "Ebenezer, be quiet," but other heads nodded, as if Ebenezer had said what they wanted to say but didn't dare.

The Warlock's eyes glittered, but his voice was smooth. "Let me remind you that the primary purpose of the Fortress is to protect the lives of the citizens of Frankland, not to enable research into historical minutiae."

Beside me Master Thomas, the librarian, snorted. I stifled a laugh. Scholar Ebenezer was digging into the life of one of the Warlocks even I couldn't remember.

"However, you need not worry about your research being interrupted by unruly children. They will be housed in one of the better-protected lower tiers, and will not be allowed in the library, where there is a greater danger of being struck by flying glass."

Master Thomas muttered, "Thank you, Your Wisdom, for that reassurance."

The Warlock added, "When the Fortress is under attack, please stay away from the windows and the glassed-roofed stairs."

That afternoon, Beorn put us to work learning a shield spell against flying objects.

At supper, Mrs Cole told me about the Warlock's visit to Blazes. "The Guild Council didn't want anybody to move until it was dead certain there would be an attack. By then it might be too late, so he went over their heads and summoned everybody to the Guild Hall. The Council members are furious, but most of the townsfolk are pissed off at the Council for dragging their feet.

"I expect I'll have my hands full finding places for everybody and helping them settle in. They should start arriving first thing tomorrow morning, and it's going to be upsetting to everybody for a while."

As I was spending most of my time in the classroom or practice room, I didn't see the townsfolk arriving, but in the kitchen and dining room the next day it was obvious things were astir. People I didn't recognise came and went. Mrs Cole bustled in and out with only half a mind on dinner, and forgot the kneading. I did it by hand, or there wouldn't have been any bread. The town's earth witch cut a tunnel from my room to the practice room so I could come and go without provoking comment. The dinner table conversation was all about past wars, speculations about the Empire's strength, and what to expect in an attack. Mrs Cole told me that most of the women with children were moving into the Fortress that day, bringing with them bare essentials, with the husbands and other adults staying behind to pack up and move more belongings later.

I asked, "Is there anything I should do when an attack comes?"

"Just do what Himself said—stay away from exposed places."

The first attack came that night, around midnight. I was jolted awake by howling winds and a rattling barrage against the castle walls, crashing blasts of thunder and lightning, and deafening clangs as the shutters slammed into place on the windows. The lightning was so close and frequent that it blinded me through gaps in the shutters. I bolted for the closet, to put the door between me and the windows. By the time I calmed down enough to use the shield spell, the attack was nearly over. I didn't get back to sleep for hours.

The scholars were in a dither the next morning, not helped by Mrs Cole's refusal to let anyone in the dining room, where the onslaught had smashed several windows before the shutters closed. People looking for places to eat breakfast milled around in the kitchen and pantry and other rooms along the corridor, making it difficult for us to get our work done.

René, when he appeared, rather later than usual, bounced into the kitchen saying, "Did you see him? He was awesome. He just walked along the ramparts looking like they weren't bothering him a bit, and snapping out lightning bolts in all directions like it was nothing."

"René, didn't he say 'stay away from the windows'? It could be dangerous with all that fire and lightning and flying glass."

"My windows weren't broken. I didn't care. I wanted to watch. I'm glad I did."

Master Sven, who was just finishing his breakfast, gave him a half-hearted dressing down for not being careful, then sheepishly admitted he had watched the spectacle, too. "Arturos and I are going to fix the dining room windows. You might want to watch."

We followed him to the dining room where Arturos was already waiting, and we, and several curious scholars, stood in the doorways to watch. They wouldn't let us come past the doors for fear the glass flying back towards the windows would hit somebody. Even René looked concerned when a shard a foot long fought to unstick itself from the seat cushion it had skewered.

Arturos explained that it was easiest to do with two wizards or witches working together. They took turns, one of them making big sweeping motions of the wand to cast the spell to bring back all the fragments of glass from a specific window. The pieces rose in a sparkling, tinkling tower up the window until each was back in the place it had come from. The other wizard would cast the spell to remelt the fragments, and when the pane had reformed, smooth and uncracked, cast the spell to cool it off again. The rough texture of the reformed panes made the repairs obvious. Many of the windows in the Fortress looked that way. Over the centuries, they must have been broken and fixed many times.

When they finished in the dining room, Arturos cast an aversion spell to keep anyone from getting too close while the windows were still hot. They moved on down the corridor towards the stairs on the eastern side, but Arturos suggested we go to the middle staircase to watch the Warlock fix its roof. We hurried towards the stairs, and found a crowd of scholars clustered at the top of the library tier, watching the Warlock working his way down. He had a wand in each hand, sweeping up the fragments with his right hand and sending them in a reverse cascade up to the empty window frame, then holding them there while he made the motions to melt and cool the glass in each pane with his left hand. He showed less strain by himself than Beorn and Sven had working together.

The next day, after they had cooled down, René and I climbed on the railings and examined the roof up close. Neither of us could see that any of the panes he fixed had ever been broken. How many times had the windows been broken, that the Warlock should get so good at fixing them?

The afternoon was more grim. A rumour spread during the morning about Warlock Nostradamus. The Warlock, looking sad and weary, confirmed it at dinner. "I have sad news. Warlock Nostradamus, the eldest of the Council members,"—he did not add 'and the most senile'—"tried to come to my aid last night, and burnt himself badly. He died of his burns an hour ago. We will light the funeral pyre this evening, at dusk.

"Also, it is now imperative that the townsfolk move into the Fortress as quickly as possible. Last night's attack was only a feint to test our defences.

An attack in earnest will not leave the town untouched."

During the afternoon, guardsmen laid the wood for the funeral pyre on the highest point of a shoulder of the mountain sticking out to the east of the Fortress. At sunset, everyone—townsfolk, castle residents, visitors, guardsmen and their families—gathered on the ramparts. We watched the funeral procession—the other warlocks carrying the bier with the shrouded body, followed by Nostradamus's widow, children, grandchildren, and great-grandchildren—make its slow way from the castle to the pyre. They laid him on it, and the other warlocks thrust their wands into the stack of wood and set it ablaze. We watched in silence as the bonfire blazed against the dark sky, and drifted back indoors as the fire slowly burned down. Over the next three days, everyone, from their closest friends down to the rawest recruit in the guards, made their way to pay their respects to the family, now safely ensconced in a suite in one of the middle tiers.

Two days later, in a snowstorm, we did it again for Warlock Venturous, whose bad heart gave out from the stress of moving.

The second attack came several days later, and lasted much longer—all night, through the next day, and halfway into the next night. It sounded more ferocious, with blasts of flame and bombardments by rocks seeming to come from all directions at once. The shutters, and the windows they covered, rattled without letup. If magic hadn't held them on, the wind would have blown the shutters halfway to Iberia.

We walked through the corridors with our hands over our ears. There was no table talk at dinner; we ate as fast as we could, with nervous glances at the rattling windows. The flashes of lightning made it difficult to see what we were eating, as our eyes couldn't adjust between the alternating light and dark.

I escaped to the practice room; it was quieter there, having no windows. I carried in blankets and pillows, and read from *Terésa* until I fell asleep on the hard stone floor.

When it was over, I thought I had gone deaf. All I could hear was my ears ringing.

The earth witch went through the Fortress healing damage to the residents' hearing, starting with the small children down below. When she reached me, she looked dead on her feet, and could have used a healer herself.

For all the heat and noise, the attack didn't seem to accomplish much other than shattering more windows. I asked Beorn about that, and he said, "You're right, we're well protected. They didn't do much to us, but they took a serious beating. They'll have to change tactics. They can't afford many frontal assaults like that."

"But, Beorn, what do they think they can do, when everyone knows the Fortress is impenetrable?"

"How do you know it's impenetrable?"

"Because everyone… Oh, I suppose I don't know that. But no one has breached it in a thousand years. That's a pretty good record."

"That's a scorching incredible record. But for centuries, our enemies were in such chaos they couldn't mount a solid attack. The Empire has been growing and hardening its armies, and has many talented wizards working for it, drawn from a larger population. If we were fighting army to army we'd never have a chance."

"But the Office—"

"The Office is unlike any other defences they've ever dealt with, and they don't understand it. They think they'll find its breaking point if they increase their firepower enough. Who knows? Maybe they will someday. The point is, they don't know that they can't. And even if they can't, they think we'll give up if they keep up a siege for long enough."

I shuddered. "It can't surrender, can it?"

"No, it can't. It'll let everyone inside the Fortress die, or kill us itself if we try to surrender. They stand a much better chance of bringing down an individual Fire Warlock. They can't attack with as much power as we have from Storm King, and as long as the Warlock stays inside the Fortress, he can keep going for a good long time before he gets too tired to fight. But if they were to catch him outside the Fortress, they could kill him. There's nothing in the way of firepower that can hurt him, of course, but if an earth wizard were to drop a ton of rocks on him, or a water wizard dropped a lake on him, they could kill him all right."

"But Beorn, why would he ever need to leave the Fortress?"

He hesitated a moment, then said, "To rescue hostages. He scared the townsfolk into moving up to the Fortress before the threat got serious. The Guild Council's argument had some merit, but keep that under your hat, if you please. The issue wasn't their safety as much as it was his.

210

And ours. If the Empire ever kills off all the warlocks who could be Officeholders, Frankland will be in one hell of a mess."

The Fortress Overrun

I perched on the edge of a chair in the Warlock's study, twisting my hands together in my lap. Would I look calmer if I sat on them? Probably not. I sat on them anyway.

Warlock Sunbeam sauntered into the study wearing his usual cheerful smile; Warlock Flint marched in wearing a scowl. The Warlock described my abilities, my lock, and the probe. Flint looked thunderous. Even Sunbeam looked distressed.

Flint interrupted the Warlock's account of my training. "What kind of nonsense is this? Do you think we will stand by quietly while you try to take over the council by putting an unqualified bootlicker on it?"

I recoiled as if he had slapped me. Arturos squeezed my shoulder.

The Warlock clipped off his words. "Did you hear anything I said? She does not appear to be a high-level talent because she is hiding her abilities under a lock. Lucinda, release your lock so they may see."

Warlock Flint was a fine example of the kind of wizard I wanted to hide my talents from. The little flame stuck at the end of the verse and refused to budge. Flint glared at me, tapping his foot, then got up and was halfway towards the door when I did manage to release it. Sunbeam gasped; his eyes widened. Flint swung around, eyes narrowed. He glared at me and then at the Warlock.

"I don't know how you did that, but you're not fooling me. I'll not have her on the council. You should be ashamed of yourself. Nostradamus's and Venturous's ashes aren't even cold." He turned on heel and stalked out of the room. The Warlock glared after him in stony silence, making no move to stop or reason with him.

If Flint came to one of our practice sessions, I would show the Warlock I could flame somebody.

Sunbeam bowed over my hand. "I'm sorry for that dreadful scene. You have impressed me, and I'm glad to know about you." He turned an accusing eye on the Warlock. "But, really, Jean, you should have told us about her as soon as you found out. Why have you kept it a secret for more than three months?"

The Warlock said through clenched teeth, "I could not trust Nostradamus to keep the secret, and I would have been remiss in putting her in danger before she could defend herself."

Sunbeam looked bewildered. "Danger? What danger?"

"Have you forgotten there is a war on? The Emperor will lavish riches on any wizard who reduces the ranks of our potential Officeholders."

"The Office is getting to you, Jean. I can't imagine they would attack a mere girl. I think this secrecy is unnecessary. I shan't allow it when I am the Warlock."

He turned back to me and bowed. His good humour restored, he walked out of the study, humming to himself, leaving the Warlock fuming, Arturos looking disgusted, and me dismayed.

I abandoned the baking. The McNamara witches vied with Mrs Cole for control of the kitchen, and made it clear I was not welcome. I was not scared of Jenny or her mother, but I couldn't tell them why, so I stayed away, only chatting with Mrs Cole over supper.

With hundreds of people living in the Fortress, the space that had once seemed huge and quiet was full of noise and bustle. We ate in shifts because the dining room wasn't big enough. Perhaps it was just as well there was such a huge throng at dinner; the Warlock and Flint never ate during the same shift. Everyone knew they had never gotten along, but that they'd stopped speaking to each other at all went unnoticed.

Compared to that breach in the Fire Guild Council, the one-sided feud that got everyone's attention was a burning twig in a raging bonfire.

For several days, Jenny threw venomous glares from across the room as I sat down at dinner with Master Sven, but she didn't come any closer and I ignored her. Then one day Master Sven left the table before I did. I was talking to Master Thomas when Jenny sat down across the table.

She smiled at the librarian and said, "It's a shame nobody likes to sit next to Master Sven."

He looked surprised. "I beg your pardon?"

"It's a shame nobody likes to talk to Master Sven."

He looked at me, eyebrows raised. I had seen Master Sven and Master Thomas talking like old friends many times. I spread my hands and shrugged. Other scholars nearby were listening, and looking puzzled, too.

Still looking at Master Thomas, she said, "It's a shame nobody could get hurt if she doesn't stay away from Master Sven."

I said, "Will you start talking sense?"

She glared at me. "Listen, Miss Butter-wouldn't-melt-in-her-mouth-who-called-herself-nobody. You're not good enough for Master Sven."

"Neither is a two-bit witch who's jealous of a nobody."

She turned bright red and raised her wand. If she flamed me I would have to let her hurt me. I flung myself backwards, overturning my chair.

A gust of flame raced down the table between us.

"Enough!"

Everyone in the dining room but me froze at the crackling fire in the Warlock's voice. I fought to regain my balance. The clatter of my chair was loud in the sudden silence.

"Is the world outside not such a dangerous place that we must fight amongst ourselves?"

Jenny's eyes rolled towards the Warlock, showing white all around.

"I do not tolerate threats to any of my guests. Any flames thrown in anger or malice within the Fortress will rebound on the thrower. Your shields will not protect you. Do you understand?"

A few voices whispered, "Yes, Your Wisdom."

The crackle intensified. "Do you understand?"

We roared back, "Yes, Your Wisdom."

The polite, urbane voice returned. "Very well. Enjoy your dinner."

No one moved as he strolled out of the dining room, then they turned as one to stare at me. I fled to my room, where I threw myself on my bed and hugged my pillow, fighting down the urge to go back and blast Jenny across the dining room.

She wasn't that important. She didn't interest Master Sven even before I turned up. He wasn't going to marry either of us. If only she knew.

My secret was still safe. I rolled over and laughed. I had done a splendid impersonation of a mundane girl running in terror from a fire witch.

The next time the enemy attacked, curiosity won out over fear. René, Master Sven, and I huddled together to watch from an arrow slit in one of the lower tiers. The fire and lightning lit up the night as bright as day, but the lightning dazzled my eyes, and the Empire's wizards were too far away for me to see. The Warlock strolled along the ramparts, wearing only a singlet and leggings despite the bitter cold. René and I laughed at Master Sven who started up with a shout the first time the Warlock dove into a snow bank to cool off.

In the distance, the forest burned. The town looked like an island with a river of fire flowing around it.

I asked, "Why isn't the town burning?"

Master Sven said, "It may yet. There are protective spells on it, but if the siege goes on for long, they may buckle under the strain. If they do, the other members of the Guild Council will be hard-pressed to keep up with putting out the fires."

After that night, the enemy changed tactics, as Beorn had predicted they would. There were no more intense, concentrated attacks. Instead, they took turns, and kept up a steady, constant drumbeat of wind, fire, stones, and hail against the Fortress. The Warlock stopped coming down into the practice room, and was frequently distracted during the brief period in the evening when we met to go over the spells making up the Office.

He reminded people at dinner to avoid the unnecessary use of magic. By the fourth time, he sounded quite testy, and threatened to start slapping down geases right and left on people who didn't behave. I asked Beorn if anyone, Flint perhaps, was trying to blind the Warlock.

He said, "No, Flint despises the Warlock, but he does, at least, take the Office seriously. Sunbeam's the biggest problem."

"Why? Because he loves to show off so much?"

"Yep, especially in front of pretty girls."

"I noticed."

Beorn laughed. "How much of what he tried to impress you with could you already do? He's been showing off all his life, and doesn't get how much the noise interferes with the Office's listening spells. He'll agree to reduce his magic use, and forget and do something huge half an hour later."

"Can't the Warlock do anything about it?"

Beorn shrugged. "He's already put a shield over Sunbeam's apartment. He's been talking about confining him there. You can imagine that won't go down well with either Sunbeam or Flint."

The never-ending gloom and noise kept everyone on edge all winter. Despite the shutters, windows shattered with such regularity that only witches and wizards capable of holding a shield spell dared walk through the outer corridors. Both Arturos's and Master Sven's repairs became impossible to distinguish from the Warlock's from more than inches away.

Wizards and scholars yelled at each other in the hallways over jostled elbows and trod-upon toes, and the earth witch had to patch up more than one hothead who forgot the Warlock's stricture against flaming other guests. The mildest of the scholars threw a temper tantrum in the middle of the library. Even the affable Mrs Cole lost her temper, and ordered several junior witches out of her kitchen.

The Warlock confined both Sunbeam and Flint to their apartments. No one but the earth witch knew what had happened in the confrontation between the Warlock and Flint, but it was rumoured she collapsed from exhaustion after patching Flint up, and one of the guards had to carry her back to her room.

Jenny didn't try to flame me again, but she and several of her friends spread malicious gossip about me, and tried to intimidate me at every opportunity. I didn't have the time or energy to worry much about the gossip, and the bullying didn't work. That set of witches was so inept I couldn't lose a verbal sparring match with them even if I tried. Many of the townsfolk gave me surreptitious thumbs-up as few of them liked the McNamaras, but none of them came out openly in my support.

I became a hermit.

I hated the jostling, and couldn't afford to lose my temper with Jenny and her friends, so I spent my time in either my bedroom or the practice room, venturing out only for meals and books. René and I both slept in the practice room to get away from the noise.

I would sit in the dark, well after René was asleep, brooding over the Fire Warlock. His every move fascinated me; his physical presence was so compelling that I was instantly aware whenever he entered a room. What would his life have been like if he hadn't become Fire Warlock so young? Would Jean Rehsavvy, Flame Mage, have still loved the Frost Maiden, or would he have married a fire witch? There was a vast, unbridgeable gulf between the Fire Warlock and me, but if he had been just Warlock Quicksilver…

Sometimes, too, I brooded about Terésa. She could have been my sister, and I thought I knew her as well as I knew myself. Often in recent years, her tragedy had been cast as a cautionary tale against women setting their sights too high. Terésa, a level three witch, should never have chased a warlock, or so the playwright seemed to say. What then, was I, a level five, to do? I could not set my sights any lower. I would terrify any man who was not a warlock.

What kind of magic would it take to hold off the fierce heat of the volcano? What would Terésa have done if she had known her shield against fire would not hold up against it? Would she have run away, determined never again to see the Warlock she loved? Or would she have stayed by his side, close enough to touch but not daring to? Or would she have dared touch him, despite the foreknowledge that it would mean certain death?

No. She wasn't suicidal. Neither was I.

Fool. The Fire Warlock wanted an orderly succession, and for the Fire Office to be rebuilt. He said so himself. Terésa's Warlock loved her. Mine needed my help. Grow up and get over him.

"Beorn," I said, "how long can the siege go on?"

"Don't know. We're in stalemate. Jean's got them boxed in so they can't break away from the Fortress and attack any of the cities, so they're not doing us much damage. The Empire's wizards are working together to protect whoever's turn it is to attack, so ever since they stopped the all-out assaults he's not gotten many opportunities to deal them serious damage either. They could keep this up for a long time—years, decades even."

"Decades? We've only been under siege a few months, and we're already at each other's throats."

The Chessmaster's prediction that I would be the Warlock's downfall was ever present in my mind. I was certain the war would not last years, much less decades.

"They're wearing him down, aren't they?"

"Yep," he said. "It's just a matter of time before they make him lose control."

Our progress on the Warlock's notes about the Office slowed, as he could not maintain his concentration on anything other than the Empire's wizards for long stretches. He would pace up and down the room while Beorn and I struggled through his notes without him, saving questions for when he looked least distracted. He developed hollow cheeks and bags under his eyes, and never got enough sleep. I watched, and worried, and daydreamed.

I ached for him, body and soul, and I wished there was something, anything, that I could do to help. How could I be afraid of him, when I was so afraid for him?

A Wish Granted

René asked, "How many kinds of shields are there?"

Beorn shrugged. "More than I can count. There are shields against just about anything that can hurt you. Knives, missiles, wasps, lava…"

My ears pricked up. Lava?

"Against lightning?"

"Sure, but like the lightning itself, you have to be a warlock to handle it. You could use it in a storm, but you wouldn't want to use it in a fight."

"Why not?"

"Because a shield against anything that dangerous is a serious drain. If you try to protect yourself in a fight against everything a wizard can throw at you, you can't keep the shields up for more than a few minutes. You'll get so tired you can't fight back. That's why we've focused on a simple mirror shield…"

There's a shield against lava? I picked up the textbook Master Sven had given us and thumbed through it. There was nothing there a level three witch couldn't handle.

The Warlock had called me a queen, hadn't he? Humbug. The never-ending exercises in self-defence and handling fire were turning me into more of a drudge than I'd been in the kitchen. If being a warlock was about being in control, it was high time I took control of my own life.

I haunted the library in my limited spare time, looking for the spell for the lava shield. If I had asked for help, either Master Sven or Master Thomas could have found it for me right away, but I wasn't willing to explain why I wanted it.

I found it after a week. Dangerous, the book said. Needs constant maintenance. Letting one's attention wander in a lava field would be deadly.

Terésa, a level three witch, would not have been able to use this shield.

The spell was more complicated than anything we had tried so far, but I understood the theory behind shields, and I was getting good at them. My teachers obviously didn't think we needed to know this one, but I wanted to see if I could make it work.

I went over the spell in my head many times in the next few days. One evening, after hurrying through supper to be the first to reach the Warlock's study, I crossed my fingers, took a deep breath, and cast the spell.

I staggered as a weight, like dozens of layers of heavy quilting, seemed to settle on my shoulders and burden my limbs. Walking to the fireplace was like wading through a sea of molasses. An hour of this and I would have nothing left for tomorrow's practice.

How could I test it? A normal fire wasn't hot enough. I was standing in the embers, feeling silly, when the two warlocks walked in.

Beorn came over to the fireplace and rumbled, "You're up to something, aren't you? What now?"

The Warlock had stopped dead just inside the door, tension evident in his neck and shoulders. I stepped out of the fireplace and dusted myself off, watching the Fire Warlock. "I was trying out the shield against lava, but I couldn't think of a way to test it."

"You're catching on fast. Jean, how about melting a rock?"

The Warlock didn't seem to have heard him. He came closer, treading like a cat stalking a bird.

Had I done something wrong? This should have pleased him. He was making me nervous.

I glanced from him to Beorn. Both men were staring at me with fire in their eyes.

The Warlock said, "Let us test it in the practice room." He led me through the fire, Beorn following. The box of magical burn treatments flew the length of the practice room and landed at my feet. The Warlock picked up one of the iron bars and held it out to me. "I will heat the iron. Touch it with the back of your hand, and pull away quickly if it begins to burn."

I held my hand against the cold metal. It warmed, became hot, then searing. It glowed red, then yellow. The Warlock seemed to be holding his breath. The metal sagged, deforming, then ran over my arm and dripped onto the floor. Through it all, the sense of heavy padding remained. My skin did not even blister.

The Warlock tossed the rest of the iron bar away, and pulled me away from the molten puddle. Before I had time to wonder what was coming next his arms were around me, his mouth coming down hard on mine.

Does a mouse welcome the attentions of the cat about to consume it? I dug my hands into his back, and answered him fire for fire. His left arm, like an iron bar across my back, clamped me against him while his right hand moved over me, exploring, caressing. I felt the heat rising in him, the mounting excitement, the inferno in my own heart responding. I was no longer thinking, only feeling.

And the shield, that precious shield, slipped, faltered under a spear of searing pain, and came crashing down. My clothes were on fire, his touch blistering me. Then Beorn was pulling us apart, shouting, sucking the heat away. The Warlock let go and I fell, slipping into blessed blackness even before I hit the floor.

Burn Medicine

Cloth covered my face, my hands. My arms and legs were swaddled like a newborn's. A burial shroud?

I opened my mouth to scream, and choked on something hard and cold.

A hand pulled the cloth away from my eyes. "Sorry," the earth witch said. "The ice is supposed to sooth your burned tongue, not make you gag."

I stared at the healer, panic forgotten. They had wrapped me from head to foot in the Earth Guild burn cloths, and still she looked as if she had fallen into a vat of boiling water. What had I looked like before they fetched her? I gagged again.

I looked around for the Fire Warlock. I had to turn my head a few degrees to see him. He was sitting on one of the metal chairs, elbows on knees, his face buried in his hands. He was as still as a marble statue. Keeping my head turned took too much effort. I went back to staring at the earth witch.

Her blisters shrank and disappeared; the angry red faded to ashen grey. Her head lolled against Beorn's supporting arm. The burns she'd stolen from me were healing, but at a cost to her.

"You'll be fine," she said, slurring the words. "It doesn't feel like it now, but you will be. I pray no more of you fool hotheads get any ideas tonight…" She closed her eyes.

If someone died tonight, it would be my fault. Comforting thought, that.

Beorn lowered the healer to the flagstone floor, and then bent over me, inspecting the wrappings. "How do you feel?"

I used a barnyard phrase that had once made my father wash my mouth out with soap, and Beorn didn't even blink. "Sounds about right."

He smoothed the burn cloth over my face, leaving my eyes free, then picked up the snoring witch. "I'll be back in a few minutes. Don't go anywhere."

As if. I closed my eyes. Keeping them open was too much work.

The metal chair creaked. Soft footfalls padded towards me, followed by a whisper of movement. I opened my eyes to see the man I loved kneeling beside me. There was no colour in his face, and when he started to talk he choked, and had to fight for control for a long moment, before saying, in a shaking voice, "I am sorry."

He knelt with his head down for what seemed a long time, moving only to draw in long breaths, hold them, and exhale, before regaining command of his voice. "It seems a pathetically inadequate thing to say. I had no right to do this to you. I knew better. I certainly had been warned."

I mumbled, "Jean, I'm sorry I couldn't keep the shield up."

There didn't seem to be anything more either of us could say.

When Beorn came back, he picked me up as if I was a goblet he might crush with his fingers, and carried me through the tunnel to my room. He put me on the bed and pulled the eider over me, then combed his fingers through his beard. "Lucinda, I'm sorry this happened. I saw it coming but I was too slow—"

"You had a vision that he would kiss me?"

"Hell, no, I don't need to be a seer to know he'd grab a once-in-a-lifetime chance. Can't blame him. I know how a man reacts to a pretty girl, and he's been stuck in that damned Office for an awfully long time. I wouldn't be as sane if I'd been there half as long.

"I meant, the shield against lava is too dangerous, but I was dolt enough to hope it would work… Now you're going to be fine in a few days. What you need now is sleep."

The ice was long gone, and the pain ebbing. I felt more like talking now. "But, Beorn—"

"Sleep," he ordered.

"But I want to know…"

I stopped. The room had been dark, but now there were shafts of light coming in through gaps in the shutters—light coming from a sun low on the western horizon. Mrs Cole was bending over me.

"I've slept a whole day?"

"Yes, honey, you have, and you look like you needed it. Arturos told me there'd been an accident, and you'd need some help getting unwrapped. I've brought you some supper, so let's deal with those burn cloths."

She helped me into the bathroom, and peeled off the burn cloths. Sheets of dead skin came off along with them, showing brand new bright pink skin underneath. She clucked over me, inspecting the damage.

"Well," she said, "that Arturos got a good look at you, that's for certain, but I'm sure it wasn't a pretty sight at the time. Looks like you were pretty lucky, honey. You don't have any scars—physical ones, anyway. The pinkness will wear off, and once your hair grows back—"

"My hair?" My hands flew to my scalp, and met bare skin. I ran to the mirror, and recoiled from the bald demon staring back at me. I threw myself on the bed and howled.

Mrs Cole tucked a blanket around me and patted me on the shoulder. "It's not the end of the world. It will grow back in time—"

"How much time?" I said, between sobs. "Decades?"

"It could have been worse. You survived. What were you doing, anyway?"

"Playing with fire."

"I can see that. No, don't tell me, I don't need to know. As smoky and singed-looking as you are sometimes when you come out of there, I've known you've been doing more powerful fire magic than I ever wanted to deal with. I just don't like that he misjudged what you were ready to handle. You can't tell me that if Himself were there he'd have let you get burned that bad."

I didn't refute that claim. I sobbed into my pillow while she fussed over me, peeling off the last bits of dead skin and reanointing my burns.

On her way out, she said, "You've earned a holiday, anyway. I told Arturos you wouldn't want to put your nose out of your room until your burns had healed, and he agreed, so you just stay here and I'll bring you your food. Now, is there anything I can bring you from the library, dear?"

Anything but *Terésa*. I named a couple of books, and thanked her. When she came back I said, "Mrs Cole, Arturos saved my life. It wasn't his fault; it was mine. I tried to do something I had no business trying yet. When you see the Warlock, please tell him I said that. I wouldn't want him thinking I would let someone else take the blame for my mistake."

"If you say so, honey," she said. "I'm still entitled to my own opinion, but I will tell him what you said. Goodnight, now."

Never, ever, lie to a warlock. What is the penalty when the warlock one lies to is oneself? I had plenty of time to contemplate that question, as I finally confessed that I had been lying to myself for months, clinging to the delusion that I was not in love with Jean Rehsavvy.

I had plenty of time, too, to remember what my mother had said: be careful what you wish for, for you will surely get it. I had gotten what I wanted, and hated myself for it. I had behaved irresponsibly, not acknowledging what I was doing, and relying on his self-control to prevent a disaster. But I had jolted him out of his self-possession, and neither of us had been in control.

I did not go down to the practice room to sleep, despite the noise, because I couldn't face René's curiosity. After four days, in which I mainly alternated dozing and crying, I had recovered enough strength to pace circuits of the room like a caged tiger. On every circuit, I stopped in front of the mirror, inspecting the hideous apparition that appeared there. Each time was a fresh shock. The bright pink had faded to pasty white, relieved only by the stubble on my scalp.

Mrs Cole spread a story that my hair caught on fire after I dozed off too close to a candle. She said I would draw less attention if she explained my burns away before I reappeared. I agreed with the wisdom of this pretence, but it added force to my stomping. I'd rather they thought I was a seductress than silly or careless. I would prefer to tell the truth, but not at the cost of exposing the Fire Warlock to ridicule.

Criticising the appearance of a person recovering from burns was bad manners. Students at the guild school suffered burns with distressing regularity, and everyone in Blazes had seen the effects, so I didn't expect much overt reaction. What they thought or whispered behind my back was my bigger concern.

The next morning, I tied a scarf Mrs Cole lent me under my chin, and crept out of my room for breakfast. In the dim light, the other bleary-eyed early risers paid me little heed as I shovelled scrambled eggs and toast onto a plate. I poured a cup of coffee and turned to leave, intending to eat in the practice room. I was congratulating myself on having escaped attention when a tug at my scarf sent it slithering backwards, exposing my bald head.

Defeat

I whirled. Half my coffee splashed across the buffet table.

"You're as bald as a billiard ball," Jenny McNamara squealed, loud enough to make heads turn. "Mundanes like you can't be trusted even with a candle."

I stared at her, breathing hard.

She gloated. "You're such a dimwit. Master Sven will gag when he sees you with no hair. He won't have anything more to do with you."

Everyone in the dining room was turning to stare. I forced my bared teeth into a smile. "You're welcome to him. I'm tired of his dithering. Besides, I could never respect someone that was rude to a burn victim."

She flushed and raised a hand as if to flame me. I swept past her and out of the dining room with my nose in the air.

Master Sven was going to be furious. I was choking down dry toast with the dregs of the coffee when Beorn stormed into the practice room, slamming the door with such force that even on the other side of the cavernous room I jumped.

He stalked across the room and came to a stop in front of me, scowling.

I slid down in my chair. "You heard?"

"Everybody in the Fortress has heard. If not now, they will by dinnertime."

He sat down beside me, blowing out through his moustache. He looked at me out of the corner of his eye. "I guess I lost my temper."

"What did you do?"

"I told Jenny if Sven took up with her I'd make sure he was never named a mage—anyone that stupid wouldn't deserve it."

I slid further down. "Beorn, you shouldn't have. Sven may never speak to me again."

"He will." Beorn grinned. "It's not your fault Jenny's a ninny."

Master Sven arrived, a bit later, with René hard on his heels. The boy bounded across the room, shouting, "Lucinda, where have you been? What—"

He stopped in mid-bounce. "Wow. I never saw anybody look like that before."

My stomach clenched. "Thanks a lot."

Beorn cuffed him. "That was rude. Say you're sorry."

"I'm sorry. I didn't mean... Why is it rude? I wouldn't mind if I got burned and she said that to me."

Master Sven rolled his eyes. At least he wasn't gagging.

René said, "That story about a candle is hogwash. What did happen?"

Beorn barked, "None of your business. No questions."

"But I want to know—"

Beorn grabbed him by the collar and snarled. "I said, none of your damn business. Do you want to practice fire magic, or do you want to go back to working in the food stores?"

René's eyes flicked back and forth between Beorn and me. "Practice magic."

"Good. Let's get to work."

Jenny and her friends ate dinner in a little island of empty space amid the jostling horde.

I was mobbed. Scholars, most with averted eyes, assured me I would feel more like myself in a week or two. Mundane staff patted me on the shoulder and whispered, "Thank you for standing up to that harpy. It isn't right for them to treat mundanes like dirt." Witches and wizards I had never spoken to before came by to tell me in gruesome detail about burns they had suffered at the school, and that accidents could happen to anybody—it wasn't anything to be ashamed of.

Through it all, Master Sven hovered at my elbow, saying little. Every time I looked up his eyes were on me, until I wanted to throw something, anything, at him. He gave us a reading assignment that afternoon, and I fled to a private corner in the dimmer recesses of the library. I was glad not only to get away from his scrutiny, but my mind was not on witchcraft. I left the book I was supposed to read on a table, and picked up a drama that I could already quote by heart, *Terésa*.

I was still trying to settle into a comfortable position when Master Sven walked through the stacks and sat down beside me, glowering.

He said, "Forgive me for following you, but I wanted to talk to you alone, without René."

"I'm sorry about what I said to Jenny…"

He waved a hand. "Don't be. You're right, I have been dithering."

I shifted in my seat, edging away from him. "I'm sorry, I didn't mean—"

"Forget it. I want to know what happened. And don't tell me it's none of my business. I love you. That makes it my business."

Now he tells me? I stared at him, my hands with a mind of their own flipping the book in my lap face down. He glanced at it, and must have seen the title. He seemed to deflate, the anger in his face fading into distress. He said, "Oh, drown it, Lucinda. Is that how it is?"

I nodded without meeting his eyes. "I tried to use a shield against lava, but I couldn't keep it up."

We sat side-by-side, alone in our own miseries. He said, "I should have guessed. I've seen how you look at each other." Several times he started to say something else, thought better of it, and lapsed back into silence. At length, he said, "I'm sorry, for both of you," and walked away, his shoulders sagging. I stared after him until he was out of sight.

I rode the stairs that evening to the Warlock's study with a dry mouth and sweaty palms. Being a warlock is about being in control, is it? How could I face him? I'd had five days and I still hadn't gotten myself under control.

He met me at the door, and we both recoiled. He looked as if he had aged a decade since I had last seen him. His eyes, always so alive, seemed dim. His face was grey with exhaustion.

He said, "Oh, my dear, your hair. I am so sorry."

I looked him straight in the eye. "It doesn't matter. Really."

He rewarded me with the old ghost of a smile that I always found so charming. "Thank you, my dear, but you are a terrible liar." The amusement faded. "Neither of us is any shape to continue these sessions on the Office. It would be better for both of us to get to bed earlier and get what sleep we can."

He paused, and took a deep breath. Exhaled and drew in another. "A change of scene would do you good. You would benefit from going to the Warren, and staying with the Earth Mother."

My jaw fell open. "You're joking, right?"

He shook his head. "Rumours about the Chessmaster's prediction will reach us any day now, and with the townsfolk in the Fortress you will be in danger even here. There are fools among them who will think they could protect me by eliminating you. You will be safer there."

My eyes stung. "I can't leave. My year of service isn't up yet."

"My dear, I have sent people all over Frankland, and even out of it, during their terms of service. The pertinent requirement is serving the Office, not where you serve it. Further, the full condition is one year, or putting one's life at risk in its service. Given that, you are free to go and do as you like."

"I would like to stay here."

He sighed. "I cannot order you to go to the Warren, but I do ask that you consider it. You are much too valuable; I do not want you to be at risk. I am suggesting this only because it is in your best interests."

"That's a, a—" I choked on the word 'lie'. What he said was true, but wasn't the whole truth. Every time he saw me, I would remind him of his own serious lapse in judgement and near-fatal loss of self-control. He didn't want to admit that. He was lying as much to himself as he was to me.

"I'm too much of a distraction, aren't I?"

He nodded without meeting my eyes.

I sagged, and whispered, "Yes, sir, I'll think about it."

I lay awake that night until nearly dawn. His suggestion that I leave the Fortress seared my soul as his touch had seared my skin, and I berated myself for prolonging my self-delusion. The Chessmaster had predicted I would claim a place in the Warlock's lustful heart. What does a century alone do to a man? He had given me ample proof of his desires, but was it love? Cold reason said, no, he would have reacted as he did to any non-repulsive woman who could hold the shield spell against lava.

I didn't know if he loved me. All I was sure of was that I loved him.

It didn't matter. I would be in danger when the rumour spread, and life here was already horrid. I had a duty to help him in any way I could, and my presence was a burden. I should do as he asked, and leave.

Ask him if he loves you, my heart said. He can't lie to you, or if he does, you'll know.

Fool, my head argued. Don't ask a question if you're not sure you want to hear the answer.

When I walked into the dining room for a late supper a few days later, the people there, mostly townsfolk, stopped chattering and turned as one to glare at me. I grabbed a plate of food and fled, my cheeks burning and my heart hammering.

Mrs Cole came to my room a little later, with red eyes and blotchy cheeks. Mrs Cole, crying?

She twisted her apron in her hands. "Honey, there's some nasty gossip going around. I've been saying I don't believe a word of it, but I thought you'd better know what they're saying."

I sat down at my desk, playing with my pen. "Are they saying I'm an enemy spy sent to seduce the Fire Warlock and steal his secrets?"

There was a brief silence. "You're not surprised."

"He warned me this was coming." I looked up to see her staring at me. "He showed me an enemy agent spinning that story several months ago." I dipped the pen in the inkwell and doodled with my head down. "The original prediction didn't say anything about destroying the Office, but it did say I would be the Warlock's downfall. Neither of us have figured out how."

"Oh, honey." The silence was longer this time. "He told me what happened."

"He what?"

"That was after I told him what you had said about taking responsibility. He said that was generous of you, but it wasn't just your fault. He said I'm going to have to take orders from Arturos soon, and he couldn't let me think it was his fault either.

"Now honey, you know I like you. I don't want you to get the wrong idea. I'd rather have you helping me in the kitchen than any of the helpers I've got now, but maybe you'd be better off if you went away for a while, either back to your village, or to stay with the Earth Mother."

I threw down the pen, and spattered ink all over the desk. "Did he tell you to say that?"

"No, of course not. I was just trying to help. Why?"

Tears splashed beside the drops of ink. "He said I should go away, too."

She came over to the desk and hugged me. "Well, it does sound like a good idea."

The walk to breakfast was an ordeal. Groups of people in the corridors stopped talking and moved aside as if I were a leper. Mrs McNamara and Mrs Cole were shouting when I walked into the kitchen. Mrs Cole attempted a cheerful, "Good morning, honey—" but Mrs McNamara overrode her with, "Go get your breakfast down in the barracks with the guards, where you belong, you brazen minx. We don't need your kind around here." She stopped cold as the kitchen door opened and the Warlock walked in.

"Ah, good morning, Lucinda, I was hoping to catch you here. Come and sit with me, please."

Turning to Mrs McNamara, he said blandly, "I am afraid I interrupted you, Helen. What were you saying?"

She had the grace to turn beet-red. "Nothing. I mean, nothing worth repeating, Your Wisdom."

He smiled, but his voice brooked no argument. "You will then assure me it will not be."

She took a step backwards. "Yes, sir."

"Good. It is reassuring to know that the kitchen is full of friendly chit-chat."

Still smiling, he held the door for me. I stalked into the dining room with my head held high. The hostile glances from other diners were more furtive with him beside me. When we were seated at the table amid friendly faces—Master Thomas and several of the more sensible scholars—he said, "I did not have anything I needed to talk to you about, certainly not in as public a forum as this, but I suspected Helen's tongue would do nothing for your digestion."

"No, sir. Thank you, sir."

Even so, my stomach was in knots. She had no right to talk to me, a warlock, like that. But none of them knew what I was, and I couldn't expect the Warlock to rescue me from the other nasty confrontations that would come. When he got up to leave, I stopped him. "I've been thinking

236

about your suggestion. I still don't like it, but I'll do it."

The sadness in his face tore at my heart. He nodded, and turned away. "Thank you, my dear."

I packed through a haze of tears. Once I left the Fortress, it was unlikely I would ever see Jean Rehsavvy again. I would not cry when I said goodbye. I could, I would, behave like a warlock. I could be in control long enough for that.

I took the two histories off the shelf and thumbed through them. He had written the text, but a printer and bookbinder had made the copies in my hands. I had nothing that his hands had touched. I put the books in my bag, and walked through the tunnel to the practice room. From there I turned around and went back to wash my face. I couldn't hide my red eyes, but I had my pride, and I would pretend I had not been crying.

He met me at the door of his study, and I walked on in, reluctant to turn towards that tunnel, closed now for security during the siege.

He said, "I will open the tunnel to the Warren long enough for you to pass through, but once out of the Fortress you cannot come back in until the siege is over, except through the postern gate. Mother Celeste is expecting you, and I trust you will be safe there.

"You need not worry about there being a place for you in the Fire Guild when the war is over. Most of the guild members respect Arturos more than they do either Flint or Sunbeam, and the Office will not allow one warlock to block another qualified warlock from having a voice in the Council. If it did, I would have thrown Flint off the Council twenty years ago. If he tries to push you around be polite but obstinate, and let the Warlock and the Office protect you. Flint will come out the loser in any such contest."

"Yes, sir. Thank you." I walked across the study, drawn by the slim volume bound in dark blue leather lying face down on his desk. I did not need to see the title—I had held this same book, or its sibling from the same printing, a few days earlier.

I reached for it, but it flew off the desk and sailed into his hands. "Forgive me," he said. "It was thoughtless of me to leave such a painful reminder lying about."

I struggled to speak around the constriction in my throat. "You were reading it, too?"

"I know it by heart, and, until recently, had not touched my copy for many years." He turned it over in his hands and opened it. Handwritten annotations filled the margins—his own copy, then, not the one from the library. "It seems strange to me that I should reread it, but I have done so several times in the past few months."

"When? After I released my lock?"

A smile flickered across his sombre face. "No, my dear, earlier, after learning you read Gibson's *History*."

I turned my back to him and walked away, the back of my hand pressed against my mouth. Drown the man, he would not make me cry. I had the answer I wanted. Why did it hurt so much? When I regained control of my voice, I said, "I want something of yours, to remember you by."

"What would you have? I possess little, other than my personal library. There is nothing I own that I would not give you."

I turned back to him and pointed to the book in his hands. "I want that."

His gaze flicked from me to the book, and back. "Lucinda, my dear, you continue to astound me. Take it, and welcome."

He held out the copy of *Terésa*. I took it from him and put it in my bag. He picked up the bag, gesturing for me to precede him out the door, and seemed at a loss as I stared at him without moving.

My careful control over my voice vanished, and I winced as it quavered. "Aren't you going to offer me your arm?"

He dropped the bag and walked towards the fireplace with his back to me, as I had walked away from him earlier. His voice, when he spoke, was thick. "I expected you to recoil from my touch."

I couldn't answer for the lump in my throat. I was not afraid of anything short of another passionate kiss, and even that had been as much joy as torture.

In a few minutes, he came back, and I clasped with both hands the arm he offered. We paced towards the tunnel without speaking or looking at each other. Once there, he held out his hand and I put mine in it. He held it for several seconds with his eyes closed, then raised it, and brushed it with his lips.

I swallowed hard. "Jean," I whispered.

He looked up. Tears in his eyes made my own vision blur. I brushed away a disobedient droplet that slid down my cheek.

"Jean, I wish…"
The world stood still, waiting.

Going to Earth

Oh, dear God, what could I wish for, that would make any difference? Jean shook his head. "No, my dear. No more ill-considered, dangerous wishes. You wished that I might have what I wanted, and it was almost your own undoing."

I bowed my head. "Yes, sir."

The feeling of something waiting passed with a great trembling sigh. I had missed my chance. What chance?

He didn't seem to have noticed. "You have made my last year worth living. Remember that, for my sake."

He released my hand and turned away to cast the spell opening the tunnel. Without looking at me again he said, "Farewell, my love."

I slung my bag over my shoulder and took two steps towards the tunnel. Coward.

I turned back, grabbed his shoulders, and kissed him full on the lips. He had little time to react—drawing back in shock and flinging out his arms to avoid touching me—before I broke it off. I whirled and ran through the tunnel, clinging to my last shred of self-control, and the memory of the emotions—astonishment, delight, yearning—that had flashed across his face.

Sunlight blinded me. I couldn't have seen Mother Celeste even if I hadn't been bawling.

She guided me through the maze of the Warren with an arm around my shoulders, tsking. "It's not healthy to be shut up underground like moles, not seeing the sun for months at a time. You'd be depressed even without any of your other troubles. The first thing you need, I think, is a good meal and a glass of wine. Let's see what we can do for you."

We encountered other people here and there in the corridors. After the jostling crowds and hot tempers in the Fortress, the calm dignity on display soothed my frayed nerves. We reached the amber chamber, where a girl about my own age joined us.

Mother Celeste introduced her, "Lucinda, this is Hazel, the finest healer in the new crop coming along. She'll be looking after you while you're here."

I wiped away tears long enough to get a good look at the other girl. She was a little over medium height, with an oval face and freckles, and looked pleased but not surprised by the Earth Mother's compliment. Someone who knew her own worth. We would get along fine.

Mother Celeste conjured up food; a meal that reminded me of fare my own mother had prepared to comfort injured spirits and bandaged knees. Onion soup with a crust of cheese. Hot buttered toast and eggs, perfectly cooked, with the yolk still runny. Strawberries and blueberries in whipped cream. Berries in winter? Why not? There was earth magic to spare here. I made a pig of myself.

The food and the wine worked their magic on me, and soon stemmed the flood of tears. The Earth Mother talked to Hazel while I ate. "She should be out in the sunshine, but we needed to come here where we won't be overheard." Her voice changed, sounding as stern as Jean sometimes did. "You are bound by your oath as a member of the Earth Guild not to divulge to anyone else what I will tell you in this room."

I looked up, startled. Hazel stared at her wide-eyed, but nodded. "Yes, ma'am."

Mother Celeste, in her usual warm voice, said, "Sorry about that, dear, but I had to say it. I know you don't give away secrets, or I wouldn't have picked you in the first place." She gave the girl a summary description of my talents and what I had been going through. Hazel's eyes, already wide, nearly bulged out of her head when Mother Celeste related my near-fatal encounter with the passionate Warlock. She ended with a brisk, "Now show her around, and help her get settled in. Lucinda, I know you're a good cook. Would you help in the kitchen?"

They didn't need my help in the kitchen. I was certain of that within minutes as I watched the efficient team of witches going about their daily business. But I understood and appreciated what the Earth Mother was trying to do—give me someone to pour out my heart to, and keep me busy so I wouldn't have time to brood—and the cooks made room for me without any fuss, as if they saw my heartache and pitied me.

Every time I saw Mother Celeste, I asked for news from the Fortress. After the sixth time in two days, she threw up her hands in exasperation. "Go away and stop bothering me. I'll come and find you if anything changes, and if you ask me again, I'll send you to your room without supper."

I followed Hazel, working outdoors when the weather permitted, helping prepare the gardens for the spring plantings. On rainy days, we worked with several other young earth witches, assembling healers' potions and elixirs. I was curious about earth magic and they were happy to talk, so we got along well. My eyebrows grew back in, and my colour began to return. Hazel taught me how to use magic to make my hair grow faster.

"An inch at a time," she said. "Don't overdo it, or you'll make yourself sick."

After a week, it brushed my collar. I abandoned the scarf, and marvelled at the lightness and freedom the short hair gave me.

I would have been happy in the Warren if I had not been worried sick. Also, the question nagged at me: what opportunity had I missed when I left the Fortress? Had I forgotten something? I searched the Warren's library for books on the Fire Guild, but they didn't have the one—Gibson's *History*—I most wanted. I skimmed other histories, but none jogged my memory. Not even my dreams offered hints.

⁂

I peeked around the corner, watching Hazel make her serene way down the corridor. When she was halfway, I scooted along, passing her. I reached the next intersection, and peered around. No danger in sight.

Hazel said, "I don't understand why you're so nervous. Even if she wanted to be offensive, which I doubt, she's more likely to snub you than make a scene."

"You didn't see how she acted when I met her."

"I'm not saying I don't believe you, but it seems out of character. I've talked to Sorceress Lorraine, and thought she had excellent manners. She's not what I would pick for a bosom buddy, but I understand why Mother Celeste likes her."

I dashed to the end of the next corridor and peeked around the corner. I had asked Mother Celeste, "Why can't the Fire Warlock and the Frost Maiden get along?"

She had shrugged. "I've wondered that myself for years. It seems to have been that way for the entire life of the Offices. It's quite a shame. I consider them both good friends. They are both lovely people to deal with, as long as they aren't in the same room together."

When Hazel caught up, I said, "What's she doing in the Warren?"

"She comes here often. The two guilds share some responsibilities, and it's easier on us if she comes here—the Crystal Palace is too cold for our comfort."

"Yes, I can see that, but spending the night?"

"Not unusual. I think she likes a change of pace once in a while."

"Fine. I hope she sleeps well tonight. I won't."

We reached the sanctuary of the library, and Hazel disappeared into the botany section. I went to the history stacks, and stood with my hands on the shelves, waiting for the quiet oasis to work its magic on me.

The chill gave way to burning in my chest and face, and I tightened my grip on the shelves. Mother Celeste had confirmed the rumour that the Frost Maiden and Jean had once been lovers, and I wanted to flame that water sorceress as much as Jenny McNamara had wanted to flame me.

If I didn't get over it, I would start burning things by accident. I snatched my hands away from the shelves. Why did it bother me so? Their love affair ended a century ago. It was silly of me to be jealous. I would not act like Jenny—I had more dignity than that.

I was still hot when I met Hazel at the librarian's desk. As we walked to the door, I plotted the shortest route to the kitchen. I would grab supper, and then dash up the service stairs to my room. If I took something for breakfast, I wouldn't have to come out again until after the Frost Maiden was gone.

We reached the open doorway, and came face-to-face with Mother Celeste and the Frost Maiden. I froze.

Shock registered on the Frost Maiden's face before the curtain of disdain dropped in place. "Well, if it isn't the Lesser Locksmith. What are you doing here? Have you run away from…Which? The war? Or the Warlock?"

I clutched my book to my chest, and glared at her without answering.

She stretched out a hand and grasped my face, the great sapphire in her ring flashing. I jerked backwards, but her nails dug into my cheek and chin.

Hazel gaped. Mother Celeste hissed, "Lorraine—"

For an instant, the first Locksmith was as strong a presence as the Frost Maiden.

The Frost Maiden examined me, no emotion but contempt apparent. "He has set his mark on you. How fortunate you are still with us."

I knocked her hand away.

She said languidly, "You do have a temper. I am making you quite angry, aren't I? How interesting, you do not seem to be afraid of me. Why not? Are you that stupid?"

"Your Wisdom, I did not insult you. The Water Office is the dispenser of justice. It won't let you kill me for expecting the same respect in return."

Her eyes narrowed. I had scored. Damn. She wouldn't kill me, I hoped, but a hex that kept me from ever getting warm again might make me wish she had.

She said, "Why should I respect you?"

No one else was within earshot. Keeping my voice low, I said, "Because someday I may be the Fire Warlock. Would you then want me asking why I should respect you?"

Her eyes widened. I turned my back on her and walked out of the room.

The Frost Maiden's touch had shocked me, and not just because of the insult and her cold hands. The sense of the first Warlock Locksmith's presence must have come from the magic making up the Water Office. He had worked on all four Offices, but I had never expected his handiwork to be so obvious. It was begging me to read it.

The impulse to read it strengthened as time passed. By midnight, I was fretting over the Locksmith's spellcraft as a terrier worries a bone. It was summoning me—I was sure of it. A clock somewhere struck half-past, then one o'clock.

I couldn't stand it anymore. I pulled on a robe and stepped out into hall.

If that spell wanted me to read it, I would.

The Frost Maiden

The conviction that someone, or something, was summoning me intensified as I tiptoed towards the Frost Maiden's door.

I shrank the flame in my mind's eye until it was the tiniest spark possible and bade it find the Frost Maiden's ring. It slipped under the door, and I surveyed the bedroom. She slept, the hand with the ring resting on top of the eider. I held my breath while the spark crept closer, to within touching distance. Her Office must be aware I was there. Would it encase me in ice crystals for committing such an outrage?

I stood with both hands pressed against the door, heart hammering, breath shallow, palms sweaty. I nudged the spark closer; it brushed against the enormous sapphire. I was not frozen to death, or drowned. But I now knew that my hunch was correct. The Water Office had summoned me.

I slid down the door until I was kneeling. I rested my head on the door, drawing in deep breaths and holding them, exhaling slowly, trying to calm my racing heart, before sitting on the cold floor. I turned and sat cross-legged, with my back to the door. I might be there a while; I might as well get comfortable. I closed my eyes, ordered the little spark to grow until just bright enough to read by, and began to study the spells.

I still had the sense of dealing with the Locksmith's handiwork, but I could not find the lock. As in the Fire Warlock's Office, there was an intertwined mess of spells, few of which I recognised. The sense of the Locksmith's presence diminished while I felt my way around. The clock struck two, then half-past. When it struck three, I gave up.

Why did I come out on such a risky errand in the middle of the night? Why was I losing sleep over this witch? Why did Jean love her? I'd like to spit in her eye.

The text of the lock unscrolled before me.

As I read, astonishment drove out the other emotions, and the text blanked out halfway through. If it had not been so dangerous I would have laughed out loud at the sheer absurdity of it, although the message it conveyed was not funny. I struggled to regain the right frame of mind, feeling wretched at the effort. Pity and horror warred with anger and jealousy. It took two more tries before I read the whole thing.

If the lock on the Fire Office was like this, Jean could not have read it even if he spent a century on it.

This lock was simple, elegant, and foolproof. The Locksmith had used the most fundamental of conditions to ensure that the lock could only be read by a level five fire witch in a jealous rage; someone, that is, nearly identical to the Locksmith herself. Everyone had assumed that the Locksmith was a man, but it was not so, and the drama the Frost Maiden and I had been engaged in had played out before, a millennium ago. Once before a fire wizard had desired a water witch, and the fire witch who wanted him had taken her revenge, locking up the water witch's heart in the sapphire Token of Office, creating the Frost Maiden—no, a succession of Frost Maidens—who could neither love nor let go of the men they no longer needed.

I pressed my hands on the cold stone floor, struggling to keep down the bile that rose as I pondered the all too human frailties of the members of the Great Coven. Had the Locksmith had any idea of how long the Offices would endure, and how many people would be hurt by her lust for revenge? If she had, would she have cared?

I cared. I might be like the original Locksmith in many ways, but this aspect of her character revolted me. When I am angry, I confront the person and thrash things out face-to-face, kiss and make up, and go on. I detested the woman lying asleep in the chambers behind me, but she didn't deserve this. Jean didn't deserve the attacks she inflicted on him out of her frustration and pain. And what had Beorn and René done to merit the abuse they in turn would receive?

That settled it. I could—I would—release this lock. There had been no one else in a thousand years who could do it; another locksmith might not appear for another thousand.

Wait. Was I making a serious mistake? The Offices and their spells are intertwined. I didn't know what would happen if I released it. Could this be the trigger for Jean's downfall?

I started up in horror, and, knelt on the hard floor, praying for guidance. I could never forgive myself if releasing this lock brought about his death, but the lock was an abomination. If he was already doomed, I couldn't, in good conscience, leave it be. I wouldn't get another chance.

The Frost Maiden didn't trust me. If I told her, in the morning, that I wanted to fix her Office, she would laugh at me—if I was lucky. And she would only be here one night.

When the clock struck four, I gritted my teeth. I had to release it, and I had to do it tonight. I settled down once again with my back to the door. Time to get on with it.

I couldn't read the lock.

How could I get back into the right frame of mind? I didn't hate her anymore. I conjured up images of her and Jean together, imagining him kissing her with the same fervour with which he had kissed me. The rage and jealousy returned and the spell unfolded, but I hated myself for it. I might as well wallow in a cesspit.

I read the spell again. A long one for a lock, it was a poem in the form of a villanelle, each repeated line hammering home the Locksmith's intention of exacting revenge.

> *You are Frost Maiden in your day,*
> *You have captured my true love's heart,*
> *For this the price you must pay.*

> *Your words, your voice, have too much sway.*
> *Each thing you say pierces like a dart.*
> *You are Frost Maiden in your day.*

> *You cannot love them in any way,*
> *Yet, many a man loves you in his heart,*
> *For this the price you must pay.*

> *You may be as beautiful as the Fae,*
> *But nothing changes what thou art.*
> *You are Frost Maiden in your day.*

A fire witch locks your heart away.
No one else can see all that thou art.
This is the price you must pay.

My anger, my jealousy, over you hold sway,
I hate you for all that thou art.
You are Frost Maiden in your day,
For this the price you must pay.

I set the flame to work at the end of the poem. It wouldn't budge. What would it take to reverse this lock? The flame grew bright enough to sear, like looking into the sun. I cowered away from it.

This was going to hurt.

Compulsion

I shoved the flame backwards through the words of the spell. Halfway through, I was drenched in sweat. Pushing the flame was like struggling with a red-hot wheelbarrow loaded down with a pile of bricks. With two tercets left to go, I was shivering as with a fever. With one tercet left, I faced possible death by fire for the third time. I lay down on the cold floor and kept shoving. My breath came in ragged gasps and my clothes were soaked through.

Why was I torturing myself?

I was doing it for Beorn and René. I clung to that thought like a lifeline. Let me stop, I whimpered, but some other part of my mind said, almost done, keep going, almost done.

I shoved the flame through the last letter. With a crack as intense as the lightning bolts the Warlock had called down on the mountain, a surge of light rolled over me, followed by utter blackness.

A worried-looking blonde woman I didn't recognise poured gallons of cold water over me, nearly drowning me. Lights appeared. People milled around, shouting. Beorn stood astride the aerie like Thor, hurling Mjöllnir at his enemies.

Which was real? Which was a fever-induced phantasm?

Mother Celeste, in a wet nightgown, cradled my head in her arms. Jean, one-eyed in a slouch hat, Hugnin and Muninn on his shoulders, brooded over the world from Mount Olympus. Blue-eyed Hera by his side waited to exact revenge on any young woman his eye alighted on.

Good grief, how did I get so muddled?

The blonde woman reappeared and put a hand on my temple. Her eyes were cool but not unkind, not icy like those of…the Frost Maiden?

"You will live," she said, "although if I had not woken you might not have. Now that you are awake, will you please tell us what in Heaven's name did you do? Something quite drastic, obviously. If you have damaged the Office of the Northern Waters you may come to wish I had left you to die, but I admit it feels more like it has been fixed than broken. Now, talk."

Talk? When I didn't know what was real? The Frost Maiden, kind to a warlock? That was an hallucination.

I looked around. I was lying in bed, dry and weak, in the room Mother Celeste had given me. From the light shining in the window, it appeared to be late morning. The Frost Maiden and the Earth Mother were both there, the Frost Maiden standing by the bed on one side, Mother Celeste rocking and knitting on the other. I tried to sit up and she waved a knitting needle at me; I couldn't move.

"Lie there, child," she said. "You are in no shape to do anything but. I'm going against my better judgement as a healer to make you talk, but it can't be helped. All the Offices are demanding to know what you've done to the Water Office. Besides, I'm a silly old woman who is dying of curiosity." She put down her knitting, and the Frost Maiden sat on the foot of the bed, where she could see my face.

"Talk," Mother Celeste said. "But don't move."

I had no hope of keeping secrets from these two witches. It didn't matter now anyway, I didn't feel anything—no anger, no disgust, no jealousy, no pain. Washed out, that was all.

I talked, describing my emotional state in blunt language. I talked about the Locksmith and the love triangle in the Great Coven, whose passions still moved us in lockstep more than a millennium later, how I had determined that I would not let it continue, and what it cost me to release the lock.

There was silence after I finished. Mother Celeste had started out watching my face intently. As I got further into the story, her gaze switched back and forth between my face and the Frost Maiden's. Now she reached out to pat my hand. She missed on the first try, fumbling around without taking her eyes off the other witch.

"So long," the Frost Maiden whispered. "This has gone on for so long, and we never even knew." She wiped her eyes, and in a few moments went on in a stronger voice. "I have read the first Frost Maiden's memoirs, of course, and knew there were jealousies in the Great Coven, but I never connected the fire witch she despised with the Locksmith, nor guessed how I was being manipulated into doing and saying things that I have been deeply ashamed of. So many times I have left meetings with Jean feeling sick of myself..."

I said, "Why didn't anybody see that something was wrong when the Offices were first created?"

She grimaced. "They may not have seen much of a change in behaviour as long as she was alive, and she lived for another century and a half. It pains me to admit it, but the first Frost Maiden was pretty much what the Locksmith seems to have thought she was—a manipulative power-hungry icicle who seduced men she was incapable of loving. There was fault on both sides, and my predecessor disgusts me as much as yours does you. Like each of her other successors, I assumed upon acquiring the Office that I would change it to be less, er, frosty, and that I would get along with the Fire Warlock when no one else had." She laughed hollowly. "We know how well that worked."

"What will you do now? I mean, do you still...?" My face got hot. What an impertinent question. She would say it was none of my business.

"Do I still want Jean? Is that it?" Her eyes flashed, but she turned away to gaze out the window. "No. That romance was over a long time ago, and some of the things I have said to him since are nigh unforgivable, even if I went and grovelled—which I suppose I must do." She grimaced again. "Even if I still wanted him, he would not want me. And you, a fire witch, are a better match for him. Not that it matters, when he is as trapped by his Office as I am by mine."

She stopped, her expression changing to astonishment. "Or was..." The astonishment changed to a faint smile. "Besides, there is another man for me now, a better match for a water witch. He has loved me for years, and I never even knew." The smile broadened until her face was radiant.

Was this the same woman? I could almost begin to like her.

She went to the door. "I must begin a full assessment of the Office, to make sure it is not damaged in some subtle way, but I suspect that even if there are other changes, overall the Office will perform better now than it has. It feels less of a burden today than it ever has before. I am deeply in your debt, Warlock Locksmith the Greater." She made me a deep reverence, and left.

I gaped after her. "Mother Celeste, did you see that? She curtsied to me. A fire witch. Can you believe…"

Mother Celeste leaned over me, hands on hips. I gulped, expecting a well-deserved tongue-lashing. But all she said was, "You are either brave or fool-hardy, I'm not sure which. Would you please avoid putting yourself in danger again while you are my guest? I would hate to have to tell Jean you died under my care after he sent you here for safekeeping."

"Yes, ma'am. I'm sorry."

"I know you are, dear, but I need to tell him what happened. I've been ignoring him ever since you seemed to be coming around, and he sounds quite angry with me. Now, sleep."

I said, "But I want to…" and talked to empty air. Early-morning sunlight streamed in my window. I would have to learn that sleep spell, and use it on one of them. See if they like it.

Hazel brought me breakfast, but sitting up made my head spin. I lay in bed most of the day, napping, worrying, and thinking hard. Something gnawed at me, something insistent demanding attention, but I couldn't put my finger on it. I worried about Jean, but that wasn't new, and mooning over him wasn't going to help.

I reviewed everything that had happened since the Frost Maiden had arrived. Did the Locksmith's jealousy infect the Fire Office, too? If she had been so obsessed with Warlock Fortunatus then why didn't she leave a way for him to retire from the Office? Too bad I couldn't talk to Jean about it.

Thinking about the lock on the Water Office led to further speculation. Beorn, René, and Master Sven had all tried both my original lock spell and the modified one that allowed me to still use my magic, but they hadn't been able to make either one work. If I combined my spell with the Locksmith's, could I create a lock that hid someone else's magic, even from that person? I played with the wording until I had something that might work.

Hazel came to take away my dinner tray. After asking permission, I tried the lock on her.

She dropped the tray, and shrieked, "Take it off."

I released the lock, and she collapsed onto the foot of the bed.

"Sorry, but you did say I could."

"I know, I just didn't expect… It was unnerving."

"Like being trapped in a glass cage, where you couldn't breathe?"

"Well, no. Is that what it was like for you? Interesting. Oh, don't get up. I'll deal with the mess." She waved a hand. The broken crockery reassembled and jumped onto the tray. "I couldn't feel anything. Not the tray, not my clothes—nothing."

After she recovered from the initial shock, we tried it again. We found, to her relief, that she could break out of it. The more power I put into the lock, the harder it was for her to break, but I couldn't summon enough power to make it unbreakable.

As she was leaving, she stopped with her hand on the door. "Promise me you'll be careful who you use that on. You could scare the daylights out of someone if they didn't know it was coming."

I woke the next morning certain that the Locksmith had left a way out. Could I find it in time?

The gnawing feeling was becoming a compulsion; an itch that I had to scratch. It was telling me to go to Jean. Why? Even if I gave in to it, how could I get there? The tunnel was closed.

Mother Celeste was out of the Warren, and wasn't due back until after dinner. By that time the itch was almost unbearable. I paced the floor at the tunnel exit, wringing my hands and fighting with myself. Hazel paced with me, a hand on my arm, helping me stay rational.

Mother Celeste and the Frost Maiden ambled in together, smiling. A moment later, they were hustling me into the amber room. The shielding in the room seemed to help. My pacing was not as frantic, but I couldn't keep still. I told them about the compulsion while I made circuits of the room, twisting my shawl into knots, trying not to listen to the pounding of my heart. The Frost Maiden did not look bored at all.

Hazel said, "There are two compulsions working on her." We all turned to stare at her. She spread her hands. "I don't know who is sending either one."

I said, "I think the Fire Office is sending one of them."

They turned to stare at me. They didn't believe me. I wasn't sure I believed it myself.

The tranquil Earth Mother looked as agitated as a temperamental air witch. "I have never heard of the Fire Office sending a compulsion. That doesn't mean it can't do it; there's lots about that office I don't know. But why would it?"

The Frost Maiden said, "Come here and sit down, be quiet." She placed the palms of both hands against my temples and closed her eyes. I squirmed and grabbed the seat with both hands. When she took her hands away, I bounced out of the chair.

"Your turn, Celeste," she said.

I groaned and sat back down. When Mother Celeste let me go, I resumed racing around the room. The two witches looked at each other for a long moment before turning to frown at me.

The Frost Maiden said, "Yes, there are two compulsions at work, and one does seem to be coming from the Fire Office. I do not recognise the witch or wizard sending the other one. I do not understand this."

Mother Celeste said, "Jean sent her here with orders not to put herself in danger, but if the Fire Office is driving her like this, who are we to argue with it?"

The Frost Maiden went to a table by the door, and brought back a large flat bowl and a pitcher of water. She said, "I will survey the battlefield. Perhaps that will enlighten us."

While she worked her spell on the water, I asked Mother Celeste if there was a tunnel that came out near the Fortress, and she said she could cut one that would come out anywhere we needed it, short of in the Fortress itself.

The Frost Maiden described what she saw in the water. "Jean is on the ramparts of the second tier. He looks exhausted, but there is no attack in progress. Arturos is in the Warlock's study, trying to read the future in the fire. Part of the town is burning. The other warlocks are reaching the end of their powers to put the fires out. The Empire's wizards are scattered below the Fortress, and on the mountain's shoulders.

"There is an unused guard tower on the way to the funeral pyre, but there is someone there. Oh, dear God. The Empire's Chessmaster enchanter is there, and he has a young woman with him, a hostage."

She looked up from the bowl, her face, even her lips, white. "The girl is one of my water witches. She's a silly little level three with no sense, I'm not surprised she walked into a trap, but she's a cousin to the king. She's royal. The Fire Office will make him rescue her."

My heart stopped. I saw black, the black of death, all around me. Beorn had said the enemy could kill the Warlock if they could force him to leave the safety of the Fortress.

No, dammit. Not while I still had magic.

The black turned to red as I burned with rage, the fiercest I have ever felt. I would have torched the Chessmaster if he had been within range.

Stay in control, girl. I couldn't help Jean if I wasn't in control.

I snapped, "Send me there. I don't know what I can do, but that's where I need to be."

The two Officeholders exchanged glances, and came to a decision. As the Earth Mother moved towards the door, the Frost Maiden stopped me and gazed over her wand, thrust at me like a sword. She said, with the bite of ice once more in her voice, "If we are wrong, and you are an agent of the Empire, I will drown you and bury you in the northern ice for eternity."

I looked her in the eye. "And I would welcome it, as my due."

She lowered the wand. "Good luck. We will help if we can."

I ran through the door and into the antechamber, where Mother Celeste was waving her wand at the wall. A tunnel appeared, and I ran through, stopping at the other end to get my bearings. The tunnel ended in the guard tower. Where were the Chessmaster and his hostage? They must be outside, on the path cut into the side of the mountain, leading down to the Fortress.

I stepped out of the tunnel. It snapped closed behind me.

The enemy enchanter stepped back into the tower, his wand pointed at me, and said, "Good day, Miss Guillierre. I've been expecting you."

The Escape Clause

The Chessmaster's smile made the hair on the back of my neck stand on end. "The royal water witch was an illusion to entice you, my dear, not your lover. I am more confident he will come to rescue you. Now you will walk ahead of me out onto the path, and I will call on him."

The Chessmaster had decades of battle experience. How could I hurt him when I couldn't even flame René? Black once more settled around me; the black of death and despair. I'd been stupid—fatally so. His prediction of the Warlock's downfall was about to come true, and I was at fault.

I snarled at him. He prodded me with his wand. He wouldn't risk hurting me; I was no use as a hostage, dead. I took my time walking out of the guard tower, and poured my rage—rage as strong as the first Locksmith's against the Frost Maiden—into the lock spell I had used on Hazel.

Fire bloomed on the path next to the guard tower and my captor whipped around, pulling me in front of him as a shield. Jean stepped out of the fire, wand raised. I snapped the lock in place on the Chessmaster and dove for the ground, pulling out of his grip. Surprise registered on Jean's face, terror on the Chessmaster's.

Hurricane-force winds hit us, knocking the Chessmaster down and slamming Jean into the rock wall of the tower. He crumpled to the ground and lay still.

The winds tried to push me over the edge of the path. I clawed at the rocks and lay flat, using my mind's eye to find the air wizards who were whipping up the wind. Two stood on the funeral pyre outcropping. As I was halfway through the lock spell the second time, the wizard I had focused on rose in the air to ride the wind closer to the tower. When I snapped the lock closed he fell twenty feet, and lay without moving. The intensity of the wind dropped by half.

Out of the corner of my eye, I saw Jean move, and breathed a silent 'Hallelujah.'

I slammed down a shield covering a quarter of the hillside, then cast the lock on the second air wizard by the pyre. Wizards in the distance turned tail, the air wizards sailing off on the winds. A drenching rain sprang out of nowhere, drowning the attempts by the fire wizards to wink out of sight in bursts of flame.

Thank God they were running. My head spun, and I was wet through with sweat despite the bitter cold. I didn't have enough power left to use the lock again.

The Chessmaster staggered to his feet. I flamed him—a feeble spurt that would have disgusted René, but enough to set a sleeve on fire. He screamed and rolled on the path to beat down the flames, then ran away downhill. Farther down, Beorn was running up the path, several guardsmen behind him.

I raised my head. Jean's left arm… I closed my eyes and rested my head on the rocks for a moment. Arms don't bend at that angle. God help me, I was not going to faint.

He made a one-handed attempt to pull himself into a sitting position. I crawled on hands and knees towards him.

He spoke through gritted teeth. "What the hell are you doing here?"

He closed his eyes and leaned his head against the rock wall, drawing in ragged breaths. Blood streamed down one side of his face. The other side was ashen, and beaded with sweat. "Never mind. Make a sling with your shawl."

"If I touch your arm, you'll pass out."

"Do as I say. I must hunt down the Empire's wizards."

"Why? The guards will be here soon, and can carry you back to the Fortress. You need a healer. You need rest. If you fight the Empire's wizards now they'll kill you."

He opened his right eye and glared at me. "If I do not, the Office will kill me, and send Beorn after them."

He leaned against the wall, unable to continue. Why hadn't the Office killed him already? He wasn't fit to fight.

He rasped, "I may die fighting, but I will die like a man. I will not just give up."

Something in my heart snapped. I grabbed his tunic and snarled in his face, "And I am not going to give up and let you die. I don't care about the damned Office and its unreasonable, idiotic demands."

He raged back at me, "And I wish I were not Fire Warlock, but wishing will not help."

But it will.

I rocked back on my heels, blinded by sudden insight. The first Locksmith had left a way out, a way that had been used, but not understood, once before. No one else had understood for a thousand years. I even knew the magic words; Gibson had given them to me in his *History*.

In complete confidence, I shouted, "Listen, you infernal Office. I love Jean Rehsavvy, and for God's sake, I wish he wasn't the damned Fire Warlock anymore!"

The world shifted on its axis. The Office had summoned me to do this, and I floated in a state of rapture, my field of vision expanding to encompass the great wheel of the zodiac making its leisurely turn.

And then I was slammed down onto the hard, rocky path. No time had passed. Enemy wizards were still fleeing; Arturos was still pounding up the slope.

But the Token of Office had slipped from Jean's finger. The monstrous ruby flashed with its own light as the ring bounced and clanged on the rocks of the path. It dropped towards the lumbering bear of a man, the new Fire Warlock, who pounced on it with a roar and vanished in a great spout of flame.

And I, the Greater Locksmith, had found the key to free my love, once more a mortal man, lying bleeding and unconscious at my feet.

The Warlock Unlocked

The guards carried Jean back to the Fortress on a stretcher. I walked through the postern gate first, and encountered a wall of hatred from the watching multitude. They were eerily silent, the men with their hats off. What was wrong with them? Oh.

"He's not dead," I shouted, "but he will be if he doesn't get to a healer soon."

Pandemonium reigned. The crowd pushed me aside as they carried him off, who knew where. I wandered through endless corridors in a daze, until Master Sven found me and led me to the kitchen. He and Mrs Cole cajoled me to eat a bowl of soup, Mrs Cole spoon-feeding me until I woke up enough to push the bowl away and ask for buttered toast. Later, she made me take a bath and tucked me into bed, then sat with me in the dark until I fell asleep.

I lay in bed late the next morning, unwilling to venture out. How could I face the crowds? Rumours would be running wild. How could I face the no-longer-Warlock, either? He had said he was tired of the Office and wanted out, but would he still feel that way now that I had forced retirement on him?

The loss of his authority didn't matter to me—I didn't need the almighty Warlock. What had I said yesterday, anyway? Did I wish that he wasn't the Warlock, or did I say a warlock? I didn't even need a wizard—I would be happy with the scholar—but could a man who had been the world's most powerful wizard for more than a century take such a comedown lightly? I buried my head in my pillow and cried.

Hunger pangs forced me out of bed. The last few days had exhausted my reserves, and I had to eat. I got dressed, and gathered my courage. Jean had said I was a queen. Yesterday, I had indeed commanded the whole board. I was a warlock, and I had earned the right to be here.

The Chessmaster's prediction had played out, and I had proved I could defend myself. I no longer needed the lock hiding my talents. I released it, and stepped out into the hall. After two steps, I turned and went back. I pulled off my supplicant's dress and put on the burgundy velvet I had worn only once.

I was a fire witch. I was going to look like one. I was going to act like one, too. Jean was always so calm, strolling down the corridors. I throttled my desire to run, and walked at a measured pace, pretending I was balancing a book on the top of my head.

People in the corridors drew aside as I walked by. The dining room fell silent when I came in. Jenny blanched and ran out the door. I was tempted to grab a plateful of whatever was closest, but I took the time to get what I wanted, then strolled to my favourite spot behind the curtains in the library.

I was choking down my breakfast when the shutters opened, folding back into their resting places against the walls in a rolling chorus of reverberating bangs. Blinding sunlight streamed in.

The war was over. My spirits rose, and I lifted my coffee cup towards the sun in a silent toast to our good fortune.

⬥

René found me a few minutes later. "Hey, what are you doing here? Why aren't you upstairs? He wants to see you. He sent me to look for you."

"Is he angry?" I asked.

René looked bewildered. "Course not. Why would he be?"

"Because the histories say powerful men don't like having their power taken away."

"Oh." He considered that a moment, then shrugged. "He looked pretty happy to me. Mostly he sounded worried about you."

Relieved, I got up and we walked out of the library, towards the stairs. He said, "What did you do, anyway?"

I shook my head. "I'm in no shape to talk about it yet. Maybe after I talk to him."

"Fine, but I've got first dibs on the story."

"Deal."

264

"He would have come looking for you himself, but Mother Celeste wouldn't let him. She ordered him to stay in the study and rest, and when he started to get up anyway she nailed him to the sofa."

"Nailed him?"

"Not nails actually, but he can't move. So he called her an officious old busybody with a heart of granite, and she called him…" He finished in a rush. "She called him a rutting old goat who's thinking with his dick instead of his head. He said I shouldn't repeat that in mixed company, but you're as good as a boy. Why does she get to say something I'm not supposed to?"

I had heard worse. I laughed, ending on a hiccupping sob. "The Earth Mother does have a reputation for being a bit, well, earthy sometimes, but they'll have to try harder than that if they really mean to insult each other. What were the damages, besides the broken arm?"

"Three broken ribs, cuts and scrapes, and some awesome bruises. But they've fixed him up. Mother Celeste says he'll be fine if he doesn't get hurt again before the bones have finished healing. And Arturos—I mean the new Fire Warlock—went off to sleep. He spent all night chasing down the rest of the wizards. He's going to summon everybody to gather in the ballroom sometime this afternoon so he can tell them what happened."

René chattered away, telling me other news. Arturos had let the other warlocks out of their apartments. Warlock Sunbeam was disappointed, but offered his congratulations like a gentleman. Warlock Flint was livid; no one dared get in his way as he stormed down the corridors. Master Sven was sitting by himself in the practice room, staring off into space.

The sea of faces packing the immobile centre stairs did not appear to bother René. My stomach began to unknot. The glances and whispers seemed more awed and fearful, and maybe even curious, than hostile. The crowd milling about on the landing at the top parted as we walked towards the door.

I stared. Two grinning guards barred the door.

"Morning, Miss Lucinda," one said. "We've got orders to not let anybody but you in. He's expecting you." The other opened the door for me.

I thanked them, then took a deep breath before slipping through.

A ball of yarn rolled this way and that across the carpet, following the motions of his wand, moving just out of reach as the cat pounced. My knees threatened to buckle under me—he was still a wizard, at least. He looked at ease, propped up on pillows against the arm of the sofa, his legs up on the seat, the arm that had been broken resting on the sofa's back.

He put the wand down and held out his hand to me. "I hope you will forgive my bad manners, my dear, but I am unable to rise to greet you. Mother Celeste—drat her—has seen to that. Come and sit with me, please."

I pulled a footstool next to the sofa, and sat on it facing him. We studied each other in silence for a moment. He looked happy but wan; his once form-fitting clothes bagged. Lines of tension in his face deepened as he studied me, and there was a reserve in his eyes that I didn't understand. A vast gulf still lay between us. My stomach lurched.

He stroked my cheek with a light touch. "I sent you to the Earth Mother for safe-keeping. You were not supposed to be in harm's way once, much less twice. I will have to have a talk with that woman." In a more serious tone, he said, "You look exhausted, my love. You saved my life. Why were you afraid to see me?"

I disobeyed orders, but let's not mention that. I studied his hand. It looked odd without the Token of Office. I took a deep breath, and said, "I thought you would feel crippled by the loss of power, when you've been used to it for so long."

"What loss?"

I looked up. His lips twitched; his eyes danced. My heart stopped. "What?"

He smiled. "My dear, you should see your expression. The Token of Office serves as a conduit that an untrained warlock can use for tapping into Storm King, but I have done it for so long that it is second nature to me. You have freed me from the dreadful burden of the Office. Without that authority, I am now merely the second most powerful warlock in the known world. Feeling better now?"

I nodded, too overcome to speak. But as my spirits lightened, he turned sombre. "But this means that I am still a serious danger to you. I…"

My heart sang. I said, "I do not fear you," and kissed him.

He made no move to hold me, and I had nothing to support myself on without leaning on either his bad arm or his sore chest. I drew back, or I would have fallen on him.

His eyes smouldered. "Fool girl. I cannot risk burning you again. You—"

I silenced him with a finger on his lips. "We can put a lock on you so that you can't draw on Storm King without intending to."

His eyes widened, then blazed. "Teach me." He followed the barked order with an abashed, "Please?"

When he was satisfied it had worked, I kissed him again. He pulled me tight against him so I had to lean on him. I pulled back after a bit because I was hurting him. Even then, he didn't want to let me go.

He still looked tired, but happier than I'd ever seen him, and years younger. His eyes sparkled, unshadowed; the lines of tension had disappeared from his face.

He said, "Too bad you did not think of that a few weeks ago."

"It's a good thing I didn't. If I had, I most certainly would be dead."

He stiffened. "Why?"

"What did Mother Celeste tell you?"

"She told me what you had done to the Water Office, but she could not explain what you did yesterday. I want to hear it all from you, anyway. Start from the beginning."

I told him the whole story, ending with my speculations about what the Locksmith had done to the Fire Office. "I think the burning is a defence mechanism she built into the Office, so that someone who was only interested in the Warlock for his power and position couldn't seduce and manipulate him. So using a lock to avoid the flames wouldn't have done any good. The Office would have overridden it, but we would have been alone when it happened. Without Beorn there…"

He shuddered, and was silent for a moment. He had relaxed, but kept a tight grip on my hand. "How could the Locksmith have done such a cruel thing? Such a terrible fate for those women who did love their Warlocks."

I said, "But if a fire witch loves the man instead of the Office, she can wish him out of it. Like the wife of the seventeenth Warlock. That story may be literally true."

"As easy as that?"

"As easy—and as hard—as that. Maybe both people have to express the wish. And I presume it only works for level four or five fire witches.

But that's why the Office summoned me to come yesterday, and why it held off on killing you even when you weren't fit anymore. It was giving me a chance to rescue you. But even knowing what I knew, it took me a painfully long time to figure out what it was expecting me to do.

"I don't know if the escape clause was forgotten, or if the Locksmith never told anyone. Maybe she intended to keep it a secret until Warlock Fortunatus tired of the Office and asked for her help, but then he never did. Maybe it was something even she didn't understand. Since we now know more about the Locksmith and her relationship with Fortunatus we should be able to figure that out."

He said, "Even if it had not been a secret, it would have been an incredible burden. Obviously one of the things you will need to fix."

"That I need to fix?" My voice quavered. I didn't relish another experience like the one I'd had with the lock on the Water Office. "You're going to help, aren't you?"

"Of course. Now free from the constraints of the Fire Office, I can pursue my real life's work of fixing it. Our life's work, I should say; you and I will form the core of the second Great Coven. With the two of us, and help from the other guilds, I have no doubt we can. I never allowed myself to conjure up false hopes by dreaming about a day when I was not the Warlock, but now…"

His voice trailed away, and he lay on the pillows with his eyes half closed. When he resumed, he seemed to be talking to himself. "It is not urgent, we have time to plan. It will take time, anyway, for the witches and wizards from the other guilds to become familiar with the spells involved…

"In the meantime, we should learn more about the experiments in governance going on in other countries. We have become too parochial here. We need to see what is and is not working elsewhere. Could we do without a king? It will be good for Beorn if I travel for a bit—he can establish his authority and his own ways of doing things. Yes, a good long vacation is in order."

Had he been alone for so long that he couldn't imagine life otherwise? Would he go away without me? No. "Honeymoon," I said.

My momentary panic melted away in the warmth of his gaze. "I cannot promise you happily ever after," he said. "Such is not often the fate of a marriage involving even one warlock."

"For better or for worse." I shrugged. "For you, Jean, I'll risk it."
"For better or for worse," he said, and smiled.

End of The Locksmith

The story continues in
Engine of Lies, Reforging: Book 2.